Windleroot

Gordon Strong

SKYLIGHT
PRESS

First published in Great Britain in 2013 by Skylight Press,
210 Brooklyn Road, Cheltenham, Glos GL51 8EA

Designed and typeset by Rebsie Fairholm
Publisher: Daniel Staniforth
Cover artwork by Matt Baldwin-Ives (model: Nick Baxter)

www.skylightpress.co.uk

Printed and bound in Great Britain by Lightning Source, Milton Keynes.

British Library Cataloguing in Publication Data.
A catalogue record for this book is available from the British Library.

ISBN 978-1-908011-70-1

To all those who laugh – at anything and everything.

FOREWORD

Everything is fair game for humour, and sacred cows make the best burgers.

Gordon Strong
Portishead, England

Halloween, October 2010

'I resemble only half the things I say I don't,' the Golux said. 'The other half resemble me.'
James Thurber

Fiction is … merely the truth liberated from facts.
John Boorman

Mundus Vult Decepi – 'All the world wishes to be deceived.'

I

2012

ec. 22nd 2012 – The date when they said the world would end. Despite numerous cock-eyed predictions in the past, this time they did get it right. The soothsayers, Sufis, clairvoyants, charlatans, flakes and fortune-tellers – all their predictions were absolutely on the money. It was there, right in your face – *The Apocalypse.*

The Four Horsemen had lined up a string of gigs – a world tour in fact, kicking off in England. They had been picky about the places they would visit so they could give them a really good kicking. Venues that many would agree deserved to be laid waste – Luton or Torquay for instance – went unmolested. Even Slough remained unscathed, which perhaps proves that nobody reads John Betjeman's poetry anymore.

The transcendental underbelly of the kingdom was definitely going to get sandbagged. Perdition had first come upon Windleroot – the jewel in the New Age crown. The Isle of Teflon, where once Jim Avabeer had hidden the Holy Pail in the Dallas Well ... where Windleroot Nob stood proud and erect over the moors ... all this was doomed to be decimated and duffed right up.

No more would Windleroot host the greatest and most grotesque carnivals of the sacred and the silly – The Bodice Conference, the Pillstown Rock Festival, The Psychotic Fayre. Never again would pilgrims from Nebraska and the Netherlands brave the journey to Windleroot, worship at the sacred shrines and be handsomely ripped off in Lowe Street. The ship of the New Age was about to sink, and it was unlikely to come up smelling of roses.

Those brave fellows and stout yeomen who manned the emergency services were the first to see the horror of it all. The sight made many of them want to retch. A tide of filth – brown and yellow, with patches of livid green – was slowly creeping down Lowe Street from Pump Hill.

The force of the deluge had torn up the paving slabs on both sides of the street. They lay like heaps of playing cards thrown aside in a casino. The town looked as if it had been disembowelled by Jack the Ripper. Among the ruins, only one house still stood upright, the gaping rents in its fabric pathetically exposing the mandalas upon the walls, the dream-catchers suspended from the ceiling.

The New Age nymph of Windleroot was expiring beneath a tide of crystals – amethyst, quartz, lapis-lazuli and turquoise – all glinting dully in a psychedelic kaleidoscope around her. The dull baubles were now as dead as the rocks that once bore them. Near them, curiously shaped jars and ornate caskets lay smashed in the gutter, unguents and potions mingled with the filth from the ruptured drains.

Angel cards, incense sticks and amulets went scattered and forlorn among copies of *The Pan Worshippers Pocket Book* and *The Wonderful World of Wicca*, their pages soiled and torn. Velvet cloaks, shawls and scarves were merely piles of rags. No more would pagan princesses and white-faced witches strut and primp down Lowe Street.

Helicopters flew over the ruins, their rotors pummelling the air. The authorities had sealed off the town with gaudy pink tape – the Isle of Teflon was now a no-go area. Burly policemen prevented anyone from going in or leaving, and officious men in fluorescent yellow jackets indiscriminately jostled both sightseers and anxious relatives. Clerks from County Hall strutted about getting in everybody's way. Inside and outside the front line it was utter mayhem.

The growing army of the media were desperate for copy – the merest sop of news that they could relay back to Canary Wharf. They would press anyone in sight for a comment, receiving only muttered gibberish in return. In vain did they aim their telephoto lenses in the direction of the carnage, but there was nothing to be seen. An impenetrable darkness had descended upon Windleroot, a black cloud that would never lift again. The vision of the Windleroot pilgrim had become as a terrible blindness.

The next morning, a pale and limp version of the sun rose, its light revealing ragged scarecrows among the ruins. Vainly did these spectral skeletons search for scraps of food in that blasted landscape. The vegans were the most feral – fighting over the crumbs of a stale sausage roll, while those who had once been strictly gluten-free contemplated cannibalism.

In the days that followed, mediums, clairvoyants and crystal healers, who had once commanded exorbitant fees for their divinations, were now reduced to whoring. Selling their favours for a pound or two, plying their trade in the crumbling alleys, the darkness mercifully concealed their sagging limbs.

Later, patrols of 4X4s with tinted windows would cruise over the rubble, crushing any bodies that lay unburied. Windleroot was nothing more than a stinking corpse, waiting to be interred.

Windleroot Nob, the conical mound that had for centuries dominated the flatlands had split in half, like a muffin struck by a cleaver. When the tower on the summit had fallen, an enormous lump of Medieval masonry had rolled with a terrible crash down Deadshed Lane. It lay in the middle of Ackwater Street, a grotesque monument to all that had befallen Windleroot in those terrible days at the beginning of the new millennium. It was a time when religion was not the opium of the people, but Fox News.

Dick Symes prodded the off switch on the remote and the TV died. With it went any trace of a present reality. He wasn't sure he believed what he had just seen, the images of the trashing of Windleroot looked suspiciously faked and photoshopped. How could you believe what you saw on the plasma panorama these days? Did Neil Armstrong ever really land on the moon except in a TV studio in downtown Burbank? Would someone who had never known of the Twin Towers, and saw footage of 9/11 think that they were only watching another disaster movie? What was reality? Weren't the media just Brain Police, with a monopoly on the way everyone was supposed to think about the world? Figures don't lie but liars figure.

The twenty-first century was all about just that – the difference between the truth and total twot. The gap between the two was now so finely airbrushed that you couldn't fit a fly's wing in there, even side-on. Everyone knows about quantum physics these days and that there are more parallel universes than blueberry muffins in Sainsbury's. Countless possible versions of what will happen in any one moment exist. Different dimensions are lined up like After-Eights in that smart, green box.

Any event is just another part of the temporal interface. Time flows, not just one way but every which way, like cream on cake. If we believe that time somehow glues us to the material world we are kidding ourselves. It may make us feel happier to have a cuckoo clock, but past and future are like different universes, infinite and eternal. Everything that will happen has already happened, and what is happening now will at some point happen again. What really went on that day in Windleroot? For all we know things might have been very different …

Dick Symes had been born into what would forever be regarded as a strange era – the forlorn and faded Forties and Fifties. The War was not long over and the old brigade were still trying to make everyone march in step. Fun had gone into hiding and would stay there until the Sixties ousted the grey and kicked ass, big time. For now, Merrie England was stuck in its own stodge and fug. It was a world of short trousers, school caps and tomato sandwiches, a world that said 'speak when you're spoken to' and 'say cheese'. Black and white, The Coronation and Brylcreem – that's what it was like. Luckily for Dick Symes he lived most of the time in a completely different world, one that he had invented for himself – an existence that didn't include grown-ups and their dreary ways.

Bill Symes – Dick's father – was constantly racked by fears that he might not be doing the right thing. He hated to be caught breaking 'the rules', and he didn't like others breaking them either. If he came to hear that someone had been wearing blue trousers and a red shirt when it specifically stated that green trousers and a yellow shirt were the order of the day, he would snarl audibly. Dick and his mother would then be forced to endure a noisy harangue concerning the slackness of 'them' – the dangerous fifth columnists who lurked everywhere, wearing incorrectly coloured garments.

Dick reacted to those outbursts in a singular fashion – his father's anger seemed to fuel his imagination. That quality had never been dormant since Symes Jr. had arrived on the planet. In Dick's inner visions his furious father would become a huge orange fruit. Rather like an outsize pumpkin, it would then bounce up and down, all the time swelling visibly. At other times Dick saw Bill Symes as a plum pudding or a bunch of balloons. His tirades would be transformed into comical music in the style of Souza, with hooting tubas, wailing trombones, and the bang and boom of kettle drums.

In those days, authority was generally obeyed, even if not always respected. If they had revealed themselves, Dick's visions would have been regarded as subversive. Humour always has an element of risk, which is what makes it appealing. Those in charge resent being laughed at, it makes them realise they're just like everyone else.

Dick was instinctively aware of the danger of his insights. Wisely, he did not share them. Being an only child, he was used to keeping his thoughts to himself.

The phenomenon that allowed Dick to 'see' wasn't confined to the family circle. On a Saturday afternoon he liked to visit the Starlight Café in the town. A mildly bohemian establishment often frequented by girls of a kind who took to wearing pink lipstick and eye shadow and Dick was constantly fascinated by these fabulous creatures. He would surreptitiously observe them while sipping at a cup of frothy coffee, purchased at great expense out of his pocket money.

One afternoon, quietly engaged in this delightful pursuit, Dick suddenly 'saw' the pubescent nymphets seated at the next table transform themselves completely. The most glamorous became dragons, with scaly talons, horny hides of gold, vermilion and emerald, eyes glimmering like crystal ice. Their beautiful wings were slowly folding and unfolding, making shadows across the sun that was beaming through the windows. Opal wisps of smoke curled towards the ceiling and torrents of flame leapt from between their fangs. Scarlet tongues, diving in and out of their vicious jaws, lashed the air. Unicorns and winged horses were among them too, strutting and prancing, their manes seeming to fill the entire sky. Dick could only stare in wonderment. He wasn't frightened or horrified at all this but he never regarded the female sex in quite the same way again.

1963

The Swinging Sixties didn't begin on New Year's Day 1960. Everyone in Coronation Street didn't suddenly go mod, or coal-miners in Yorkshire start wearing bells and beads. Change came up behind Britannia and very slowly pulled her knickers down, but once they were off she was a different woman.

In those days not many people had their lives completely turned around when they were sixteen. Dick Symes didn't really recall the particular event that juggled with his brain and turned it inside out until half-a century later. When he did remember, most of the details were still there, but the memory banks were short on funds.

When the snow came on Boxing Day in 1962, it hung around almost until the Spring of 1963. The previous generation reckoned it was even more harsh than the cold spell of 1947. Dick was a scrawny kid, without much real flesh on his body, and that Winter he felt almost sick with the cold. Every morning he would look out of his bedroom window at the opaque whiteness. It had been there the day before, stretching out across the landscape, and looked as if it might stay forever.

When he saw the spaceship, he was at first merely curious, content to gaze at this strange spectacle. It seemed to hang forever in the grey skies, the silver hull just visible in the gloom. He didn't actually want to believe that he was seeing it – that would have been too much to take. Dick read comics, like everyone else in those days, and that's where he preferred any weird stuff to stay – inside the coloured panels of Dan Dare. He didn't want to be seeing flying saucers and Men from Mars in his own garden, thank you very much.

But Dick had to admit to himself that right now he was watching this graceful aerial galleon sliding out of the clouds. Just when he thought he could see some of the details of the gleaming apparition more clearly, it disappeared. No matter how many times he would scan the darkening skies, he did not see it again. That was, until the seasons moved along and it became Summer. In those days in England, Summer always meant cricket.

Dick's dad played for the second team in Nimble, the town where they lived. Bill Symes liked to refer to himself as a 'middle-order batsman' and a 'useful bowler'. Dick, not being very interested in the ancient and noble game, did not know what any of this meant. He usually kept quiet when his dad talked about cricket, or anything else, it was easier that way. It also meant he could engage with his own thoughts. This was an advantage when his father embarked on one of his lectures. The one that came up most frequently was about 'getting on' in life, a rather lacklustre collection of what Mr. Symes considered to be terribly worldly observations.

" … pulling strings … that's the way to do it … knowing the right people … tackling them … getting a word in on your behalf … pulling the right strings of course … "

The last bit always confused Dick. What strings? Where did they come from? Did they always hang straight down, or occasionally swing about? How hard and how often, were they supposed to be pulled?

In the car together, Dick realised that his father had abruptly stopped talking. They were at a cross roads and his dad was trying to remember which road he should take, he had a horror of looking indecisive in his son's company. The crisis quickly over, Dick resumed reviewing one of the odd ideas that was currently in his head. Always there, these thoughts waved their arms about, constantly seeking attention. As has been noted Dick was an only child, and his point of view tended towards the subjective. Right now, a lot of what was going on his head, and increasing daily, revolved around *girls*.

The away fixture, the last one of the season for Bill's team, was to be held in Windleroot, the small town where they had now arrived. Dick's dad drove into the cricket ground and parked his Morris Traveller next to the other cars lined up by the pavilion. As soon as he took his leather cricket bag out of the back Bill Symes became a different person. He started hailing other members of the team and being very chatty and friendly with them.

'Tommy' Thomas, 'Taffy' Edwards, 'Fruity' Rowntree – apparently not one of them could escape without some silly sobriquet. Dick knew that at any moment his dad would start smoking his pipe, something he did when he was being convivial. Dick also knew when he was being ignored, so after muttering about seeing his dad later, he wandered off in the direction of Windleroot Nob, the steep mound that dominated the landscape.

He walked along narrow streets, past houses built of neat red brick, until he reached the edge of the town. A path led through an archway of trees. Many of them had lost their leaves and he trod upon heaps of gold and brown. As Dick emerged into the sunlight, Windleroot Nob rose up in front of him. On its summit was a ruined tower, all that remained of a Medieval castle.

Dick was aware of music in the distance, soft at first but growing louder as he climbed up the steep slope. Soon he recognised the melody – the Beatles. At the same time he saw someone dancing to the sounds coming from a transistor radio. Somehow, it did not seem incongruous to Dick, just an open celebration of joy. He was close enough to see the whirling figure was a girl about his own age. She was dressed in a red sweater and jeans, apparently so involved in gyrating to 'She Loves You' she was oblivious to his presence. Even when Dick sat down on a bench quite close to where she was performing her ritual, she did not acknowledge he was there. Not for some moments anyway.

Dick tried hard not to stare, though he was fascinated by the sight before him. The song swirled to its end on a celestial G6 chord. Realizing she was no longer alone, the girl deliberately switched off the radio. The silence that followed still seemed to contain some memory of the music he had heard. Suspended in the air, the final cadence – 'Yeah, Yeah, Yeah' – echoed for long minutes over the fields and in the sky.

Both of them waited for the enchantment to fade, as if they were engaged in something almost religious. The girl then sat down next to Dick. The deliberate way she did this made it seem as if she was acting out a part. Dick watched her and every movement she made. He had never been this close to a girl before.

"What's your name?"

"Dick."

The girl appeared to consider this.

"I'm going to call you Richard."

"My mum does that sometimes."

For some reason this caught the girl's interest.

"When does she do that?"

Dick pictured one of those occasions when it happened. He had a talent for always being able to rerun the details of any moment in his life.

"Probably when she likes me a lot."

The girl's eyes glittered, though Dick didn't see this as he was looking down at his feet when he spoke.

"I'm not surprised she likes you – I do too."

Dick didn't say anything.

"You're very shy."

"Am I?"

"Yes."

She moved closer to him and stroked his hair very gently.

"Look at me."

Dick did as she told him. Her face was now very close to his, he could almost taste her breath – it was sweet. She was smiling. Her lips touched his and all at once he realised that he was kissing a girl for the very first time in his life. It was strange, very different to how he had imagined it would be – like walking barefoot on jelly.

"Do you like kissing?"

Dick tried to be matter-of-fact.

"Oh, yes."

She kissed him again, and this time he took a much more energetic part in what was going on.

"There … you're not so shy now are you?"

"No, you make me feel like that I think."

She laughed, and held his face in both her hands.

"Oh, you are so sweet. I've never met any boy like you before."

Dick suddenly felt a terrible pain, presumably where his heart was. This girl, who he had only just met, had caused a strange sensation to go right through his whole self. Even though it was overwhelming, and accompanied by such hurt, he wanted this feeling to go on for ever. The thought that it might not do so was too much to bear. He was suddenly aware she knew what he was thinking. She kissed him again, slowly and tenderly, as if she really meant it.

"You are so funny."

Dick put his arm around her. She didn't appear to mind, and put her head on his shoulder and left it there. He could feel her long, dark hair on his cheek when the wind blew. But even as all this was happening Dick knew something was wrong. With no warning at all the girl suddenly jumped to her feet and began to run off down the slope. Dick leapt to his feet, hurrying after her.

"Hey, what's the matter?"

She was running as fast as she could, it was extraordinary that she did not tumble over and over on the grass.

"I've got to go now."

Dick watched her figure becoming smaller and smaller. He shouted desperately, as loud as he could.

"What's your name?"

No answer. Until, as if caught on the wind, he strained to hear the sound.

"Janice."

Dick continued to watch her until the figure disappeared through a gap in the trees. How he felt right at that moment was entirely new to him. Tides, swollen with strange and unknown feelings, begun to sweep over him. Such swirling, uncontrollable forces inside him he had never known before, probably because he did not realise they existed. Dick's brain struggled to find some way of describing them. Was this what being in love was like? Dick didn't know how that was supposed to happen. Hadn't he read in some book that it could happen at any time … always possible … often completely unpredictable …

With his soul bouncing round like a yoyo in a thunderstorm, he turned round and walked back up the top of the mound. Right at that moment the spaceship appeared. It swung round out of the air and floated neatly down onto the lawn-sized plateau on the other side of the tower. It remained there, its hull gleaming dully.

A lot of utter twot is talked about aliens; it always has been, since the first time humans encountered them. Most people are frightened of aliens too. The very word hints at things we would rather not know about – people who are not like us. 'Space Travellers' is a tad better but still doesn't quite make the grade. Not that Fantuk and Zavrod were really bothered what anybody thought about them. They had surfed over the time waves from the planet Xog in the Twenty-Seventh dimension, in a way that said, 'we do this kind of thing every day'. Beings that possess the technology to blast planets into mint-sized meteorites in one zap, aren't easily intimidated.

They released the front hatch of the craft and the two Xogs stepped out onto the grass. They appeared to be casually surveying the scene, while all the time they knew that an earthling was peeking at them from behind one of the walls of the tower. Dick was also nearly peeing himself with fright, but the Xogs didn't know about that, or were too polite to mention it. They did however announce their presence, pretty loud and clear.

"Good afternoon, Mister Symes, Fantuk and Zavrod at your service. We mean you no harm and would be delighted to meet you."

A slight hint of a Twenty-Seventh Dimension accent did not disguise a genuine friendly tone. Dick emerged from his hiding place.

"Hello."

He wasn't quite sure how you greeted eight-foot tall creatures with emerald skin and amber eyes encased in platinum–coloured space suits. After all, Dick had no previous experience of these things. He need not have worried; Fantuk extended a short flipper in Dick's direction.

"Pleased to meet you I'm sure. I'm Fantuk, and this is Zavrod. We're Xogs from the Twenty-Seventh Dimension."

Warily, Dick took the pseudopodia and gripped it with a couple of fingers. It was like handling frozen cod.

"I, uh, didn't know what you would look like … "

Zavrod's eyes flashed like traffic lights on speed.

"What were you expecting? Some sort of Steven Spielberg special?"

Dick looked genuinely puzzled.

"Who's Steven Spielberg?"

"Ah, yes, he's not known here yet is he ... quite a few more years to go ... he's probably about the same age as you are right now. I always forget you still have *time* here on Earth."

Dick looked even more perplexed.

"What d'you mean? Time's everywhere ... isn't it?"

Fantuk seemed to find the idea amusing.

"Not in the Twenty-Seventh dimension, no. Our consciousness has developed far enough to conclude there is no distinction to be made between any state – past or future."

"Wow! When did you find out about all this?"

Zavrod made the kind of noise an old sofa would make if it was being shagged by a set of bagpipes. It was the Xog version of laughing.

" ... I was going to say 'a long, long time ago'. Shows you how easy it is to forget how far our technology has advanced when I'm back in a place as primitive as Earth."

Dick thought this was probably some kind of mild insult, but he ignored it. He considered that there were more important things in life than getting uptight because of what people (including those from the Twenty-Seventh dimension) said to him. The thought that Zavrod probably had the power to turn him into a Uranian cider mug had crossed his mind as well.

"Um, how did you know my name?"

"We have all knowledge in the entire universe stored in our cerebral data-banks. All that has ever happened, will happen and even things beyond that, is digitally filed."

"Everything?"

Zavrod was inclined to be slightly patronizing, pompous even.

"All wisdom, theories and hypotheses, proven or not – every piece of information stored in the human brain since the dawn of time, and a lot of other stuff that even the smartest people on *this* planet couldn't imagine."

"Double wow!"

Zavrod did the best imitation of a smile that a creature who had nothing whatsoever resembling a mouth could achieve.

"We have been visiting Earth since man first ceased to crawl on the ground like an animal – that was over two and a half million years ago. He's been living a more or less settled life for around ten thousand years, that's less than 0.2% of the time he's been here. And actually *thinking* probably even less, and what he thinks about never seems to amount to much … even after all this time. Sorry, that wasn't very nice of me to say such a thing, but it's absolutely true … "

Dick folded his arms and prepared to make a few comments himself. He felt he was at that moment a representative of Earth and he had to jolly well speak up a bit for his own kind.

"Are you more clever than a computer or a robot?"

Zavrod bent down in order to examine Dick more closely.

"How do you know of these things? Personal Computers and Artificial Intelligence were not developed fully until the Twenty-First Century … "

"I read a lot of comics … "

Dick was aware that Fantuk, who had presumably been content to stay silent all this time, was now looking at him. The Xog had assumed an expression that was difficult to identify because of the way their faces were made.

"Remember this, little earthling; the brain is much more powerful than any machine."

"Is it? I can never remember my French verbs when there's a test in class."

"You may manifest anything you wish. Watch … "

His right flipper turned into a round paddle. Dick saw something appear in the middle of it – a transparent Cuboid that gave off a pale pink glow. Fascinated, Dick watched as it spun slowly on its axis. Somewhere in the middle of his head he was aware of Fantuk's voice. He was asking him something – a question that to Dick's ears sounded very strange.

"You think God is invisible do you not?"

Dick, although surprised, was still inclined to talk back.

"I've never really thought about it. My mum goes to the Methodist Church in Station Road. My dad always tells everybody he's an atheist… "

"What's that?"

"Somebody who doesn't believe there's a God."

It was Fantuk's turn to sound like the erotic sofa and bagpipes combination.

"It seems to me that a lot of people on Earth have spent thousands of years wondering about God. As well, a lot of them have been busy insisting that their own idea of Him is right, and He wants them to do this or that. So I thought that you ought to see Him for yourself and make up your own mind, then at least one person on this planet will be a bit more informed."

Dick could only stand and stare.

"Am I really going to meet God?"

All this talk of higher things made Dick think of the time when he was a little kid. One Sunday, he was watching people coming out of St. Edmund's church and noticed that all the men were wearing a tweed jacket and flannel trousers. Putting two and two together – and making five and a half, as he often did – Dick came to certain conclusions. Assuming that the church was 'God's House', it followed that the supreme deity must also wear a striped tie and hoof about in Heaven in a pair of brown brogues. This was as well as insisting every pronoun referring to Him had to have a capital letter.

The Cuboid had begun to get bigger. Or was it that the world was getting smaller ... Dick had no way of telling. Now he was surrounded by so much pinkness it was as if he were sitting inside one of his dad's roses that had become a cloud, or the other way round. The sensation was pleasant enough and he was just getting used to it when it all changed. Now he was in a turquoise world, one with the occasional streak of mauve. The edges of the cloud had become harder too as if they were part of a celestial city, one with pointed turrets and castellated walls, set upon some steep escarpment.

Beams of light began to strobe playfully above Dick's head making fractal patterns that melded into endless curlicues of miasma. Not that Dick would have put it like that – SFX in movies, or patterns on a computer screen – would be how he would have described it fifty years later. But Dick somehow knew that the Cuboid wasn't some cheesy pop concert, it was something else – a gateway to other worlds, or a path that led to the infinite galaxies and beyond. Perhaps it was a stairway to heaven, and one day would have a song written about it.

Dick, like many an initiate experiencing enlightenment, found it impossible to describe exactly what he was seeing. The whirling maelstrom then calmed down a bit and from its vortex began to emerge a wondrous face. The features were so incredibly perfect as to be unbelievable, but there they were so he had to believe in them. Dick realised he was looking into the face of Creation. Hadn't he read somewhere that gods – like Sumo Wrestlers and Afghani tribesmen – didn't like being stared at? And this was GOD – not just with one capital letter but *three*, the jackpot of Jehovahs – the top celestial banana. Dick concluded that looking too hard at the Almighty was about as smart as chewing on a chain-saw.

Dick being the kind of cheeky little chappie he was, just had to have a peek. He had a friend called David Tree who used to say that life 'was only material for reminiscence'. He wanted to tell old Tree that he had seen God. After all, this was the Almighty, the One who invented the Venus Fly Trap and the Monkey Puzzle Tree, both extremely impressive things in their way. Not to mention mountain ranges, arctic waters, blistering deserts, jungles and limitless oceans. Oh, and *man* – the Clown of Creation.

This God he was gazing upon was definitely the real thing and no cheap imitation – Dick could tell. For a start, His eyes were radiant like a million suns, each one brimming with the brilliance of molten gold. It suddenly occurred to Dick that if he could see God, then God could see him too. This all seemed terribly profound and important, and Dick believed he shouldn't waste this great opportunity.

He ought to talk to God and ask Him a few tricky questions. God obviously wasn't the sort of chap who would hide anything – you could tell that by just looking at Him – as honest as the day was long. And He had decided how long that would be, hadn't he? His heavenly aura was like nothing else – well it wouldn't be, would it? So, like the late, great Hurricane Higgins, young Dick set up his first shot.

"Why has there got to be Good and Evil?"

Dick thought he might have been shouting. It was difficult to tell when you were in the presence of the Almighty, the prospect of thunder and lightning never seemed to be very far away. God looked quizzical, if that was possible for The Ultimate Wisdom.

"You gave the words capital letters, just like Me, I wonder why? Now then, *Good* and *Evil* – they do look impressive in italics don't they? Much more important than they really are you know ... why they have no more significance than a peduncle."

It was Dick's turn to look quizzical.

"What's a peduncle?"

"It's that purple flowery bit on the top of a leek."

"Oh."

God carried on. He was being quite chatty and friendly really, Dick thought.

"Yes, *nothing* is any more important than anything else. I made sure of that."

Dick thought that probably his time was running out, like ringing

Australia from a call-box.

"What's the *secret of life*?"

Dick knew he was bellowing, he almost frightened himself with the noise he made.

"If I told you, what you do with it? Have your own website? Sell it on e-bay?"

Dick didn't know what he meant but he carried on.

"But, if everybody knew … then, uh, the world would be a better place."

God looked very serious, quite an easy thing for Him to do.

"Do you really think that's true?"

Dick, surrounded as he was by the ineffable, gave up as quickly as he had begun, there was nothing else he could do.

"I don't know … p'raps it's just a nice idea."

God was encouraging.

"Some ideas are."

Dick tried again, for the last time.

"So, all things considered how d'you think things have turned out?"

God looked pensive.

"With the universe you mean? Well, depends on how you look at it I suppose."

Dick wondered if this wasn't God simply being a bit evasive – avoiding the issue, sort of – but he didn't like to say so. Any more theological speculations were interrupted by Fantuk's voice, almost singing in his head. Dick realised the Xog must have been tuned in to his exclusive interview with the Almighty as soon as the programme began.

"God can't delegate. If you are God then you can do anything you want. I would have thought that followed … it seems quite logical to me."

One tiny part of Dick thought there was something that wasn't right with that argument. Was this being irreverent? He had once heard some old man shouting on a street corner about blasphemy, but he hadn't understood what he was saying then, and it was unlikely he would now. Whatever was happening, God certainly wasn't anymore. He had simply moved off – in mysterious ways his wonders to perform, no doubt. A pity really because Dick still had a lot more questions to ask. More than in the final of a pub quiz.

The pink cloud had disappeared. Dick found himself looking at the strange but not too terrifying features of Fantuk, the Xog from

21

the Twenty-Seventh Dimension. Ah, well, all in day, thought Dick. Suddenly he really did have a thought, a big one – about Janice and the kiss, and the ache went and started up again. Dick decided it would be better to think about something else, so he asked a question out loud.

"Did I really see God then?"

Fantuk was mater-of-fact.

"No reason why you shouldn't have done, I'm sure He's got his own dimension – as many as he wants, I expect."

Dick nodded his head, more absently this time ... he rather considered he'd had enough weirdness for one day. It just happened there was more to come, but he didn't know it.

"Here."

Zavrod handed him the Cuboid. Dick was amazed, a state he was sort of getting quite used to. At least he wasn't inside it any longer, very definitely not, because he was holding it – unless this was some profound metaphysical point he hadn't come to terms with. The Cuboid fitted nicely in his hand – it was about the same size as a packet of tea. Dick began to wonder if it had really been responsible for doing the things that he had seen about five minutes ago. He carefully put the Cuboid in his pocket.

"It's a present – from me to you."

"Thanks. That's a song, you know – the second Beatles Number One ... "

"We know all about them."

But they didn't let on about what happened to John Lennon – that would have been cruel and unnecessary.

"Can this really do anything?"

A great big thought had just come into Dick's head about the Cuboid.

"What were you thinking of ... ."

Dick looked, not slightly embarrassed, but totally as the tomato in all its redness.

"There's this girl ... I only met her this afternoon ... I want to see her again ... can you make her come back?"

Zavrod shook his head.

"No, can't be done. Mustn't alter destiny – not part of the deal we've made with God. All sorts of problems come up ... like the possibility of killing your grandfather and then the possibility of you not being born ... you know ... all that sort of thing."

"But I don't want to kill grandpa, just see Janice … "

The Xog shook his head, and Dick suspected there was more to all this than he knew, and he was right. He would find out all about quantum physics and parallel universes when he gave up comics and started to read science fiction. The idea of time not existing and other extraordinary notions were not on Dick's mind right then however. His concerns were infinitely more practical; down to earth, you might say.

"Thanks very much for the Cuboid thing, but I really have got to go. They'll be having tea in the pavilion about now … and my dad will be wondering where I am."

As soon as he said this, Dick wondered briefly if they played cricket on the planet Xog. But Fantuk had other matters of import to impart. He looked at Dick and the amber eyes glowed even more brightly.

"We have scanned your cerebral cortex and found you have an abnormally high P.S.I. faculty … "

Dick looked anxious.

"Am I going to die?"

For the first time the Xog looked puzzled.

"I have absolutely no information concerning that question. Perhaps you are unfamiliar with the term P.S.I.? It occurs in the study of parapsychology and simply means this, you are inclined to be extremely sensitive and intuitive. Zavrod, in his way, prefers to describe you as 'irrational.' "

Dick said absolutely nothing, mainly because he didn't have anything to say.

"You are inclined to a transcendental view of life and your consciousness is full of dreams. Be careful that you do not confuse *imagination* and *fantasy*, the one is creative the other merely wanting wishes to come true. The two terms have become confused, particularly for those who regard all the transactions of the brain as merely the mundane exchange of one thought for another. I do not want to confuse you, but I must stress that *imagination and fantasy are different creatures.* I will quote from ygypWt the great writer of the Neptunian galaxy,

Imagination has bright plumage, sings of beauty and dreams beyond joy, and creates swirling patterns in endless skies. The other is made of some artificial stuff, is tawdry, its brittle words are no more than lies and nightmares. The imagination blossoms and fills the air with

23

sweet scents; fantasy turns weevil-ridden and evil-smelling within a moment.

Dick didn't know what to make of that, *English* Literature was hard enough, how could he be expected to understand the classics of Neptune? Fantuk was looking hard at him.

"Mister Symes, I would advise you to stay away from drugs, particularly of the psychedelic kind, when they become extremely fashionable in a few years time. I would also recommend that you do not wear flowers in your hair … they just look very foolish … neither would I recommend you going to San Francisco."

Dick was inclined to be a bit cheeky.

"You sound like a gypsy fortune teller."

"The best one you'll ever meet, kid, 'cos I know where it's at, and what's happenin', babe. Oh, and one more thing … "

Dick looked wary and maybe even a little weary.

"What's that?"

"My advice for dealing with what goes on here – on Earth, I mean – is very simple. Just accept that everything that happens is completely insane but don't let on to anybody that you know."

Dick nodded.

"Okay."

The two Xogs started back towards their spaceship. As they waved farewell Fantuk called out something. To Dick, the words sounded believable and not so, all at the same time.

"You'll forget all this in precisely two Earth minutes, but I promise we'll see you again in fifty years."

Like a silver fish, the spaceship slid into the atmosphere and travelled on into the infinite blueness. Dick didn't have to do any sums on his fingers. Fifty years? That made it 2013 – a long way off. He continued to stare into the endless skies until his thoughts returned to right now and all that had happened to him. Unfortunately the two minute deadline that Fantuk had mentioned was now up and running. When Dick tried to rummage around in his brain for any details of what had happened his neurons became slippery and wouldn't grip on what he wanted. They did grab onto some other stuff though.

He did remember that he had kissed a girl for the first time. When he reviewed a list of his friends, wondering if there were any candidates for him to share this gem with, the prospects weren't encouraging. He started back down the slope, retracing his steps. As he approached the cricket ground he wondered if his Dad had enjoyed anything like such an eventful day as he had. Apparently, Bill Symes had scored thirty-seven not out, and Dick was there to clap him off the pitch. Thus, father and son were both in quite a jolly mood on the drive back home, though Dick was a little wistful to say the least.

1967

Ignoring the advice of the Xog folk, Dick did wear flowers in his hair in 1967. Some hippie, more hip than the rest, named that year 'The Summer of Love' and it has remained so ever since. A lot of people were claiming to have seen God too. This usually came about from imbibing what the British Government chose to call 'dangerous drugs'. Obviously they weren't that dangerous or so many people wouldn't have tried them, even coming back for second helpings because they liked the experience so much.

Dick left school and home at the same time and went to live in London. His parents, rather naïvely, believed that he was engaged upon his studies at the L.S.E. Dick quickly found more fun was to be had away from the confines of being a student.

He began to spend most of his time in the Kings Road and Portobello Market. Having discovered an entrepreneurial spirit lurking in his wallet, he had quickly realised that an income was to be made selling antique gear to pop stars and their groovy chicks. Military jackets, furs, boas and velvet, all was grist to the mill of Sixties fashion. Dick had no objection to hanging out in Ladbroke Grove with the rich and famous. If you were a provincial boy in London, it was always better to blow your cool, and your mind, in swinging company.

The usual crowd were gathered in *Finches* that particular Friday night when the plan was hatched. They left Hammersmith at midnight and drove through the night. By the time they got to the West Country, dawn was breaking over the moors. A portable tape recorder guaranteed that the strains of Pink Floyd would sweeten the mood of the drowsy travellers. Pop music was different back then, it actually meant something. Now it is aural wallpaper, toilet paper even.

The weekend exodus from the metropolis had become quite an event. Dick was happy to be in the company of these artists, writers, poets, and musicians and join in their revels. These 'beautiful people' as they were known (usually by themselves) regularly congregated around the town of Windleroot, anxious to live out the rural idyll. With a sprinkling of the English aristocracy to add spice to the mix, the fashionable elite were regularly to be found sitting around a campfire at the foot of the Nob. In that blissful Summer, troubadours, sages, and many a princess danced in a world of sunshine and sweet reveries. They it was who on starry nights evoked once more the fairies on the hill, and told tales of wizards in secret caves and kings who rode upon the grassy downs.

The L.S.D. was probably in the orange juice that they had all swigged down so heartily in the early morning light. Dick, no stranger to this particular drug experience, was taken by surprise on this occasion at how quickly it rocketed him into loopy land. Suddenly fascinated by the sparkling dew on his *Anello and Davide* boots, he knelt down to examine this kaleidoscopic phenomenon and was sent further into Technicolor Dreams by the laughter of those around him. Climbing to the top of the Nob in Cuban heels was also a pantomime, but nothing compared to what he saw when he got there.

Buddha and Jesus Christ fell out of the sky while the Goddess stretched out her palms to embrace him. The tears fell from his eyes and streamed down his face. He realised someone was staring at him, not unkindly. For all he knew it might have been Brian Jones or some other pop princeling. They liked slumming it with the plebs in those far-off, far-out days. Words floated in the air like silky doves.

"You're a Pisces like me man, they're spaced out all the time."

Dick wandered away from the tower; he had seen enough coloured balls and rainbows whooshing into the clouds and wanted to see if there was any other strange stuff that might take his fancy. He found what he was searching for in the person of King Arthur and a brace of knights. Friendly enough they were, and only too willing to show him the cave where Excalibur, the Holy Grail and the Ark of the Covenant were all hidden. It flashed across Dick's synapses that The Cuboid wasn't among the treasures. Right on cue, came the flying saucers.

Three this time, flying in formation out of the sun as Dick emerged from the mouth of the cave. They circled in the air then flew away from him till they were merely dots over the horizon. Dick heard a voice in his head.

"The time when you are in need of us we will come again."

When he saw the film of the U.FO.s a few years later – three minutes of Super 8 – it was remarkable. It appeared so mainly because of the photographer's desperate attempts to keep the image in frame. The camera jerks around, reflecting the puppet-like movements of the stoned youth pressing its trigger. As he focuses on what he is seeing through the view-finder, the poor guy is trying to control his astonishment at the same time.

When the tweed jacket appeared round one of the curved paths that circulated the Nob, its owner saw Dick first. Continuing to look ahead, making sure he would maintain his balance on the uneven ground, the gentleman spoke cordially, each word measured and precise.

"Hello, there. Fine day, don't you think?"

"Hi. Yeh."

The smiling face above the old school tie was friendly enough. But there was something about the eyes that caused Dick to readjust his already high-wired perceptions. It was as if he were looking into deep pools filled with glistening diamonds.

"Why do ye seek?"

Attempting to reply, Dick discovered he could hardly put one word in front of another, let alone one foot, something he was also attempting to do at the same time.

"Well, you never know what you might find."

The man laughed out loud; the sound almost knocking Dick off his feet. It was like thunder trying its hand at ballroom dancing.

"Good. Good. That's very true."

Dick felt compelled to ask the stranger the same question.

"Why do ye seek?"

Dick was not certain that the reply was actually spoken. But the meaning was there, in letters ten feet high – in the air in front of him.

"I seek in order to serve."

Raising his stick in a gesture of farewell the man continued along the path. Many years later Dick was to discover that what he had been given was the only true response to that magical question. He also had the strange impression that somehow he would meet Mr. Tweed Jacket again, but in different circumstances. Dick was absolutely right, but in another star system far-removed from his own galaxy.

Later, Dick found himself in the town walking along Lowe Street. In those days, the shops were a sublime mix of butchers, bakers and wurzlestick makers. Some of the locals stared at the dandy in snakeskin boots and a brocaded jacket. When he tried to talk to anybody he couldn't decide if it was him or them who wasn't making a lot of sense.

Don't you want to bicycle our Thursday umbrella sandwiches? Very pretty very on elephants exactly.

Dick floated back to the Nob to share the company of his friends, all in a similar state of mild psychosis. It wasn't always going to be this way; he knew that only too well. As the man had insisted a few years before, times were already changing. Dick realised that what he wanted was very different to the pageant that was daily acted out in front of him. Sometimes the two coincided, but less often now. He decided that real reality wasn't such a bad state after all. That too had its own novelty and variations.

The way ahead was to work, travel, and then work some more. When he went out into the world again it didn't take Dick too long to realize that many of people he met were sound asleep. He also learned to avoid those who talked nonsense, unless it was humorous twot of a very original kind. Those who met him in the decades that followed probably saw only the smallest fraction of his real self. Like an iceberg, nine tenths of Dick Symes was hidden from view, he made absolutely sure of that.

Part of Dick's memory was tucked away in the Twenty-Seventh Dimension with the Cuboid, a state of affairs that didn't bother him, as he wasn't consciously aware of it. And thus life for him continued, largely uneventfully. Things were not to change until fifty years later – right where we're going now. So that's very handy and dandy, isn't it?

II

2012

Vargle Snipe was the sort of operator who was always on the lookout for anyone who might be useful to him. Coming across young Beans, he had approved of what he saw. Straightaway Beans had received the summons, one that he knew it would not be sensible to ignore. The room where they met was at once faceless, and easily forgotten. Invariably these are the surroundings preferred by men who do not want to be noticed – those beyond the law.

The Fulham traffic could be heard from the street below, faint but insistent. Beans waited. Vargle Snipe was in a league far removed from his own, he knew that. He made his play – Beans listened.

"I like the way you do fings, son. I can use you."

"Fanks."

With that, Beans agreed to be used.

"That's right then. Now, I got a little project coming up I want you to sort out for me. I'll give you a bell a bit later on."

Beans went on his way, certain he would be called again very soon. He was right, this time he went to Holland Park. In a hotel suite that smelled faintly of disinfectant, Beans met Colin. Cropped hair, a smile so false it might as well have been pasted across his face, he owned a voice that was tailor-made for making announcements about late trains.

"Colin's a planning consultant ... he fixes fings up for us, y'know in those circles where the big wheels turn."

Such arch phrasing might have given the impression that Vargle Snipe was merely an eccentric. Beans, who was a shrewd judge of the criminal fraternity, knew better. Snipe was the sort who would dispose of – permanently if necessary – anyone not fulfilling his expectations. When Snipe spoke, Beans listened. Just as carefully, he agreed with whatever was proposed. Not once was Beans asked for his opinion, and neither did he volunteer it.

Finally, he was given 'the list' – the names of a dozen characters currently 'useful' to Snipe. It was his habit to compile a different version each time he started on another 'project'. Those selected came together briefly, and parted company just as quickly. Beans was given his orders.

"What I want is for you to get a nice little place for my guests. You're *Mr. Jackson* when you're settin' it up, alright? Conference room … nosh … and a bit of quality *entertainment* … you know what I mean … afterwards. Your job on the day … remember this … make sure all the business goes the way we want it to. That way I'm happy, and so will everybody else be too."

Beans agreed and a moment later was left in no doubt that the meeting was over.

"Give me a bell after it's all done and dusted. Good boy. Now then, Colin, we've got a few little things to sort out."

Colin Sopwith smiled in vague farewell. Beans went down in the lift and walked briskly away from the hotel. As soon as he got in his car, he started to jab numbers on his mobile. While negotiating the streets around central London, he issued his own commands.

"Rove? You and Goldie get over to the shop soon as y'can. Alright? Make it 'alf-two."

At noon Rover picked up Goldie from the *Plum and Wallet* in Brentford. As soon as he got a text from Rover, he left his drink on the bar, twisted his tie back into shape, and went out into the street. Goldie buttoned his jacket while glancing up at the skies – rain, any minute. Rover, was parked on double yellow lines, two wheels on the pavement. Goldie loathed the black BMW with tinted windows, but he got in it.

"Alright, Rove?"

"Not so bad, Goldie. 'ows yerself ?"

"I'll get over it."

"Well, yer gettin' on a bit now enncha? Eh?"

"Fink you're clever doncha? You'll be fifty one day."

"Yeh, bet I won't be like you though. They'll have some wonder drug by then, stop people gettin' old and miserable."

Rover grinned and started off. Gunning the motor already, thought Goldie – flash. They turned into the one-way system on the main drag. It was Saturday, and the good citizens of Brentford were already clogging up the pavements, eddying in and out of the shops. Goldie thought it was as depressing a picture as anyone could ever wish to see. Even being at one remove, behind a shield of glass and metal, wasn't enough – he still felt part of it.

Goldie's mood, never light, moved downward a few notches ever nearer to the slough of despond. It was a destination that was never far away these days, and the two pints of lager he had sucked down in the pub didn't help. He should have gone to the Gents as well.

A maze of roads led onto the M25. Rover headed east, manoeuvring into the fast lane and turning up the radio at the same time. Mildly squittering before, the volume was now loud enough for Goldie to be annoyed by it. He didn't say anything, just added the sensation to the list of inner complaints that always stacked up as his day continued. Rover stared straight ahead, a small vein in his neck intermittently keeping time with the music.

Here comes the static
Just like automatic
I can no longer talk to you
Like I wanna do.

"...The Tantric Grasshoppers ... remember ... real cool sounds ... all through the day and night ... all the time ... on Estuary radio ... Estuary the sound of Ecstasy ... the sound around...

"Good that one ennit. I like that. Gets yuh."

Rover switched lanes and took something out of the pocket in his leather jacket – a joint the size of a roll of wallpaper. He lit the twist in the end and inhaled deeply, as if he was doing deep breathing exercises. After a few more Herculean tokes he waved the spliff in Goldie's direction.

"Have a blow on this, mate. Cool you out."

"No, fanks."

"S' good gear."

"Nah. I'm too old for that game."

"Beans told me you're too old for *this* game n'all."

"Yeh?"

"Only tellin' yuh."

"Right. Fanks for that."

Rover went back to fiddling with the radio, finding another station that spewed out the sort of pop music he liked.

"That was Bobby and The Beasts ... You're so Beautiful ... everybody here at Estuary loves that one ... we sing it round the place all the time ..."

Goldie watched the M25 unrolling like a strip of black lino into deeper suburbia. Maybe Beans was right – call it a day. One more job – this one perhaps. What would it be this time? Probably the usual – putting the frighteners on some geezer, keeping on doing it again until things were sorted.

"Wot we doin' on this one then?"

Goldie had to shout to be heard above the music.

"Wozzat?"

"Where we gotta go for this number comin' up then?" Local? What?

"Dunno. Beans didn't say nuffink abaht it."

Rover threw the roach out of the window. Goldie reflected that it didn't matter whether he smoked the stuff or not, he always ended up feeling doped when he got out of the car. They left the motorway at Junction 24. The sky was now the colour of polished pewter.

Beyond the Leisure Centre in Potters Bar were the edges of a faceless estate. Blocks of flats, the colour of raw pastry, lurched into the air beside the road. Here, the urban sprawl had seeped like an oil-slick, leaving behind the sort of housing that might have been designed by a serial-killer. Rover followed a narrow track between two rows of garages, stopping in front of the green metal doors of a warehouse.

Goldie got out and looked about him. Since the last time they had been here more rubbish had piled up. It was like wading around in a huge skip. Rover flashed the central locking on the BMW while Goldie prodded the bell push beside the sign that read *Milton International Importing*. He had often wondered who Mr. Milton might have been, if he had ever existed at all. A shadow appeared behind the reinforced glass door, remaining there for a moment, then disappeared. Rover and Goldie waited, the older man's patience speedily becoming as thin as rice paper.

"Woss goin' on?"

Eventually the shadow returned to open the door. Shaved head and a blue suit, several gold chains quite visible beneath the shirt. Goldie was looking at someone he didn't know – didn't want to know.

"You the new geezer?"

"Might be."

"I'm Goldie, son, and that's Rover."

"Yeh?"

Goldie stared.

"Woss your name then?"

"Farver Chrismus."

Goldie stared even harder.

"Right. Clever."

The geezer in the blue suit grinned impudently. His collar shifted an inch or two, revealing the tattoo on his neck – a livid green butterfly.

"Derek."

"Right."

They followed Derek to the top of the stairs. Immediately in front of them was a room so small it must have once functioned as a cupboard. Three chairs and a low table took up all of the space. Goldie sat down on one of these, while Rover looked out of the afterthought of a window. Derek was now nowhere to be seen. Goldie looked at his watch – ten to three. This is what it was all about. Sitting around, waiting for someone – then get up and go and wait for someone else. Most of his life had been just that.

The room was hot, the air as thick as raw pudding. Goldie didn't think the window had ever been opened since the place was built – probably in the Eighties. A small pool of sweat was gathering at the base of his spine – it would mean the tail of his shirt would have a stain on it. The thought made him twist his lips in the way he did when he was annoyed, which was most of the time. Rover carried on staring out of the window. If anyone had asked him what he was looking at he would not have been able to answer. Rover only noticed what was important to him, and he always kept quiet about that.

Beans came into the room. Goldie didn't notice him. Beans had a way of being able to slide along walls, over floors and ceilings. He always had a sly grin, which made people think he knew something they didn't. Never telling anybody anything, just suddenly announcing what was happening, that was another of his tricks. Beans turned other people's way of seeing things upside down. It put people on edge. Beans knew that, and he worked on creating that kind of tension. He could usually do it just by being there. His kind of control was based on fear, not strength, and he needed to have that power more than anything else. It fulfilled all his needs – his pleasures, his ambitions, everything.

Rover and Goldie turned to look at Beans, but he didn't respond. He knew he had that effect on people; he watched them watching him all the time. They thought by doing that they would know what he was going to do next. Beans knew that too, and he then did something they wouldn't have expected. Then he went back to doing what they thought he would do – for a bit. That way he always kept people guessing and second guessing as well. It made them tired very quickly – doubt is a very powerful weapon. Make someone not sure he can trust what he's seeing and you always have the advantage. Conjurers do it all the time.

The silence went on. It seemed to make the air even thicker. Goldie twisted in his chair; his shirt was definitely damp now. The sound of his voice when he spoke was like steam escaping from a kettle.

"So woss 'appenin?"

Beans appeared not to hear the question. At least, he did not reply, which was very different. Another silence followed. Rover continued to stare. Goldie was finding it more and more difficult to breathe. Suddenly he realised Beans was speaking.

"Nuffin' 'appens, Goldie, until I say it does, awright?"

"So, what we doin' 'ere then?"

Beans came up and stood close to Goldie. He looked down, leering at him.

"What you're doin' 'ere right now, Mister Goldsmiff, is gettin' up my nose. I don't like that. I don't like people who work for me gettin' arsey. I'm runnin' this show … *me* an' not no one else … you understand? I don't want questions, Goldie. I got enough trouble gettin' the answers I want. When I need you, or any uvver geezer, to tell me what they fink about summink, I'll give you a bell, awright."

The look Beans turned on him made Goldie seem to shrink into the chair. His shoulders hunched up and he had the look of a dog that will do anything not to be beaten one more time.

"Alright, Beans, me and Rover was just wonderin'…"

Beans had teeth that stuck out over his bottom lip. Nature's warning to the world they were dealing with a dangerous rodent.

"That's the difference with you and Rover, Goldie, or hadn't choo noticed? He keeps his gob shut … you don't."

Beans shouted the last few words and as quickly as he had come in, slipped out of the room. Goldie was starting to look like a punctured beach ball, shapeless and slowly deflating. Rover stopped staring and looked round at Goldie.

"Oh, dear, Goldie. He's right ennee? You are too old for this game."

Goldie felt as if he were in a trance, he was gasping for breath and wondered, as he often did these days, if he was going to have a heart attack. He sat, unable to move, for what seemed an age. Then he was aware that somebody else had come into the room. Goldie jumped in his chair – the thought that it might be Beans terrified him. It was Derek who, in a casual way, handed Goldie a thin wad of money, crossing the room to give Rover the same.

"Beans says bofe of you gotta get new whistles, then be at the *Arcadia Relax* 'otel, next Saturday mornin' 'alf-ten…"

34

Rover looked enquiringly at him.

"Flash gaff off the Brentwood roundabout."

Rover nodded. He waited for Goldie to get up out of the chair. Derek and Rover glanced at each other as Goldie, now looking old and defeated, almost fell down the stairs. On the way back in the car, it was no better; he was silent, hunched in his seat. Finally, he spoke.

"He shoulda never spoken to me like that. Woss 'is game? I do me job, do what I'm told, always 'ave."

"Beans is the gaffer, Goldie. The old criss-cross. Don't say nuffin' till he does. Bit like the Queen, mate. Speak when you're spoken to. Know what I mean?"

Goldie was holding his hands over his head, like a child desperately praying for sleep. Outside, the rain had begun again, falling gently at first then with a dull insistence.

III

For Dick Symes nothing much else happened in the twentieth century. He had to wait until the next one before he was served a big slice of good luck pie. It was worth the wait. An aunt in Hampstead, who he had barely known since his time at Digbeth Junior School, popped her clogs. After the lawyers had clawed their own share out of her estate there was still a lot left over for Dick. No other claimants coming out of the woodwork, he was left holding a cheque as fat as Fred Emney.

Dick had always liked the idea of owning a house in Clinton, the posh part of Barstowe. Since the 1990s, properties there had cost rather more than a king's ransom – the price of an entire royal family would have been nearer the mark. No. 30 Richardson Gardens was a cornucopia of lofty ceilings, alabaster fireplaces and ornate plaster work. It always surprises our American friends that we have so much of this stuff left in England. What astonishes them even more is that we don't take it all too seriously.

Dick bought the place in the Spring of 2012. He dealt with Mr. Kyte the solicitor, representing Mrs. Dolores Peabody his client. It was agreed, for a consideration, that what furniture there was could remain, and Dick was grateful for that. The first night he went to sleep in a brass bed and, for a moment, believed he was some Edwardian Grandee. He felt differently when the springs began squeaking tunelessly in the small hours.

During the night Dick's brain had been peppered with one thought. A name – *Standley-Strange*. To Dick it seemed oddly familiar. Wasn't there some Marvel Comics character called Dr. Strange? But, with a long list of chores to get the house ship-shape and Barstowe fashion, he forgot about it. Standley-Strange, however, had not forgotten about Dick Symes.

While investigating the rooms in the basement he discovered the brass plaque. Tarnished and dusty it was, but a firm wipe with a piece of rag did the trick. Dick's rudimentary polishing seemed to make the metal sing, as if rejoicing in its new life.

Dr. H.M.Standley-Strange BA. MA.

When Dick held it in his hands, the light coming through the gap in the basement shutters splashed onto its decorative font. Just the sight of the name transported Dick into another time and place, one that for some reason he rather liked the feel of.

He went out into the street and examined the pillar on the left of the front door. The four screw holes where the plaque had originally been fixed were still there. Without quite knowing why, Dick rummaged around, found a screwdriver in a cupboard and restored the plaque to its setting. He stood and admired his handiwork, and as before the metal seemed to glow with a celestial light.

Whatever Dick's view of its transcendental quality, it was not one shared by the vandals and varlets skulking in the shadows of Clinton. Twice in one week, the plaque was levered off the wall, and thrown into the private garden opposite. Dick was not be deterred; he had the metal parts of the sign ingeniously wired so that the owner of any errant jemmy would receive a 240 volt shock. Result – the sign stayed put, and a pleasing patina began to form about its bevelled edges.

When Dick had discovered his prize, wrapped about it was a newspaper of comparatively recent date. The name 'Standley-Strange' was at the head of one page. The article was sub-titled 'A memoir of a great man and a dear friend', and was written in a style known to men of letters as 'purple prose'. After reading it Dick detected more than a whiff of lavender …

Hector Milverton Standley-Strange (1914–2010) was renowned as a devotee of metaphysics. Yet, behind the mysterious mask and occult dabbling lurked a very typical Englishman, one of a kind no longer encountered, and great is the loss to all of us in this nation. Hector was the sort often to be seen sporting a paisley cravat while breakfasting on Oxford marmalade. If the mood took him, he would also sport white spats and cane. He was a figure who represented an era long gone. Standley-Strange belonged to that singular breed of gentlemen, at one time often seen in our University towns, or at Lords Cricket Ground who invariably wore a boater, a striped blazer and immaculate cream flannels.

His was the cultured voice to be heard often on the wireless. One promoting a view of such infinite wisdom, yet seemingly so obvious, that a dozen pundits would snarl because they had not thought to make the same point themselves. His kind are now rare; society no longer has a place for the urbane eccentric. In our increasingly conformist society he would be regarded as unacceptable, even a danger to the false democracy that passes these days as civilization. The twenty-first century is one quantitative in its values, dull in its aspirations. Standley-Strange's idiosyncratic personality could not have been encapsulated in a sound bite, or come handily wrapped, intellectually sanitized, in cling-film.

A man of many parts, as many as the mind could invent, in turn serious and surreal, he was like many of our island race – an enigma. No man can totally free himself of his personality; he will always play a part in the drama that is his own life. It is also true that few of us choose the character that we will play, and often it is thrust upon us. Those that are content with the part they are assigned are fortunate, for they are at ease with the world. Standley-Strange was not one likely to rail against Dame Fortune for long.

To visit him in his house in Clinton would always be a delight! How glorious would be the garden on a May morning! Roses, white, old-fashioned, with petals as soft as maiden's cheek, broadcast a scent as intoxicating as fine wine. Irises would stand aloof from the rich beauty of the camellias, and the gorgeous pink of azaleas would harmonise with them. Narcissi would be peeping out from behind crowds of columbine while foxgloves stood seductively among them.

Oh, the timeless atmosphere in that secluded place! The backdrop of the play, enacted for the visitor's pleasure, was the old garden walls covered in clematis and honeysuckle. Above the stage were the trees – benign and, protecting. Pastel and chartreuse magnolia, golden laburnum and plum, the leaves already hinting at copper tones to come – the garden was always majestic! A statue of Pan playing his pipes sported with Venus in one corner, and songbirds clustered about the little table that resembled a Greek temple. Mauve Wisteria clung to the pillars of the verandah and the wall of the house – all was idyllic.

Although he possessed a worn copy of Mrs. Beaton's Book of Household Management and several other tomes of the culinary art, Standley-Strange would never have considered consulting them. To him, cooking was akin to alchemy – intuitive and redolent with arcane secrets. Ones that could only be revealed to the worthy adept. He often remarked that in England the spectacle of a man dining alone inspires pity, in France – never. La vie est trop courte pour boire du mauvais vin.

I was honoured to dine with him more than once. One particularly splendid meal I shall always recall. The weather was warm and the various courses were served in the glorious garden I have described. During proceedings, Boswell, his devoted cat, was curled up beneath the hollyhocks, his tail twitching gently. The fayre was gazpacho and French bread to start with then poached salmon and new potatoes with parsley and an English salad. Standley-Strange could never be enthusiastic about what he considered was the bourgeois habit of serving melon; he remarked that to him, 'it had all the attraction of wet cardboard'.

It was known that the most extraordinary parade of characters came to consult Standley-Strange on matters supernatural and arcane. To ordinary mortals, such as myself, these things were also unremittingly opaque. The study where Standley-Strange took his clients was as formal a room as the one that he set aside for dining. It did however have certain exotic features – a chaise longue, an Oriental carpet and glass case filled with stuffed birds, apparently an heirloom.

The mahogany desk and revolving bookcase gave the space the air of a Gentleman's club. Various plants in pots were grouped by the windows. A group of prints featuring Bedouins and camels hung upon the William Morris wallpaper which, over the years, had faded becomingly.

The library, with its fireplace and the leather armchair next to it, was a scene that hinted at quiet evenings in utter contentment. Bookshelves covered every wall, and loose volumes were stacked on the floor and in any corner where there was available space. A scholar's paradise, but more than that, here the soul of Standley-Strange roamed freely.

It is a rare thing if at some time in his life a man does not realise he has become as a caricature of himself. We will always be actors, and often so well do we play the part assigned to us that we cannot assume another character. The most impressive of those who choose to take the stage are magicians, and magicians are the most compelling performers of all. They deliver their lines, make their moves, in as many dimensions as there are possible to imagine and make their final exit with a bow and a flourish. They leave only impressions – perhaps the echo of a voice that lingers in the air, a certain look, perhaps. Standley-Strange, as he would occasionally reveal to me, believed himself most sincerely to be a magus.

The actual performance of the magician is his gift to this plane – an attempt to define the indefinable. Such men create a world about them, and in doing so become the closest to the gods as it is possible to be. The soul of Standley-Strange always sang, a celestial melody was constantly in his heart, and it was not impossible that cherubim and seraphim regularly joined him in a glorious descant. It was not difficult to imagine Standley-Strange walking with angels, gazing upon endless horizons, and being intimate with the brightest of stars. It had once been remarked that his tenacity to solve a particular knotty problem in the astral realm for his client was on a par with Sherlock Holmes. My readers will be relieved to hear that my subject never, in my experience, *had recourse to pipes of black shag, or a five-per-cent solution of cocaine. His was a talent nurtured in a realm beyond our vision of the heavens.*

Accompanying the article was a grainy portrait of an imposing gent in formal evening attire. The features were welcoming, but those of a man who definitely could not be taken for granted. Meeting him, Dick thought, would have been akin to coming across a bear in the woods. He had the oddest feeling that such an encounter had already happened at some point in his life but the details were, for the moment, lost in some distant mist.

That night the moon was almost full, with a solitary star next to it. Over the rooftops of Clinton was an eerie silver light speckled with blue. The alchemy of the hour made past ages mingle with the present, and at the same time the landscape of Dick's dreams became equally mysterious. Another age began to dominate the usual panoply of images he experienced when asleep. These became so vivid that Dick wondered if he had suddenly mastered the art of time travel. The images came as if he were reading from some novel written in the late nineteenth century.

Philomena looked out onto the great expanse of lawns that, with the immaculately kept gardens beside them, were the great feature of Brenton House. One of the jewels in the crown of Victorian England, now bathed in June sunshine, it stood as a monument to all that the Empire had achieved. Philomena decided that a walk around the lake before luncheon would please her. She knew that the talk later would be only of Brunel's great ship being launched from Bristol. The prospect did not bring as much joy to her as did the morning air.

Philomena returned to witness one of those domestic mishaps that precipitate a drama. Earlier, the windows in the drawing room had been opened by the maids, and a thrush had flown into the room. Vainly endeavouring to regain its liberty, it had flung itself, first at the walls, and then at the ceiling. The efforts of a quartet of domestics to capture it had merely reduced the poor creature to a state of near terror. The situation seemed hopeless.

At that moment a figure passed by the window. Captain Standley-Strange, gorgeously attired in a red uniform, his whiskers immaculately curled, responded immediately to Philomena's summons. Entering the house by a side door, he marched into the drawing room and within moments, the gallant captain held the bird in a firm but gentle grip. Bowing to the company he returned once more to the garden.

Philomena rushed to the window. There before her was enacted a scene as if from one of the fairy tales that had so delighted her as a child in the nursery. The Captain, such an epitome of beauty and strength, held his hands aloft, and released the bird into the air. With its flight went Philomena's heart, soaring to the heavens. She thought she had never seen anything so wondrous in her entire life.

The Captain, aware that a pair of beautiful eyes were fixed upon him, turned and smiled. Philomena flushed becomingly. It was as if Aphrodite, that most benign goddess, had answered the peal that rang out so clearly from two hearts. Hardly aware of the ground upon which she walked, Philomena joined her beau upon the lawn. If any words were spoken, neither of the pair remembered them in days to come.

Thus, Philomena Hillsborough-Gresham was, soon after, wed to Lancelot Standley-Strange. The Captain, upon the very day of their meeting, had intended to take ship to India to serve with his regiment in the Punjab. Instead, he remained in England, and a week later resigned his commission. It was always said that any member of the Standley-Strange family had a purposeful air about them, as if always certain where their destiny lay. Such a resolute act, although not upon the field of battle, brought Captain Lancelot Standley-Strange the greatest happiness any man could ever know.

Dick woke to the absolute conviction that the demigod so described by the ephemeral narrator was the father of Standley-Strange. He had, on waking, also plainly heard a voice. What it had said to him did not make a lot of sense, but he knew that it was not to be ignored.

Save Windleroot! Go its aid! Great danger surrounds the sacred Isle of Teflon!

As a gesture more charitable than sensible, Dick took on the services of Mrs. Wolynyski to do a little light dusting once a week. As luck would have it her closest friend had once 'done for Mr. Strange' as she quaintly phrased it.

"It was not long before that chentlemun he went to his maker, God rest his soul I'm zinkin'. Basha she say he talk all the time of that town

41

... some place ... Vinklepoot ... Vendlerood ... Vindlerottle ... I dunno, Mister Seemes ... "

The roar of the Dyson drowned out any other confidences Mrs. Wolynyski might have shared with him. Curious, Dick looked up 'Windleroot' on Wikipedia where, with nefarious links, he was directed to other more obscure sites. What came to light was that 'Windle' was Old English for a basket, that 'root' was from the Old Norse *rot*, and a 'windlestraw' was the name for a thin and unhealthy person. He gleaned also that in the Middle Ages the peasants would have sounded a long 'i' in *Wyndleroot*.

The sound of the front door closing told Dick that Mrs. Wolynyski had left. The telephone then rang, and something very extraordinary happened. Dick Symes experienced an uncanny transformation in his character when he answered the call. He wanted to be someone else! He picked up the receiver to hear the strident tones of Morley Trumpton, a man he had never met.

"Hector! Morley here. How's tricks with you ... been exorcising any interesting incubi lately?"

Several things happened simultaneously in Dick's brain, and all in the space of a nano-second. The victor in this skirmish of the synapses was a notion that then transformed itself into a performance.

"Trying to sell me a book, old chap ... "

Morley Trumpton was an exotic creature in the cultural jungle of the twenty-first century. A breed that has become almost extinct – a bookseller. A misanthrope early in life, but one who still gained a modicum of amusement from the vagaries of humanity. He was a *littérateur* with no ambitions to write, but one who possessed incisive views upon writing. When a lugubrious individual suggested that everyone has a novel inside them he remarked that, with very few exceptions, it ought to stay there. And here was Dick Symes talking in a voice that was not his own and believing he was Hector Milverton Standley-Strange B.A. M.A. And the extraordinary thing was – Morley Trumpton was totally and utterly convinced.

"Sell you a book, old man? Thought never crossed my mind. Except ... Can I not tempt you, with some little volume of *belles lettres* combining history and astronomy, perhaps? Got an absolute glut of those at the moment for some reason ... *Orion in the Iron Age* ... *Uranus in the time of Coriolanus*? Suit you, guv? See you right, squire. No? Ah ... well ... no one can say I don't try."

"You never cease to impress me, Morley. You never lose your touch

... the well-honed patter."

"Don't I? Hang on I'm going to get in a more comfy...that's better."

Dick could clearly see Morley in his imagination. Generous of girth. Collapsing into a well-cushioned armchair ...

"I did want to ask you something ... "

"Ask away ... I never refuse money if offered ... and waffle is absolutely free. But tell me first ... have you been waving your wand at witches in Windleroot?"

"The very place I wanted to ask you about. After all these years, you now turn out to be psychic."

"Don't be impertinent."

"Perish the thought. Tell me all."

"About Windleroot? The New Age Nirvana? Not much to tell, really. Old Jimmy Jamerson runs *The Maze*, the only decent bookshop in the place ... pops in here sometimes ... he just about gets by ... like all of us. Stocks a lot of bilge ... has to ... and shifts it too ... sometimes got a few interesting bits. Go and see him sometime, he'd be pleased if you did. Had some flaked-out floozie in tow last time I saw him. Anyhow, why all this sudden interest in the crazy world of crystals?"

"Curiosity mainly. Tell me what Windleroot's like now ... remember I haven't been down there since the Sixties."

Morley wheezed a little before answering.

"Some of those little villages round there are very snootsville. You still get some old Colonel type asking you to pop down and sniff about round his library. It's either the Peninsula Wars or moth-eaten porn. Some of those old boys got hold of some pretty fruity stuff in the old days. But, to keep to the point ... something which I rarely do as you know ...Windleroot ... because it wasn't snooty ... got easily taken over by the Fascist Freak State. A lamb to the slaughter really ... mint sauce included."

"I think I'm getting the picture."

"In our day it was the underground, now it's the alternative society, in my view, still run by dictators and dick-heads."

Another name came unasked into Dick's mind.

"I see. Do you know somebody called Hobbit Socks?"

"*Who*?"

"Something like that anyway...Nibblet Oxo...?"

"Oh, you mean *Rivet Boxer*? He's the mayor. Old hippie type – minus any of the love and peace. That went long ago, if he ever had any of it in the first place. I've an idea he was once a copper or a bookie's runner or something. Jimmy's mentioned him once or twice ... he runs one of those ghastly little emporiums down there ... places that sell tripe to the tourists. The thing about bloody Windleroot ... I wouldn't mind if it was just plain vulgar ... like Weston-Super-Mare ... it's all that pompous piety. You know, we're enlightening your soul at the same time as we're nabbing your cash."

"Is it really like that?"

"Worse. It's all turned full circle, like the Middle Ages all over again – the devoted pilgrims on their knees in front of the bejewelled casket. Inside ... the monks solemnly swear ... is the shrivelled Bobby's Helmet of some pious saint ... the poor sods then unloading their very last groat for the privilege of sniffing it."

To Trumpton a tangent in the conversation was always to be savoured.

"And Mr. Boxer runs the Tescos of Teflon?"

"Now who's being cynical? Anyway why do you want to know about him for? Is he a celebrated necromancer as well as being a nerd? Is there to be a magical battle at dawn on the top of Windleroot Nob? Choose your weapons ... pentagrams or pea shooters..."

An old-fashioned bell went a-jingle-jangling.

"Sounds like you've got a customer."

"Hope springs eternal. I may yet eat today."

"Best of luck, and thanks for your help."

"Tootleoo, Hector. Keep your wand strictly beneath your robe ... there's a good chap."

The visitor turned out to be a Jehovah's Witness. After dismissing him peremptorily, Trumpton was aware that distant parts of his mind were receiving urgent signals, at a speed quicker than he could process them. He launched himself at the laptop on his desk and began to Google furiously.

Hector Milverton Standley-Strange b. August 15th 1914 – d. 2010 – aged 96.

Trumpton read this gobbet of information twice before he would accept its veracity. Hector had died two years ago. Fair enough, it was certainly possible. He had only been in touch with him on rare occasions in the last ten years. But that did not answer the question now burning in his brain. Who the hell had he been talking to just now? Trumpton, although an authority on the supernatural, was pragmatic. Somebody was winding him up – tighter than a bloody top.

IV

Since the 1980s Windleroot had been the Demonic Disneyland of the New Age. It would have been better for the world if it had suffered the same fate as many a medium-sized country town – having a by-pass and a pedestrian precinct foisted on it, or being in the grip of *Tie-Rack* and *Next*. That would have been a simple fate compared to hosting a den of thieves outside the Bodice Temple. It was all a tawdry façade, The Quest was merely a sight-seeing trip, the Holy Grail yet another rip-off. The arrogance of the ignorant held sway in Lowe Street. The cafés – Huckleberry's and the Red Lettuce – along with the pokey little stores that sold the trappings of the New Age – were like an unsightly rash on the face of Windleroot.

Covens of commerce were lined up along the street like cheap Parisian whores – *Mytheltoes, Krazy Krystles* and *Paganorama*. This last emporium was managed, in a loose sense, by Rivet Boxer – the mayor of Windleroot. He held court as the Demon King in the palace of gloom, while his wife Squiddle and the assistant Zeep played the part of the Ugly Sisters in this grotesque pantomime.

Once the premises had been an honest ironmongers; there was nothing straightforward about the place now. In more innocent times, Durston Biles, the khaki-coated owner, had weighed out nails by the pound, dispensed paraffin, and sharpened spades for a shilling. Once, merry banter over the price of clothes pegs, bean canes and bales of chicken wire was to be heard. No more. Rural chaff had been ousted by an Estuary whine, or the rarefied jargon of sallow-faced fakirs in open-toed sandals.

The intended ambiance of Paganorama was Gothic, the reality Hammer Horror with lashings of sleaze. A jumble of dusty debris, concealed morbid visions and nameless things dangled like blood-sucking bats from the ceiling. Shapeless garments, black or bilious green, hung in a dingy alcove. Books with lurid covers, caskets embossed with meaningless symbols, phallic candles, lewd statuettes – all were displayed in all their ugly splendour. The price tags attached to this plethora of piffle displayed illusion and insolence in equal measure.

Upon a stool, perched like an arthritic crow, was something female. A few centuries before, looks alone would have guaranteed Zeep to be a certain candidate for the faggots. She would have sizzled at the stake in the market square, whilst pustular peasants gawped at the spectacle. True to form, this apprentice crone dabbled in witchcraft, and 'did the cards'. In the hierarchy of Windleroot society, Zeep Delly held the rank of a scullery maid.

The absence of any heating in the shop meant the girl shivered involuntarily on that chill Spring morning. The door suddenly clattered open and Zeep trembled, this time in apprehension, rather than an impending approach of hyperthermia. Her employer, the aforementioned Rivet Boxer, resembled an oversized gnome with the gait of Quasimodo. Greedy and lecherous in equal measure, his clothes were shabby and shapeless. His outfits were frequently stained with the greasy sweetmeats with which he constantly stuffed himself.

"Morning, Zeep, how are we? Any punters about this morning?"

Rivet shuffled about while his eyes went flickering about the shop, as if making sure that none of the plastic bats had taken wing since the previous day.

"See my email about the Satanic incense holders? No? So, obviously you didn't see the other three I sent about new stock either … sort of important, actually … like urgent … things have got to be sorted out today or we might be in big trouble with our suppliers … "

Over the years, Rivet had honed the techniques of the tyrant. Keeping several steps ahead of anyone he was talking to, never revealing what he was thinking about or doing, these were essential tactics. Shrewd enough not to be caught out telling outright lies, but always misleading others – in this way he sought to rule the world of Windleroot. To Rivet, other people were always the enemy, particularly anyone to whom he owed money, including his staff. This consisted solely of Zeep. By using expressions such as 'our staff', Rivet convinced himself he was running some multi-million pound corporation, rather than a third-rate junk shop.

He shuffled behind the counter, leaning over Zeep to reach the till, his breath reeking of the fried bread and black pudding that had featured large in his breakfast. When opened, the till, like Mother Hubbard's kitchen units, revealed little abundance. Rivet slammed the drawer shut in irritation. He took to leaning morosely on a cabinet stuffed with cheap rings of ugly design and worse execution. Zeep watched his fingers straying towards the buttocks of a *deshabille* witch about to be rogered by an obviously excited Beelzebub. That this shiny, polyurethane figure bore a strong resemblance to her employer seemed somehow inevitable.

Zeep cowered in her employer's shadow – fear, and a curious longing, fought for dominance in her doughy breast. Rivet was an arch druid, and that sort of stuff made a huge dent in her very impressionable mind. Rivet himself was all too aware of the effect he created on the girl, and took advantage of her as much as possible. Mainly, he ensured that she worked for starvation wages. The other intention, carnal in nature, he intended to bring to fruition as soon as the opportunity presented itself.

"Right … well I have to go off and see a few people. If you can sort out our mandrake root, and pack up the herbs this morning, that would be a good thing. See you later."

Rivet slouched off, sending a lascivious wink in the direction of Zeep. The enamoured girl pinked, her heart fluttering momentarily beneath her black nylon blouse. After a moment or two of vacant reflection, she eased her ample buttocks off her stool, and ascended the stairs to rummage around in the stock room. After some minutes she returned with bags of pungent smelling greenery, and a sheaf of transparent packets. Her task was to divide, weigh and pack the 'sacred herbs' into saleable portions. Zeep did not know, or chose to ignore, that she was intimately involved in dealing a Class 'C' drug.

Peddling marijuana was the only line in Rivet's business that consistently showed a profit. Taking risks was as the act of breathing to Rivet. If things went awry and the Law stepped in, he intended that Zeep would take any rap. A conscience would not be found among a list of Rivet's personal possessions. Zeep, the willing maid, toiled diligently until lunchtime, uninterrupted by the rarity of a customer.

Dick was gradually getting used to the idea that he lived in a haunted house. He did not recall the solicitor – Mr. Kyte – mentioning the presence of any spooks when he showed him round the property. Perhaps 'haunted' was too strong a word, suggesting an Elizabethan nobleman, head beneath his arm, or the sound of rattling chains. This phenomenon would be filed under 'presence'. It still had a marked effect on Dick, who took to poking about in odd corners of the basement or sitting in particular rooms just to see what might happen. During this period he became mildly eccentric and did not shave for a fortnight. Such personal neglect didn't make him look dashing or glamorous, just a bit rough round the edges.

And Dick pondered, mostly, on the nature of fate. Why had it been him who had bought the house? A man had lived there for sixty-odd years and, quite reasonably, had died on the premises. But did he not have the good grace to remove all of his mortal self from the planet? The spirit of Standley-Strange lingered. Drifting, floating and to Dick's current state of mind – insidious.

Apart from the furniture the only other tangible legacy of the previous owner was a large black cat. Realising that his owner was on this plane no more (cats being acutely aware of these things) Boswell had sought out new quarters. Periodically he kept an eye on the garden at his previous abode and, sensing that Dick was now in possession, returned. Dick was first aware of him one morning when he appeared from behind a stone urn. Slowly and deliberately the cat made his way towards Dick in order to establish if he was worthy of anything approaching friendship.

He was certainly an imposing creature, as is a bald eagle or a Great White shark. Not that Dick yearned to share the sofa with either of those particular creatures of an evening. Dick noticed that Boswell was always purposeful. He had the air of some consul on a mission in the Gilbert and Ellis Islands sorting out a little local trouble between warring tribes.

With staring eye and strident gait, Boswell advanced until he was less than a yard away from Dick. He then halted and lay down. It is said that a dog looks up to you, a cat looks down on you, and a pig looks you in the eye. Boswell must have inherited a few porcine genes, for he regarded Dick in a way that the latter found eminently disturbing. The cat's eyes appeared to grow larger, filling with emerald fire, and though he tried, Dick could not avoid their gaze.

Boswell raised himself up on his haunches, his front paws splayed out in front of him. Very deliberately, he opened his jaws wide to reveal rows of murderous teeth. These jagged peaks seemed to grow larger until they were those of a ferocious beast. Dick's whole body trembled … he was about to be attacked! Rigid with terror he waited for what he was certain would be a bloody and painful death. As that thought entered his head, another quickly followed. A voice, measured and reassuring, came to him.

"Nothing you can see is worthy of fear."

The words echoed for what seemed an eternity then slowly died away. Dick was in a walled garden in Clinton, watching a cat scuttle behind a bush. If this phenomenon happened again, Dick was determined to be more prepared. There had been two images and the more Dick looked the more they became each other. One moment he saw a cat, the next some lion-like beast. By turning his head slightly Dick was able to locate the exact point where the change happened, simple as that.

But that was only the beginning of the questions he wanted answered. Which of these impressions was the real one? His reason told him one thing, another part of him said otherwise. And why had this all happened anyway? The voice again.

"All is possible."

"This is magic isn't it..."

No reply.

" ... how does it work?"

"There is an old saying, 'He who hath the how is careless of the why.' "

And Dick had to make do with that ... for the time being.

It is a fact that the indeterminate, shifting nature of our world has always attracted the artist and the thinker. Such individuals are fascinated by ambiguity and oblique ways of seeing the world. The artist and the philosopher consider the very uncertainty of perception to be its greatest fascination. The multi-faceted crystal that is existence also shines the brighter when wit and jest are reflected in it. The essence of humour is the 'hidden variable', the spontaneous reaction. The only ambition of the jester is to make us laugh; he mocks us when we take life, and ourselves, too seriously. Humour reflects the ultimate in detachment from our situation, and as such has the highest spiritual goals. It has no ties with the mundane and desires none; the world is solely there as the raw material for amusement and jolly japes.

V

The *Arcadia Relax* lay between Barnet and Watford. Part of a development conceived at the fag end of the Thatcher era, that time when the Iron Lady was no longer rust proof. The design, of purple pillars and screeching yellow plazas, might well have been conceived by a six-year-old playing with yoghurt pots. Towers of black glass lurched into the sky from green concrete rhomboids, chrome fountains pointlessly squirted water into fetid pools. Jagged shapes of pipe and girder randomly stabbed the horizon, while inches from the grumbling traffic, stunted and sickly trees struggled for life.

To the hotel management, Snipe's 'project' was just another gig. The buffet had been hauled out of the deep-freeze and laid out on tables in the Falklands Suite. The Spring sunshine washed through the plate glass of the conference room slowly thawing the vol-au-vents and scotch eggs. In the foyer Beans loitered in the shadow of a giant bamboo plant anchored precariously in an inadequate pot.

M'bouto, one of Snipe's regular stooges, greeted the guests as they arrived. His glistening pallor challenging his shiny suit in brilliance, he directed them to the second floor. Yes, Mr. Jackson of Golden Trove Investments would welcome them all there at noon. The trickle of arrivals turned to a substantial tide. Soon a dozen or so men in suits, some carrying briefcases with intricate combination locks, were gathered in the suite. Moving among them was Julius Gowley, a man so unctuous as to make Uriah Heep appear aloof. He introduced them one to another and a certain amount of small talk ensued – much of it so small as to be almost invisible.

Ensconced behind a two-way mirror in a room adjoining the suite, Beans checked off 'the list'. The two lawyers – Sibe Schwab from New York, and his English counterpart Roger St. John-Pemberthy: Athel Pumnik representing financiers Plattel Rhomber: Colin Sopwith MP: property developers Atherton Hook and Dowie Ringle and a few moneyed gentlemen from the Middle East. Rover and Goldie, slightly too conspicuous in their new suits, hovered.

Beans' focus zoomed from one to the other. Speedily he came to his own conclusions – to a man, bent as a nine-bob note. He said as much to Gowley when he joined him.

50

"Y'know, all that rabbit aht there don't mean nuffink. But, we got 'em all 'ere togevver Mr. Gowley … an' what we gotta do is make sure they do what Snipey wants 'em to. You and that MP geezer get that sorted, right? We pays 'im to impress … an' you…to be a king-size creepass, right?"

Gowley winced slightly at this impromptu job-title.

"I'll certainly be as persuasive as I possibly can, Mr. Jackson."

"Oos that bloke wiv yuh – the shine?"

"Stan M'boutu? Oh, he's a good lad, Mr. Jackson, very much one of us. I can vouch for him … been with us for a very long time."

"Kosher is 'e?"

"Really, Mr. Jackson, both of us always give of our very best…"

Beans' eye was steely.

"You gotta do better than that, treacle. Two 'undred per cent Mr. Snipe wants…"

Gowley loosened his collar a little.

"I assure you, Mr. Jackson…"

Beans cut him short.

"Right, yeh. Now listen, sunshine, when the 'ole fing's in the bag, an' they been good boys, then they can 'ave their little treats. Dere's booze, coke, tarts, porn videos, everyfink, in them private rooms downstairs. But they ain't 'avin' a shake of none of it till you gimme the wink they've signed up to everyfing, alright?"

"I certainly understand, Mr. Jackson."

Beans jerked the curtains across, obscuring the mirror. He moved towards the door.

"Right, let the dog see the rabbit."

At precisely noon, Gowley and Beans slid into the suite. Some of the guests stared inquisitively but it was as if they looked upon a mirage. One moment Beans was flitting among them the next he was not there. Beans knew them for what they were – hard men – and he was as flint himself.

When Gowley introduced Athel Pumnik he was almost as oily as the curls in the other's hair.

"Plattel-Rhomber are not just part of the money-market … they *are* the money-market. Mr. Pumnik is the UK's top…"

Pumnik, slight and slick, was not content to listening to anyone else for long. He was used to flying the plane not being a passenger.

"At present we are involved in 98% of all major trade transactions throughout the world. *Ninety-eight per-cent.*"

Beans' expression did not change. He regarded Athel Pumnik as if he were no more important than the water cooler in the corner of the room.

"That's a lot then innit?"

Pumnik continued, as if he had not heard.

"Our daily turnaround is several *billion*, and that is in all recognized currencies. The market rises and falls totally on how we ourselves do business."

But Athel Pumnik was addressing an audience that had dwindled to one – himself. Beans had moved, figuratively, to the Middle East. Gowley followed, catching the attention of the most prominent member of the group.

"Mr. Jackson, may I introduce Mr. Izal?"

"'ullo. Alright?"

"Mr. Izal owns several hotels in Riyadh."

"That's nice then."

"Nine to be precise, Mr. Jackson."

"Nine? Right. Lovely."

Gowley was watching the conversation slowly expire in front of him. Desperately, he oozed the more.

"And one of them is rated at seven stars is that not correct, Mr. Izal?"

"Soon another will be the same. I have to speak with the people in my country who arrange these things."

Gowley was relieved when a smiling Colin Sopwith came over to join the group.

"You manage to arrange things so perfectly where you are located, Mr. Izal."

The other flashed a set of teeth, riddled with gold.

"Of course, Mr. Sopwith, it is the way of things is it not?"

"Ha, ha, but it takes someone as *expert* as yourself to bring about so much success."

Izal's tone was one of perfect reasonableness.

"In my country, we have a saying that 'no man can stop the ocean'. It means that one cannot halt the advance of progress forever. Sometimes we find there are those who in their ignorance protest at some development. It might be some new building perhaps ... they believe it will change the lives of the people in a bad way. These types are a danger to the government and also to the rest of our people. Our rulers have a simple solution to the problem. It is like this, if there are reports of wolves being seen anywhere we send men with guns to exterminate them."

Sopwith nodded encouragingly. Izal turned to see what impression this remark had made on Beans, but he was no longer there. Mr. Izal looked momentarily disturbed. Such a phenomenon reminded him of the fakirs and sorcerers he had seen as a child in the square in Marrakech. Mr. Izal did not think Morocco was a good country; it was not modern – not forward-thinking, like his own.

Conversation flowed more smoothly with the lawyers. They recognized Beans as being of a familiar ilk. He was the kind their colleagues often defended in court. Atherton Hook and Dowie Ringle, the developers, were already succinctly bonding with them. Has this not been so for fellow capitalists ever since the Industrial Revolution? Sopwith too knew that once the money men were squared, then the deal would gather its own momentum.

The MP noticed that Pumnik, Izal and the rest of the moneyed set had moved into a corner. They were intent only on exchanging tales of wealth, moved and manipulated. With the aid of Gowley, Sopwith ushered the rest towards the replica oak table. On it was laid out a detailed plan of the town of Windleroot and the area round about. They clutched their drinks, looking interested.

"Firstly, to give you some history … Windleroot is a rather, shall we say, quaint little place. It has a reputation for ancient traditions … history and myth that sort of thing. You may actually have heard of it … Certain landmarks … old ruins etcetera attract a substantial amount of visitors, particularly in the summer months. The most famous is Windleroot Nob…"

Sopwith speedily turned to more secular matters.

"For this site we have in mind a commercial development … on the scale and conception of the American model."

Sopwith nodded in the direction of Schwab, who patted his briefcase encouragingly. On the plan Sopwith's finger traced the yellow line that represented Lowe Street.

"At present, there are a number of small businesses – mainly located here – retail … catering … food outlets … this will all go, naturally … consumer and tourist demands being met entirely in one location. Now, gentlemen, we come to our vision of the twenty-first century – maybe even the twenty-second."

Sopwith revealed his prize with a flourish. They gazed upon it and a detectable buzz went around the group. The sight was certainly impressive – a monumental piece of modernism. Coloured with a palette generated by digital alchemy – teal, sea green, aqua, plum, lavender, rose and tan – glowing incandescently. Sopwith's voice, like a surreal Santa Claus, provided an echoing soundtrack.

"Basically, it's a giant shopping mall – three hundred and thirty-five square metres – so it will rank in the world's top five. Parking for ten thousand vehicles on the perimeter … apart from specialist boutique installations … a giant food court. The big boys … McDonalds, Starbucks, Subway, naturally, plus all the anchor stores – Tesco … B&Q … Argos … Do-it-All. It's deliberately not your Waitrose and Benetton … because it's been shown … again and again … they're not the big money spinners. This is mainstream not exclusion we're going for … and our site houses all the major natural attractions in the vicinity under cover."

They liked what they heard – ideas that were all about power, ownership, and profit. Control was what they wanted, and expected.

"All the shopping malls in the entire world are owned and managed by only two companies. For us … it's ours and it isn't. What that means is it's underwritten by the big boys but actually owned by the shareholders. This whole project is self-funding. Every quid that goes in any till in the whole of this mall is ours. Parking fees … rents … everything scrap of income … one hundred-per-cent profit."

Spontaneously, they applauded – this was even more of what they wanted to hear. A golden future for them all – paradise, anything and everything. Sopwith gave them a look that said 'and there's always more'.

"I wonder that nobody has mentioned that evil word – that old party pooper – 'planning'. Well, as nobody has mentioned it then I will."

He grinned, and they all grinned back. He'd got them now.

"In the UK, legislation was passed in the Nineties to restrict the construction of Shopping Malls in cities."

Dramatic pause – a smile of triumph.

"We've got planning already."

Another pause.

"How have we managed that? Because we have English Heritage … the most powerful rural lobby in the country on our side, gentlemen. Lord Sturmington has deemed us to be 'a benefit to the community'."

The light from Sopwith's beaming features could have illuminated a small town or two for over a year.

"And, here's the real cream on the cake, the ratable charge is set at zero. The local council, and the county council as well, have in effect waived those charges by agreeing to return our contributions at the end of the financial year. We involved the Tourist Board in all negotiations. They have convinced local government that the revenue we will generate in other areas is well worth the rebate."

On the plan, Sopwith pointed to what looked like coloured sugar lumps.

"Apartments. What is called these days 'hybrid housing', provided at an adjustable tariff, for any of the local inhabitants displaced by the development. Again, the council are with us on this one too."

Sopwith turned and faced them – they were converts, disciples to a man. He gave a 'thumbs up'. This was no random gesture to the crowd, it was a sign to Gowley who immediately whispered into his phone.

"Things are going very well indeed, Mr. Jackson."

Beans agreed.

"Once Sopwith nails them two what's still ditherin' abaht, we're laughin'"

Gowley passed instructions to Sopwith who in turn confided to St. John-Pemberthy the approach he would employ towards Izal and Pumnik.

"Financiers are only glorified accountants … they spend their time doing bigger sums that's all. If the numbers work they say 'yes' … they're trained … like Pavlov's dogs. Show them, not 2+2 = 4, but 2+2 = 25, they don't know what to do. If then you say – 'the other nineteen is your profit' then they savvy and don't argue with anything after that. How can they?"

St. John-Pemberthy smiled and said things like 'absolutely' and 'brilliant'. And Sopwith was proved absolutely and gratifyingly right – the money men agreed immediately. The lawyers looked on as papers were signed. Effectively it was all over – a coup for Beans and his cohorts.

At that moment he reappeared in the room, congratulating them all for being so sensible – so wise. They didn't feel patronized, just immensely grateful to Beans to allow them to be part of such an occasion.

"… and fank you for coming, gentleman. I'm very glad indeed to hear all our arrangements have been satisfactorily concluded. Now … I expect you would like to 'ave yourselves some sorta…relaxation… after bein' so busy 'n' all that. You deserve it … if I may so."

One of the Saudis started to perspire. His eyes began to jiggle like hard boiled eggs on an ice rink. Beans slipped away, Gowley in tow.

"It's two o'clock now. Give 'em till six. Then chuck 'em all out and clean the place up."

"Six o'clock, Mr. Jackson? Of course. Stan and I will make sure everything's neat and tidy."

"You better."

"You can rely on us, Mr. Jackson."

Beans handed him a thickish envelope.

"That's for the tarts and you two…"

"Thank you, Mr. Jackson."

Gowley was almost bowing as he took the money. Beans walked off in the direction of the restroom. He was drying his hands when the Saudi who had been noticeably sweating came in. Treating Beans as if he were an old acquaintance, he called out to him over the roaring blast of air from the blower.

"Will you be joining in with the entertainment, Mr. Jackson?"

The leer on his face was like a cut melon. Beans brushed a speck of fluff, visible only to him, from his jacket.

"No fanks, mate, I gotta bitta paperwork to catch up on … know what I mean."

In the foyer, the girls had arrived – fantastic creatures, encased in leather and fish net stockings. Petite and Amazonian – in their eyes were the prospect of unspeakable delights. Mr. M'bouto courteously ushered the giggling gaggle into the lift. Upstairs the party began to grow restless. The buffet had remained untouched almost from the beginning.

VI

Rivet Boxer pulled on a shabby coat over his striped pyjamas, squeezed into his wellington boots, and prepared to take the dogs out for their morning walk. Once outside, he realised that the air was certainly more appealing in the middle of the orchard than inside their dwelling. The rumours of the squalor in which Rivet and Squiddle lived were surprisingly accurate, considering that most loose talk in Windleroot was positively free-range.

The home in Badcorn, a village some miles from the town, was more than a blot on the landscape, it was an overflowing inkwell. At its rotten heart was an old scrote-weaver's cottage. To this, several caravans and an old Winnebago had been affixed to make a mini shanty town. The fabric of the whole thing, particularly the original cottage, was in a parlous state.

Of the interior, it could only be said that housework was not a talent Squiddle excelled in. A blind man, finding himself in the kitchen, might have believed he was in the elephant house at Barstowe Zoo. The décor in the dining room might have been designed by Miss Faversham, and the rest of the rooms looked like the Somme after a night's heavy shelling. Interesting-looking fungi had for some years been growing up the walls in the bathroom. Rivet's previous wives had put up with him and his pad until they could stand it no longer. Squiddle, it appeared, did not even notice.

Rain in the night meant there were several small lakes to be negotiated in the lane. Rivet and the dogs trudged on, their owner intermittently calling to his charges.

"Bastard! Here boy! Come out of it!"

Rivet was the sort of wiseacre who thought it amusing to name a dog that way. Much of his life was spent guffawing loudly at his own feeble jokes. The popular consensus, that he was a tiresome bore, had permanently eluded him. Like Bastard, his own animal instincts had rewarded him with a certain amount of success. Minor conspiracies were always jostling for attention in the Boxer brain. He conceived enough plots to fill several allotments. Recently, a brace of schemes had occupied him. The first was immediate and carnal; the other meant sailing even closer to the wind than he usually did. Rash Rivet always went where no self-respecting angel would dare to venture.

It had started to rain and Rivet, feeling the splashes upon his balding pate, chivvied the dogs in the direction of home. Both had contrived to wallow in mud and other things even less salubrious, and it was a sodden and smelly trio that arrived back at the house. Rivet noticed that an entire row of slates was missing from the roof, and a length of guttering was hanging precariously from its fixings. He made no mental note of the fact. Dismissing from his mind anything that did not appeal to him was a habit he had acquired early in his life. Abandoning the dogs in the hall, he made straight for the kitchen, intent on making a pot of tea. As the kettle slowly came to life, he could hear Squiddle's snores from the bedroom upstairs.

Rivet took a tray on which was piled a small mountain of burnt and leathery toast, into the lean-to – fantastically referred to as 'the conservatory' by Squiddle. The toaster had ceased to work some months ago and he had been obliged to employ the grill, the result not being a great success. Equally disturbing to Rivet was an odour he did not immediately recognise. It was different from the usual stench that hung over the house. Decidedly more offensive, he suspected it had a sinister origin.

Rivet's instincts were correct; Squiddle's penchant for ritually sacrificing small rodents had left its mark. Next to some shrivelled nasturtiums was the evidence of her unholy pastime – the stumps of several black candles, an iron pentacle and, more alarmingly, a putrefying heap of fur and bones. Rivet decided to finish what remained of his breakfast in the study. At present that room was mercifully free of death and diabolism.

Deciding to get dressed, he ascended the stairs to the bedroom. Opening the plywood door of the wardrobe woke Squiddle, who turned a bilious eye in his direction. Even a voyeur in shades would not have found her an attractive spectacle.

"Do you *always* have to make so much noise clumping about? Wozza time?"

"About a quarter to ten."

"Bollocks! I was going to have bath … I haven't got time for that now."

Rivet was engaged upon putting his legs into a pair of only slightly soiled flannel trousers. He grabbed a shirt that had not enjoyed the attentions of an iron for some time. Intending to pull on his socks, he sat down on the end of the bed. A tide of fury came from its present occupant.

"Can't you do that somewhere else? I need to find something to wear and I won't be able to do that if you're hanging about up here getting in the way."

Rivet retreated down the stairs with a gaping fly and grasping one of his socks. He poured himself another cup of tea, and was taking a goodly slurp when Squiddle's fantastic form filled the doorway. She was attired in an outfit rather more off-the-wall than off-the-peg. It would definitely have won all the prizes in a fancy dress competition.

Encased in a pair of purple culottes which clashed blindingly with the turquoise top, all notions of colour-coordination were radically challenged. A pattern of scarlet balls of differing sizes covered her scarf. To further enhance this freak show of fashion, she had added lemon yellow leggings. Squiddle had surpassed herself; she resembled a cross between Humpty Dumpty and Guy Fawkes Night. Even Rivet, who was used to her bizarre dress sense, was taken aback. To take his mind off the sight before him, he offered a remark or two.

"Those guys from Essex have been in touch again."

This was part of Scheme Number Two, although dodgy, it held less risk than Squiddle discovering the details of Scheme Number One. Keeping his wife informed about some things and not about others was a tactic he always employed.

"Really. And what did they have to say?"

Rivet adopted the air of some priest dispensing indulgences.

"I think, mainly, they just want to keep in contact. They want to get a foothold down here and I might be able to help them out if need be."

"More to the point is … what can they do for us?"

"I think, darling, they could be extremely useful in our future plans. They'll want a slice of the pie … naturally … but I think it's worth giving that to them."

Squiddle's eyes narrowed until they were like gun slits.

"How big a slice?"

"Er … I'm not sure exactly … we haven't gone that far with any negotiations."

Squiddle deftly inserted the stiletto.

"Isn't that just like you, sweetheart, all mouth and no trousers. Much more important at the moment is you making some more tea … as you've just emptied the last drop out of the pot … I'd be extremely grateful if you'd do that."

While filling the kettle, Rivet continued.

"I'm certain they've got big London money behind them … and want to start up a business here. Now … you and I know that isn't easy. Nobody in Lowe Street is turning over much…except us, of course. That's why they've sounded me out. Anyway, wearing my other hat, as the mayor, a sizeable investment in the town would be good for everybody."

Squiddle snorted audibly.

"That sounds like the sort of twaddle I'm always hearing you coming out with at the Merchants Association meetings. If these guys want to invest in *us*, that's much more like it. Frankly, I don't give a stuff if everybody in Lowe Street goes bust tomorrow. Live in the real world, Rivet! No one in their wildest dreams would describe *Paganorama* as a going concern. Why don't you big up the shop, then flog them the lease, lock, stock and bloody barrel?"

Rivet looked hurt – a mediocre performance as always.

"I don't think that's very fair, sweets. I've put a lot of hard work into that shop … it has the potential of being the most successful place in Windleroot."

Squiddle was short and to the point.

"But it isn't, is it? And as for the 'hard work' you've put in, I for one have never seen any evidence of that. The place still looks like a tip … exactly as it did when you moved in on the first day. You talked that daft cow Fanny Jangle into putting up the money for the first year's rent … and I know she's never seen any of that back."

"Cash flow, darling. Speculate to accumulate. I've just bought in a lot of new stock…"

Squiddle stamped her foot and banged her fist on the table at the same moment – a bravura performance.

"You can't make any money and you can't make the bloody tea either. You useless fucking idiot…"

Rivet attempted for the umpteenth time to pacify his wife, a technique he had yet to master.

"Just coming. I did make tea earlier you know, darling, when I took the dogs out."

"I was up late last night … doing things…"

Rivet spooned some heaps of bargain box blend into the pot. He had his back to her when he spoke.

"I thought so … I had to clean it up…"

He came back to the table with the tea. Squiddle's eyes, lit like twin braziers, drilled into him.

"Have you been messing around with the altar?"

Rivet attempted to be nonchalant, though he knew he had wandered, unarmed, into dangerous territory.

"There was a ghastly whiff in there, darling. I had to do something about it."

Squiddle was now the hue of a very ripe tomato.

"I said...*Did you touch anything on my altar?*"

"You know I wouldn't do that, sweetie. I just got rid of the crap that was around those pots."

Without a word Squiddle got up from the table and marched off to investigate for herself. She never believed a word Rivet said about anything. However, she would have been most surprised if he had openly admitted to doing anything that he knew would annoy her. That was not his style; it was one based on cowardice and deviousness. Satisfied that his meddlings were inconsequential, she returned to the kitchen. Rivet, quickly assessing that he had escaped any severe punishment, was chatty when Squiddle sat down and took up the tea pot once more.

"I thought I might pop into the shop this morning and sort out a few things there. That vampire stuff from Budapest still hasn't arrived yet, and there's some other stuff I want to check up on."

"Right."

Squiddle slurped her tea a bit more, anticipating what Rivet would say next. She did not have to wait long.

"What are you up to today? Got anything special on?"

She chose not to look in his direction.

"Not really ... but sort of ... if you know what I mean."

Rivet smiled indulgently.

"That sounds just like your sort of day, sweetheart."

He might have attempted to kiss her fondly if Squiddle hadn't abruptly left the table and stomped off upstairs taking her tea with her. Rivet looked at his watch. He was behind schedule. No time to lose. He stood at the foot of the stairs.

"See you later, then, Squid."

There was no answer, and picking up his briefcase, which Rivet carried more for appearance than anything else, quit the house. He narrowly missed colliding with something *doggish* on the floor in the ill-lit passage, but unscathed, he made it to the car. Noisily he drove out of the yard and into the main road, nearly running down the postman. Oblivious, Rivet accelerated towards the town.

Upstairs Squiddle sat in front of her dressing table and scowled at her reflection. She knew Rivet was up to something, and had a shrewd idea what that was. For no longer than the merest second was Squiddle ever taken in by her husband. Swiftly, she made her own plans.

Meanwhile, the focus of her reverie sped towards Windleroot. The grass in the fields glistened from the rain that had fallen during the night. The ultramarine of the skies bore a passing resemblance to an early Constable. Not that Rivet's thoughts were in any way aesthetic, today they were undeniably carnal. His lust was growing more savage by the minute. By overtaking dangerously on a few bends he gained a little time. The clock on the dashboard showed half-past eleven. Rivet reflected that, if he scored this morning, that would set him up nicely for lunch in the Chuff and Peacock.

Zeep was polishing a brace of fibre-glass dwarves when Rivet, carrying an enormous bunch of flowers, came into the shop.

"Hello, darling. Now don't say I never think of you."

The bundle of blooms was shoved unceremoniously in Zeep's direction. Before she could mouth any thanks Rivet launched into his well-prepared spiel.

"I do have an ulterior motive actually."

Rivet attempted to appear coy and failed, his sly leer always taking precedence over anything subtle that he attempted.

"Oh?"

Zeep, in the grip of confusing emotions, merely stared.

"I desperately need you in the stock room in a minute or two. Just give me time to get ready."

With that, Rivet almost sprinted upstairs. Zeep stared at the plethora of chrysanthemums, retrieved from a florist's bin had she known, and wondered, in some trepidation, what was going to happen next. She did not have to wait long to find out.

"Zeep, shut the shop and come up here, will you?"

Her voice sang out in cheery reply like a young maiden in the meadow.

"Okay, Rivet."

She hurriedly locked the till, came out from behind the counter and turned the key in the shop door. She made sure to reverse the picture of the green demon, the inscription 'CLOSED' drooping from its mouth. She climbed the stairs, at the same time holding up her voluminous skirts as best she could. A little flushed and trembling from the climb, she peered into the gloom. The only light came from one of the phallic candles burning in a corner.

When her eyes became accustomed to the gloom she beheld an awesome sight. Rivet stood *sans culottes*, his member stiff enough to have supported many flags of all nations. He was staring hard at her, a curious expression on his face, one of abject determination. Zeep quivered like a sherry trifle.

"Come over here, love".

Rivet, ignoring the puzzled expression on her face, simply bent her over the desk, and none too gently either. In one movement he pulled up her skirts and removed a pair of rather voluminous undergarments. Zeep suddenly wished she had chosen to wear more chic lingerie that morning. More immediate was the sensation she felt when Rivet plunged his engorged joystick into her most private parts. At no stage of the proceedings had he enquired if he might avail himself of the privilege.

It was true that she had, on occasions, imagined what the experience of being rogered by Rivet might be like. The reality was more astonishing than anything else. Rivet was ramming her vigorously, while all the time grunting and rasping as if he was manhandling heavy furniture up a narrow staircase. He was determined to prolong the pleasure for as long as possible. So desperately was he concentrating on this end, that he did not hear the sound of footsteps coming up the stairs.

Unknown to him he had been followed. Squiddle, pedalling furiously on her bicycle from Badcorn, had arrived in the alley behind Lowe Street. She had unlocked the back door of the shop and silently made her way up to the stock room. Reaching the top of the stairs, she impassively regarded the tableau before her.

Her husband, staring fixedly at a tattoo of The Grim Reaper on Zeep's ham-like buttocks, was about to climax noisily. Zeep, as unaware as was Rivet that they had an audience to their frolics, let out a yell – one not entirely prompted by pleasure. It was more astonishment, at the sheer volume of Rivet's seed as it gushed fervently into her. The sound of ironic applause was heard.

"Very good, darling. A great performance. I'm glad to see you keep the staff satisfied in every way possible. I'm glad to see that our girls are happy in their work as well."

Mortified at the sound of Squiddle's voice, Zeep froze with shame. With razor-like inflections, Squiddle continued.

"Why don't you pull up your knickers and pop off downstairs, Zeep sweetie. Rivet and I have a little business we must see to up here … haven't we, dear?"

Almost in a trance, Zeep did as she was bidden. Retreating downstairs, her boots could be heard clonking on the stairs. Squiddle then put her arms about Rivet's neck. In anyone else it would have been a gesture of affection. Being Squiddle, it was nothing less than a threat.

"I don't see why the staff should have all the fun, do you, Rivet?"

It seemed that Squiddle was massively turned on and was enthusiastically removing those parts of her costume she deemed necessary. The next moment, she had splayed herself over the desk in the same position that she had observed Zeep adopt minutes earlier. Rivet sighed deeply before concentrating on achieving a reasonable erection necessary for the task that lay ahead. With some relief he watched his member swell until it resembled the dimensions of a saveloy, while Squiddle waited, none too patiently, for this miracle to transpire.

"Hurry up, Rivet, I need a fuck!"

In a resigned fashion, Rivet set to work once more. On the floor below, Zeep, after adjusting her costume and sensibilities, reopened the shop for business. Taking up her usual place on the stool behind the counter, a sudden marked tenderness made her realise it would be more comfortable for her to stand. A moment later a pair of punky pagans came into the shop and began to examine the wares. One of them was idly sniffing some pyramids of goat dung – 'essential for evoking Pan' – when noises off began to markedly intrude. She stared inquisitively at Zeep.

"What's that?"

With mounting horror Zeep was aware of an unmistakable sound. Increasing in volume, it became a protracted squealing – like a sow in the throes of producing a generous litter.

"What is it? What's going on up there?"

Zeep thought quickly.

"It's a healing ritual … very intense … what you're hearing is the sound of the negative vibrations leaving the aura and going back into the uh, earthly plane. Very powerful energies they are."

All three listened intently until, with a deafening yowl, it ceased. The two girls stared at each other and hurriedly left the shop. After some time, Squiddle appeared, flushed and grinning like a Barbary ape, closely followed by haggard-looking Rivet. Squiddle took her husband's arm with a flourish.

"And now you're going to buy me lunch in the pub, aren't you, darling?"

Rivet, absently nodding in agreement, allowed himself to be led off into the Chuff and Peacock. As he went out of the door, he tried not to catch Zeep's eye.

VII

The headquarters of Plattel Rhomber took up most of the floors in a giant tower block overlooking the Thames. In Pumnik's room the pile of the carpet eddied like a beige tide. The meeting in progress was not going well. Already, Vargle Snipe and Athel Pumnik were at odds. The financier, feeling more than secure on his own ground, was inclined to be bumptious. Snipe was not one who took well to being patronised, and the atmosphere had quickly soured.

St. John-Pemberthy, having casually taken the temperature of the situation, had made camp next to a window. He appeared to concentrate on observing the traffic that meandered through the city streets below. Pumnik's piping tones continued, an accompaniment to a vain attempt to coerce Snipe.

"I admit your terms seem generous but those at director level, who naturally I am answerable to, apparently see the offer differently."

Snipe's mouth was a thin pencil-line. "Not sure where you're coming from. Half as much again coming back on your dosh, and you want more? That's *greedy*...I don't think I like that."

Pumnik's reaction to this was to puff himself up even more.

"The market situation determines the acceptability of the figures put on the negotiating table."

Snipe could feel the rage beginning. It always started with a cold stab deep in his gut.

"You're not listening to me are you? Trying it on, is what you're doing. Nobody does that to me."

Whether through arrogance or ignorance, Pumnik obviously chose not to see the warning signs. He continued to employ a condescending tone.

"Broad money growth, through asset purchase via investment, is always unpredictable and never guaranteed."

Snipe could not believe this was happening. With his other investors – namely the Izal contingent – any agreements were now a matter of formality. A steady stream of Putney hookers in their direction had successfully eliminated any difficulties there might have been with negotiations. This was how Snipe liked business to be done – ask what a man wants and give it to him – simple as that.

He believed, almost with religious zeal, that if he had to explain that he liked things to be done his way, the situation was not as it should be. Snipe had a habit of reducing to the status of puppies those who considered themselves to be top dogs. His standing in a world where having power measured the gap between success and failure, was high enough to matter. When Vargle Snipe won the game, others lost – heavily. Curbing his temper only by a hairsbreadth, he responded bluntly to Pumnik.

"Right. I didn't come here to be told this sort of crap … I don't want to hear no more of it."

Pumnik, unaware that his continuing existence upon the planet might be seriously in jeopardy, merely smiled beneath his tan. Snipe moved away from him as if the financier had suddenly become radioactive. For the first time in the encounter Pumnik's confidence wavered slightly. Snipe continued; his tone was acid, it bit deeply.

"I'll deal with you later Pumnik. Now … if you don't mind … I'll just be having a quick word with Mister Pemberfy here. So … what's 'appenin' then?"

Almost languidly, St. John-Pemberthy left his post at the window. He could sense Snipe's icy anger, always the most dangerous kind to deal with. It would not abate for some little time, but the lawyer had the advantage of being more circumspect than Pumnik. Neither was he one to be easily intimidated – attending to business was his only concern. He always addressed his clients as if he was totally *au fait* with the matters that really concerned them.

"Regarding the Windleroot side of things, the searches pertaining to the properties in Lowe Street have come up with quite a number of deeds of covenant … something I would naturally have expected. I don't see any problem there, but what is slightly puzzling are some of the legislative documents, supposedly held in the Council chambers in the Town Hall. I have seen copies of these and they are … to say the least … written in very archaic … and thus convoluted … terms. It will take some time to actually clarify what our obligations to the town council are … if we actually acquire these properties that is."

A slight twitch of the lips indicated to him that Snipe's patience was wearing thin to the point of being threadbare. St. John-Pemberthy coughed apologetically.

"It must be very frustrating and equally annoying for you to hear all this but I am duty bound to inform you of all the facts. Every other aspect of this business has gone extremely smoothly … far more smoothly than ever I could have expected…"

Snipe broke in sharply.

"That's 'cause I invest heavily in *co-operation*, Mister Pemberthy. I *pay* people to make things go smoothly."

The lawyer bowed, almost imperceptibly, and continued.

"I'm sure you do ... but this is not an ordinary matter of conveyance ... it requires rather more ... how shall I say ... *application of law*. These things cannot be dealt with using quite the methods that you might wish to employ."

"No?"

St. John-Pemberthy was quietly firm.

"Definitely not. We cannot afford to be *unorthodox* at this stage. The only way is through the proper channels ... and that takes time ... I'm afraid. Dealing with legal matters in rural areas often means moving at the pace that people there are used to, probably have been since the time of Elizabeth."

Snipe looked suspiciously at the lawyer.

"Elizabuff? What's the flippin' Queen got to do with all this then?"

St. John-Pemberthy raised a finger or two in mock apology.

"You misunderstand me. Elizabeth The First ... Good Queen Bess."

Snipe was in no mood for a history lesson.

"Right. Let's have all this wot we been talkin' abaht sorted then ... sooner the better."

"Absolutely. I shall be driving down to Windleroot myself tomorrow. I have to look a few things up in the Record Office in Barstowe on the way. Hopefully ... that will hurry things along a bit as well."

He looked purposefully at his watch.

"... unless there is anything else ..."

Snipe knew instinctively he could demand no more of the lawyer. St. John-Pemberthy accepted his curt farewell gracefully and, with some alacrity, left the office. Downstairs, he passed Beans in the reception area, and automatically touched his hat.

"Mr. Jackson."

Beans did not respond. The lawyer took no offence, always acknowledging another's desire for anonymity whatever the reason. He walked briskly out of the building, his mind exclusively on his own affairs.

In Pumnik's office, Snipe casually sat on the corner of the financier's desk. He picked up a pencil and tapped it lightly on the walnut veneer, his tone when he spoke was even.

"Mr. Jackson's coming up here in a minute...you met him already I think. He wants to have a little word, make things a bit clearer…very persuasive…very reasonable he is…my advice…you be reasonable too."

A light tap on the door meant that the secretary, rather nervously ushered Beans into the room. Pumnik licked his already dry lips. Vargle Snipe slowly removed himself from the desk.

"There are we are then, Mr. Pumnik. I'll leave you two together. I'm sure it won't take too long before you see our point of view."

As Snipe left, the silence that remained spoke of many things, none of which Pumnik wanted to hear. Half an hour later, in the car park of Plattel Rhomber, Beans could be seen in conversation with Snipe.

"Alright?"

"I fink he knows a bit better how we like to do fings, Mr. Snipe."

"Good boy. Quick word … all was needed, wannit?"

Beans nodded. Snipe pulled a fattish, buff envelope from the inside of his jacket.

"Token of my appreciation. Very pleased with the way you been 'andlin' my business. Very professional."

"Fank, you very much, Mr. Snipe."

Beans waited, he knew the conversation was not over.

"Windleroot – that place in the sticks I told you about. Fings are moving along down there … but not quite quick enough for my liking. I want you and your lads to 'ave a word with the mayor bloke dahn there – Mister Boxer. I fink he's amenable to 'elpin' us aht … if you know what I mean. See what you can do … "

"No problem, Mr. Snipe, just gimme the word."

"I knew you'd say that, son. I can rely on you – I like that."

"Anytime, Mr. Snipe."

Once more the slight movement around the mouth, the attempt at a smile.

"Give you a bell."

Beans nodded and walked away he always knew the exact moment when he had been dismissed.

Dick Symes was also interested in a trip to Windleroot, a place he had not seen since the psychedelic Sixties. A 'trip' meant something entirely different then. As Dick recalled, psychedelic drugs were employed to squeeze the brain into strange shapes and reassemble it later. The instructions for restoring that organ to its original state were invariably upside down too. Dick soon realised that driving to Windleroot in the twenty-first century was an experience quite as mind-blowing in itself.

The motorway resembled a dodgem track. It seemed that today impatience was considered a virtue as cars flitted from lane to lane and kamikaze motorcyclists leapt into spaces that existed only in an X-Box. Abandoning this three-lane circus for the A-roads brought little relief for Dick. Other drivers overtook with lethal promiscuity or pursued him relentlessly, inches from the rear bumper.

At Farkle there were temporary traffic lights and a bright red sign announcing 'Road Works'. Nothing that could, even in the loosest sense, be regarded as industry was taking place. Dick waited with that particular resignation the English have adopted, probably since the time of the Norman Conquest. On the lights turning green, progress was once more impeded by a scaffolding lorry parked unrepentantly in the middle of the road. The scaffolders themselves were engaged in hauling pipes about and paid scant attention to the chorus of honking horns. Dick contented himself with surveying the delights of the countryside – a fridge and a cluster of black rubbish bags abandoned in the hedge.

Still, June was the most delightful part of the English Summer, the time before the Solstice, when Mother Nature was quietly informed that the game was up for another year. July was often too blowsy and overblown, but now all was fulsome and bright. Haymaking had begun early, and the swathes lay like glistening emeralds upon the earth.

The tawny corn stood majestically in the fields. Swans, like the slender white stems of some exotic plant, lay among the spiky grass of the moors. Beneath a bower of ash trees, elderflowers clustered, creamy on the verge. Passing through the village of Duggett, Dick saw bent ancients chatting over a gatepost. The land became older, as if dark gods were jealously guarding their dank world. Suddenly revealed was the heart of the Isle of Teflon.

Leaving his car by the Old Chapel, Dick walked to the foot of Windleroot Nob and gazed at the sight before him. The mound seemed to be pulsating with energy, fuelled by the devotions of pilgrims over many a century. He walked among clouds of butterflies, afloat upon the early summer haze. Dick was aware once more of voices, and distinctly not mortal. The sacred mound of Windleroot was speaking to him.

More sounds came as if floating upon an eddying breeze. A woman sobbed for mercy and guidance – old priests, warriors weary of battle – their words all mingled with her cries. In the distance came the calls of the stones that had once made up the tower, and these, though barely audible, were just as potent.

Dick sensed that the spirits of the place, those eternal beings who had seen much and wondered more, were troubled. Their very reason to exist had been challenged, and they felt unwanted. The world they knew was about to fade and another take its place. It was not the inevitable rolling of the wheel of time they feared, but the knowing that those who came had no sympathy with their ways. If the spirits had been the guardians, these newcomers were the destroyers. They would lay waste all that had in ancient times meant peace and concord.

Dick had little time to take all this in as he was aware of other voices, distinctly terrestrial and nearby. They belonged to a noisy claque of tourists jostling each other as they passed through the gate, some waving cameras, all festooned with digital whatnots. Were they aware of him? Dick rather thought they were not. This was his first taste of magic, and the power to manifest it had been given to him by the spirits within the sacred mound. Another voice came to him too …

If he is wise, during his training the magician masters the technique of becoming invisible at will. It is not too difficult a procedure – the essential elements being a combination of practice and faith. Hamlet hints at the principle when, in the noblest soliloquy Shakespeare ever wrote, the prince reflects upon the essence of existence – 'to be or not to be'. By concentrating upon 'not being', the portion of space that we usually occupy is no more. No longer having a part to play in the conscious world, the individual is as good as invisible. By this method, whole kingdoms may be concealed – the Isle of Teflon, for instance, could at one time be whisked away into the aether at the command of the sorceress who resided there…

No one could see him! Dick was now as one of the spirits that resided upon the Nob. He was like them, a denizen of the otherworld. The conscious plane had no hold upon him, for it was the nature of magic not to consider the confines of time and space. Dick instinctively knew that even if he chose to return to the real world, it was unlikely he would be noticed. He would have been as a moonbeam mirrored upon the surface of a lake.

Dick's return to the conscious plane coincided with the weather becoming capricious. The charcoal-coloured clouds mobbing the horizon were assuming a darker grey by the minute. Dick drove along the curving lanes, once nearly colliding with a jogger in luminous shorts. Around one corner he encountered a pair of women, one sporting hair like a worn mop, the other with features the texture of pickled cabbage.

The storm announced itself with little ceremony and by the time he reached Furlong Street it was raining heavily. Dick pulled up outside the Maze bookshop and, remembering his conversation with Morley Trumpton, nearly went in. Hail was lashing the windows of the shops on the opposite side of the street and making a sound like gunshot. After a time the storm lost its anger and the sun returned.

On cue the endless parade began again in Lowe Street, menopausal matrons, weighed down with crystals the size of jam tarts, straddled across the pavement. A flower-crowned goddess or two mingled with gurus in moth-eaten Tibetan hats. Unshaven Antipodeans loitered outside The Bushwhackers Hotel while twisted figures cavorted in the churchyard of St. Geoffrey's – creating an animated version of a Hieronymus Bosch painting. Shamanic staffs clattered upon the pavement, the swish of shoulder bags providing a harmony to a drunk's mouthings at the passing traffic.

The slovenly and the tawdry, masquerading as the transcendental, celebrated its victory over the true and faithful pilgrim. It was smugly reflected in the cheap trinkets, graveyard black and medieval maiden's rags that were everywhere on display. The path to enlightenment had become overgrown and obscured by foul creepers. The map had been lost, and the one that replaced it now showed only false trails. The guides that had once aided the travellers upon the Quest had fled, taking the fingerposts with them for safe-keeping.

Dick turned his back on all this mayhem and drove back to Clinton. As he went past fields, newly ploughed and chocolate brown in the early evening light, the nightmare of Lowe Street was left behind. The essence of Windleroot Nob stayed with him however, and he felt as if only the thinnest of veils had separated him from this previously unknown kingdom. Other screens, more dense and opaque, would have to disappear before he could know the brightest light it was possible for any mortal to know.

72

VIII

In the dusk-filled garden Boswell was asleep beneath the azalea, his tail twitching gently. Dick sat on the verandah and watched the bees playing kootchie-koo around the flowers. When it got too dark to see, Dick went inside and called Morley Trumpton. It was time for him to lay his cards on the table – this time the whole pack, including the Jokers.

"Mr. Trumpton?"

"Speaking. Loud and clear."

"My name's Dick Symes. You phoned me the other night and we talked for some time. I think you were under the impression that I was an old friend of yours ... Mr. Standley-Strange."

Trumpton was used to dealing with all manner of rum coves. He thought this one might turn out to be more rum than that imbibed by Nelson's crew before Trafalgar.

"Ah, yes ... and now I am informed he happens to be the *late* Standley-Strange. My own fault for not checking up that my old chum wasn't actually brown bread."

"I bought the house from his sister ... "

Trumpton's tone was matter-of-fact, with just a hint of the stern and stiff.

"I see. And might I enquire *why* you pretended to be Standley-Strange? You certainly fooled me, all ends up, by the way ... "

Dick paused. Understandably, this wasn't going to be easy.

"I didn't actually *pretend* to be Standley-Strange. If you can believe this, I actually thought I was him ... um ... sort of felt his presence around me so strongly that it was as if I was speaking from a script he had given me ... "

A pause, probably the longest in the history of telecommunications, followed.

"... does that make any sense at all?"

Morley Trumpton sighed, it had to be wearily.

"All things are possible ... a few probable ... and nothing is absolutely certain. I have spoken. So the answer to your question seems to be 'yes' with reservations ... of course. I'm a man who likes to keep his options open."

Dick had a go at a bit of sighing himself.

"I hope you're not too pissed off about it all."

"No ... not at all. Take a lot to make me lose me rag these days ... well that's not strictly true. Dealing with the tosspots who try to tell me what I know already still gets me going. That sort couldn't find their own arse in the dark with both hands."

Dick was keen on asking a few questions himself, and started right in.

"How well did you know Standley-Strange though? I mean ... I've read some kind of obituary of him that I found knocking about here but ... what did he really get up to? For various reasons I really would like to know."

Trumpton took a moderately deep breath.

"Not sure anybody *knew* Hector terribly well ... or what he got up to come to that. He wasn't the kind of bloke who let people get that close to him. Oddly enough you found yourself telling your secrets to him but I'm damn sure he never confided any of his. I mean, he was twenty years older than me ... that's virtually an entire generation ... so he may well have had a circle of friends that I didn't know about ... though somehow I doubt it. He was a bit of a hermit when I first knew him ... more than a bit ... he was a bloody recluse."

"He never talked about what he did in his life ... in the past?"

"He lived in Paris in the Thirties I know that ... hobnobbed with some odd crew who called themselves *Les Enfants du Paradis*. I'm not quite sure who they were. I know he went out East ... Lhasa ... Kabul ... stayed for a time in an Ashram in India ... he used to say to me 'the world itself is the greatest of all teachers' ... in that way he had.

"But what about his family? He must have had some means to be able to do all these things?"

Dick remembered the vision of Philomena at Brenton House, the heroic knight, saviour of the drawing room – falling in love in an instant.

"Army I think. Father was well-to-do ... big place in London in Edwardian times. Kensington Gardens ... very swish ... loads of servants and all that sort of lark. I got the impression he was fond of his mother ... and his grandfather was a consul in the Punjab or somewhere. Mother inherited a gift for getting on with people ... comes of chatting a lot. I have some sympathy with that ... I can never willingly avoid a digression myself even if I can spot one coming ... "

"And the sister was the only sibling?"

74

"Dolores, yes … "

"Who I bought the house from … "

Morley was suddenly waspish.

"I bet you don't know how much Hector paid for it in 1948?"

"I hate to think."

"Five hundred pounds."

"It's funny that during all the time I was dealing with that solicitor bloke Kyte, Dolores never ever mentioned he was her brother."

"That's not totally surprising … she was quite a lot younger … ten or even fifteen years between them … and they were never that close. She didn't understand him … and certainly wouldn't have approved of what he got up to. She was a rip-roaring born-again Christian, and a Jehovah's Witness for a time too I think."

"So what *did* he get up to?"

"I'm coming to that. 'Don't be so hasty', as the tortoise said. It was Hector's mother who really went a long way to shaping who he was. She kept – a *salon*. The people who came to that read like a who's who of the metaphysical arts back in those times – Hayleyfont Topham, Mary Poole, P.G. Booth and Chester-Black … Hector once told me that for him knowing about the occult might have been the same for other kids as having railway engines or collecting stamps."

It was a long speech, one that had within it all possible openings, rather like a Swiss cheese.

"So what did he do with all this knowledge … "

"Simple. Wanted to be a magician from about the age of twelve …"

"And he was one?"

"Does the Pope wear a funny hat?"

Dick pictured someone with long white hair dressed in black with a big silver pendant dangling on his chest. It was an image that stayed with him for a long time – that was until he knew more about these things.

"Was he a Freemason? All that rolled-up trouser leg stuff … "

"A lot of people wanted to bag him … as one of their particular lot … these people do. The Grand Lodge claimed him … so did the Rosicrucians. The Theosophists wouldn't have anything to do with him, put it about that he was a black magician. The remnants of the Golden Dawn who were still active in Barstowe said he was a member of some very arcane inner circle … but nobody knew what it was. He was a bloke who got associated with the sort of magical society you read about in these flaky exposés and conspiracy theory things people write these days ... about cults so secret that nobody believes they exist."

Dick let that particular hare go, but started after another one.

"And what *is* going on in Windleroot?"

Trumpton wheezed with some exasperation.

"I don't know ... I really don't. Hector did, and used to mutter darkly about it all ... but unless you're gifted in spiritualism you won't find out. There is one thing though ... "

"What's that?"

Trumpton wheezed again this time in amusement.

"You were asking me about Rivet Boxer. I remembered after we'd been talking ... he was at Bumbles."

Dick wasn't sure he had heard right.

"Bumbles?

"My boarding school ... he was a fat little junior tick. Sort of kid who sneaked to our housemaster if anything went on in the dorm. Got me the whack many times. Vile little beast ... his nickname was 'smellyarse'."

"Very traumatic. No wonder he's like you say he is."

"Quite. I feel more sorry for the wives, he's had three already. This Squiddle is number four ... though I don't feel sorry for her ... let me see, Jamerson was telling me the names of the other three...Doob, Lilt and Scrag ... that was it."

"I don't believe it! You're making that up."

"Extraordinary, isn't it? Nobody ... even if they were writing some way-out novel ... would dare to use names like that. Talking of names, Hector once told me his nickname when he was at Eton ... slightly more salubrious than Rivet's ... it was 'Battleship'. "

"Why's that?"

"Initials of his name ... Hector Milverton Standley-Strange ... together they make H.M.S ... His Majesty's Ship."

Trumpton was obviously playing his favourite game of tangents, the conversation into other channels – babbling brooks even. Dick politely wound it up.

He opened the French windows and went to sit on the wooden settle that stood against the wall in the verandah. The moon was up, illuminating the bamboo against the garden wall. It swayed hypnotically, its narrow leaves making limp gestures towards him. The mauve tints of the lavender bush made the very air soporific, and he felt himself sinking into a kind of oblivion. Macbeth had it down ...

Out, out brief candle!
Life's but a walking shadow, a poor player
That struts and frets his hour upon the stage
And then is heard no more…

Old Bill certainly knew what he was talking about when he wrote that, Dick thought. He was no stranger to fairies and the like – and a lot of them in the theatre it is has been rumoured. Dick reflected, as one might under a waning moon, that there seemed to be a very thin line between life and death. And what is one supposed to achieve before all this candle-snuffing business? Happiness? Fulfilment? The man on the Clapham Omnibus would say that Dick had a toe in both of these ponds – living in a posh house in Clinton, and with plenty of change in the bank.

Dick was wafted away to another time and place. Was it Standley-Strange who he had met on Windleroot Nob that morning of mirages in 1967? Was his knowledge of magic the thing that would help Dick? He knew the greatest rewards had to be truly earned. As for discovering the Grail, he was most certainly a knight upon the Quest, but the nature and the timing of that great adventure seemed to elude him at this moment.

Hidden in the darkest corners of the cosmos are places that Time forgot. Empty hours, lost even to the most diligent memory wait, lying idle among abandoned aeons. These are the real wastes of time – absolute ages when nothing much has ever happened. The universe just continued without them and they dragged along behind it like a kid trailing his coat in the mud. In adolescence they turned churlish and resentful, having no desire to be part of any future. Eventually they joined the lifeless part of Time's web, burrowing deep inside its twisted spirals, determined only to cook up a vicious circle.

It was here, in the deepest parts of hyperspace that Fantuk and Zavrod were travelling. They had recently visited the planet Vood where life consists only of small luminous clouds interacting with each other by changing their shape. The two Xogs had to be extremely careful that no juvenile member of the population strayed within range of the spaceship's air conditioning. An accident like that would have prompted an intergalactic incident.

They had also journeyed to the double moon of Glemtard, a place inhabited by the Squagbo – creatures that have as many eyes as a King Edward spud. It had always been rumoured too that the Budfon birds in those parts fly upside down in order to display the crimson tufts on their forelegs. The two Xogs, no matter how much research they ventured upon, could shine no light on this question. Some forms of life they encountered fell within spheres beyond reason, and would turn the beholder's brain to bubblegum given half a chance. While compiling their reports, it was inevitably difficult to organise these impressions into any holding pattern. To persist with the gum analogy, some would remain forever attached to the underside of the cosmic pilot's seat.

After a week of all this zapping about among distant galaxies, Zavrod was as tense as a surf-board. Fantuk, being of a mercurial temperament, never tired of the diversity of creation. His insatiable curiosity made him eager to investigate inner space as well – those dusty sub-basements that held data of the most obscure kind. It was well-known that the richest vein of *cerebral imprint and posited thought* resided in a dimension parallel to the Twenty-Seventh. Fantuk thought it would be eminently worthwhile to make a diversion there on their return to the planet Xog.

Zavrod was less than keen on the proposal and, when this was suggested, protested vehemently. Fantuk waited until this fit of the sulks had run its course before quietly setting the controls for the heart of the sun – sort of. Fantuk had not forgotten the promised reunion with Dick Symes. That day and hour approaching, he was curious to discover what had elapsed in the fifty Earth years since their last meeting.

Xogs have no concept of forenames or surnames. The notion of a 'Christian' name baffled them even more than it does the members of some religions on Earth. Accordingly Fantuk referred to Dick as 'Mister Symes' – rather quaint and Victorian. He was at that moment collating a great deal of data concerning Dick and, like Sherlock Holmes, could not resist making the odd deduction. He was also thinking out loud, his remarks half heard by Zavrod. His fellow traveller was still miffed and thus not a Xog not at his best. In these moods he inclined to apply his gigantic intellect in a picky way. Fantuk was busy checking the screen once more.

"Is it not interesting that Mister Symes' life has not followed the usual pattern that these human creatures follow. He has not mated."

"Don't be disgusting."

Fantuk waved a flipper airily.

"I wasn't trying to offend, I merely mentioned that humans have a convention of pairing off with one of the *opposite sex,* as they are wont to refer to the difference in gender among their kind. After some arcane ritual, where they profess loyalty to each other, they live together in a domestic situation and then produce offspring. It is the method they use to guarantee that their race may ultimately continue."

Zavrod' eyes spun round like a crazed kaleidoscope.

"Just imagine participating in such a revolting exercise. Did you tell me once that they get pleasure from this activity? That is so *extraordinary.* I just can't believe it, they really are the most irrational creatures."

Fantuk looked arch.

"Apparently they think about this mating activity constantly. On Earth there is 'porn' ... "

"What can that be?"

"It is an industry which makes vast wealth selling moving pictures of individuals engaged in all sorts of mating acts, some of them totally unimaginable."

"If anybody else had told me this I would have said they ought to have a brain transplant. Talking of that, when was it we Xogs were implanted with hermaphroditic genes?"

"About fifty thousand years ago, I think."

Zavrod shook his horned head.

"Earth is just so appallingly primitive. If they didn't indulge themselves with this mating nonsense then they would all die out. That would be much the best thing. Their planet would then return to being a wild life park and that would be that. I would be much more inclined to visit the place if that happened – at least some of their animals and birds are reasonably attractive. More than could be said for *homo sapiens* ... most of them are incredibly ugly ... and the rest are just vicious and stupid."

As he was talking Zavrod deftly inserted a plastic tube into an orifice in the upper part of his body. A device in the craft then dispensed the juice of many exotic fruits into his body which then mingled with his own vital fluids.

"This is why I'm so fascinated as to why our Mister Symes is such an exception."

Zavrod shrugged, a few tentacles writhing in sympathy.

"Is it so important?"

"Although the Xog race has provided an answer to every philosophical and ethical question ever proposed ... there is still one aspect of existence that remains unknown ... even to us."

Zavrod's jolt almost detached the tube, which would have resulted in many colourful liquids being squirted all over the cabin.

"There can't be. I'm sure you're wrong. What is it?"

"The solecism ... the unaccountable exception ... the random aberration ... and that is what Mister Symes personifies. At one time on Earth society used to refer to his kind as bohemians ... artists ... eccentrics and the like. He doesn't show any particular aptitude for being creative ... though I did carry out a thorough examination of his cortical potential. He could have been ... in Earthly terms ... a great artist if ... "

Fantuk's attention was suddenly caught by an image that had appeared on the screen in front of him.

"Aha! Here's 'the blonde' he met when he was twenty-four ... from somewhere called 'Hawaii' apparently. This liaison may tell us a little more about Mister Symes' character."

An image flashed on the screen of a woman with a bright smile, obviously in her twenties. She was wearing shorts and a top so thin that her breasts could clearly be seen through the material. It seemed she was acutely aware of the effect she would have on horny young men, and revelled in it. In the next picture she was entirely naked and had chosen to display her tanned body in a most provocative manner.

"I think Mister Symes and her spent some time together. There doesn't seem to be any record of her name though."

Zavrod regarded the lithesome figure with undisguised distaste.

"How could he wish to *mate* with that revolting object? There's not a trace of colour in her entire form ... "

He flounced away from the console, the purple scales on his secondary tentacles flashing in the light from the craft's wall illumination.

" ... I'd rather handle a Querb if it was *absolutely necessary* to have physical contact with another creature."

Fantuk did not respond. A dense chunk of text had appeared on the screen and he was concentrating on reading it.

"It seems she was keen to settle down and mate with Mister Symes but he wanted to hitchhike … that means travelling in the most uncomfortable way possible … around the world instead."

Zavrod made a grunting noise, employing the leathery flaps that hung from his snout to achieve this end.

"What is there that anyone could possibly want to see on that dreary planet anyway? The inhabitants have turned most of the land into industrial wastes and polluted the air and the seas. They spend most of their time killing each other … and those who are not victims of some oppressive regime are dying of starvation. The methods of food production are cruel or corrupt … their economy is designed to make a minority rich and the rest to live in poverty. Society and culture are on a par with a mollusc colony … need I go on … "

"I'd rather you didn't as I've heard it all before … and after a time it gets rather boring."

Now in even more of a bad mood, Zavrod stumped off on his rear pseudo podia and contented himself with pulling a tray of space rations out of the modal dispenser. Under the Sellex wrapping were various globs of multi-coloured gunk set out in small plastoid compartments. The set-up looked like an artist's palette. To the untrained eye, painting a picture with the stuff might have been more suitable. Zavrod thought wistfully of how he would like to have been back in the Twenty-Seventh Dimension consuming a platter full of Zorp Cheese and pickled Orms but he contented himself with what was on the tray before him. Wodges of purple, orange and dark blue …

"Ah, now we come to the mysterious Janice … "

"Not another 'blonde' … "

Fantuk enlarged the very small image on the monitor in front of him. Enlarged, the face pixilated until it resembled a melting mosaic. Fantuk fiddled with various functions on the visio-monitor but to no avail.

"Difficult to tell with this very sub-standard resolution … but I don't think this attraction was ever trivial … the emograde response is way above average. I think Janice was the great love of Mister Symes' life … "

Zavrod sneered, outdoing early Elvis.

"Love! Pah, the delusion that accompanies biological necessity in the brain of prehistoric beasts!"

Fantuk ignored this outburst and continued to study the elusive image before him. He suspected that its enigmatic quality was somehow bound up with the whole notion of love. When he resumed conversing with Zavrod he was in a reflective mood, something unusual for a Xog. Creatures of unsurpassed intellect in the known galaxies they may have been, they were not so well-renowned as philosophers or poets.

"True love ... rather than infatuation ... seems to be the zenith of happiness upon Earth. Not experiencing that ... and many appear not to do so ... is considered a tragedy. Mister Symes would consider himself fortunate that this experience has happened to him ... even though it may be his love went unrequited."

Zavrod owned a monopoly in cynicism; he could so easily have been a hot-shot movie guy in Hollywood.

"It never existed in the first place! Illogical malfunctioning of the neurons ... the detritus of illogical thinking ... "

Fantuk was not to be put off from these speculations upon romance, he was rather enjoying himself.

"Exactly my point! Earth people don't want to acknowledge that falling deeply in love is something that actually exists ... they fear that losing control of their emotions ... something that accompanies this experience is damaging to their individuality. Often they are embarrassed or made angry by the prospect and totally deny it. Perhaps deep in their hearts they do know it is the most priceless gift given to the human race but they are so blind ... as they are to the beauty all around them in the universe."

Zavrod was forced into silence by this amalgam of illogical and unreasonable concepts. He contented himself with snorting like an old steam train.

"To Mister Symes ... who is a poet and a dreamer ... though he may not realise it ... love is the very breath of life."

Zavrod was scandalized.

"It seems to me that you rather admire these low forms of metazoan and their bizarre habits."

"The case of Mister Symes has its fascinations certainly. I am intrigued that he has not found another mate after all this time."

"Back to mating! What about this ... this ... *Janice* did you say she was called ... has she remained in the same state ... *in denial?*"

"Apparently not. Janice seems to have done her fair share of mating ... nature's way of making up for Mr. Symes' reticence in that area no doubt. There have been several children from two different fathers ..."

"Appalling. They all ought to be exterminated."

Fantuk laughed.

"You sound like the Daleks."

"Who?"

"Haha! Exactly! The Good Doctor … no, I won't prolong the joke, it would be cruel … like telling children there's no Father Christmas."

Zavrod looked totally perplexed, affronted even.

"Well, there isn't any such person as Father Christmas … I know that. You keep returning to these aberrations of the unconscious mind as if they somehow existed! Myths, legends, fairy stories … your Mister Symes … and those types similar to him … seem particularly prone to these kinds of chronic psychoses … "

Fantuk was inclined to want to tease his comrade. A long journey of several light years back to the Twenty-Seventh Dimension was ahead. Any kind of mind games would liven it up.

"What about magic, then? Mister Symes seems to have something of a penchant for that … "

"Isn't that yet more hocus-pocus? The sort of thing even more primitive peoples on Earth than those of the twenty-first century got up to?"

"It seems to have been a powerful force for thousands of Earth years. Recently it's rather been mocked because the Earth people have developed a scientific view of everything. I know theirs is rather basic knowledge of physics compared to our own … "

Zavrod took the bait, as Fantuk knew he would.

"Very basic indeed! They seem to think by discovering the microchip they've reinvented the wheel."

Fantuk returned to his original thesis, like a dog with a bone that was at least a week old.

"This New Age thing has diluted the beliefs that are at the centre of their being. That Windleroot place was once pulsating with magnetic energy … now it has almost faded away. A negative force is there now … I felt it … and it actually registered on the ship's monitors too. I didn't like it – very similar to being near to the Chaos Zones of the Forbidden Land.

"The what?"

Zavrod looked anxious. The small tentacles in his mid-section seem to writhe around like pasta doing the Hully Gully.

"Don't worry, I just made it up."

Zavrod glared, and all his eyes, including the secondary and concealed ones, turned a fetching shade of vermilion.

"Why do you say such ridiculous things?"

"I don't know, perhaps I'm tuning in to Mister Symes ... with that English sense of wit and waggishness."

Zavrod tried to be sensible; anyone could have told him that would be a losing game in the mood Fantuk was in.

"The Cuboid has the power to reproduce any of these extraordinary 'magical' states that you are describing, surely that's enough? Why are you trying to denigrate our superior science in favour of the superstitions of savages?"

"But the parallel between the Cuboid and magic is that they both have at their centre a paradox ... "

Zavrod was desperately confused, poor thing.

"What do you mean?"

"As I understand it ... to be successful ... magic depends upon the magician being aware that his power depends upon realising he has no personal power at all."

Zavrod was squelching furiously in utter frustration.

"How do you expect to ever think logically when you utter such convoluted claptrap?"

"The forces that the magician evokes are from a place beyond him ... he is the medium and merely uses his will to bring about any changes in consciousness that he wishes."

Zavrod began to sound like a jellyfish trying to be a ventriloquist.

"Where do you get all these extraordinary ideas from? You must be investigating some very obscure data-banks on the galactic information interface."

"Yes it is amazing what you can find when you start looking. Mister Symes is currently occupying a residence where the previous owner ... now deceased ... was a certain Mister Standley-Strange. Even after his death his cerebral traces are still so strong that they are capable of being interpreted and converted into a causal input recording. His knowledge of metaphysics is extraordinarily vast. He is a kind of unconscious mentor to Mister Symes ... one 'beyond the grave' ... as humans would say ... "

Zavrod was dismissive in the way only he could be – coldly.

"The blind leading the blind I would suggest. And where is the paradox in the Cuboid ... or have you conveniently neglected to include that in your mystical speculations?"

"Not at all, I was just coming to that. We offered Mister Symes the Cuboid. He still possesses it ... but all memory of his meeting with us has been erased ... in accordance with Galactic Law. Thus he knows he has it and yet he doesn't – a neat little quantum puzzle, worthy of Schrödinger and his theoretical cat."

"Just as well perhaps. He obviously hasn't the intellect to use it … like a bicycle would be of little use to a fish … if we want to be even more ludicrous."

Fantuk was on a roll.

"Interesting isn't it? If he had been aware that he had the Cuboid he could have used it to change anything and everything in his life. In the 70s he could have been all four of the members of Led Zeppelin … their Manager … and all the groupies as well if he'd wanted to. In the Eighties he could have been Margaret Thatcher or – worse still in the eyes of some – Ronald Reagan. In the Nineties … Donald Trump or Cher … but he didn't."

"He was 'fated to take another path' … I suppose you're going to say some twot like that … "

Fantuk was still cooking, in the groove he was.

"I think he was born for a purpose. The one meant to save Windleroot from its fate. Standley-Strange might have done so … but he died before he could."

"So what does this great saviour have to do?"

"Reinstate to the present various events that happened in the past … and at the same time cause others to be removed. Standley-Strange is training him to be able to do that by slowly teaching him the art of magic. He isn't aware of that … but it still goes on happening to him. Wait till he experiences the spiritual epiphany that every magician … and many artists … have to go through."

"I don't believe he will acquire these 'supernatural powers'! He won't get anywhere … "

" … without us. Exactly. He might just achieve what usually takes a lifetime's training and dedication for a magician to achieve … but we're going to give him all the help he needs. When his mission is over, his life will change again just as it did when we met him fifty years ago. Also, I promised him … on the last occasion we were in Windleroot … that we would see him again. To someone on Earth, fifty years must seem quite along time."

Zavrod hung his horny head in despair.

"That means we have to go back to that dreadful Earth place again."

"It's not that bad. Anyway … I'll go on my own if you don't want to come."

"You can't! That's breaking Intergalactic Rules."

"That's what rules are for. 'You are remembered for the rules you break.'"

"You were quoting then, I could see the actual punctuation when you were speaking."

"Quite right. General Douglas MacArthur said that."

"I won't ask who he was, but I'm sure he's on your personal data banks."

Fantuk didn't answer immediately as he had realised it was exactly the appointed time to programme the lateral flip across the time wall. They were approaching the Twenty Seventh Dimension and the space continuum had already been reversed. The manoeuvre Fantuk intended to perform meant twisting the parameters of space into a nice neat knot. In practical terms it also meant a bunch of light years trying to squeeze into a space where there was only room for a Thursday afternoon. It was the only way to do it; they had to slip through a very narrow time tunnel, one of the billions that perforated the walls of the parallel dimensions. *Zzzphoottt!* It worked! They got bounced out of there faster than a pork pie out of a synagogue.

IX

Sound advice for any visitor spending an English summer in that country would be, 'never go beyond your garden gate on an August Bank Holiday'.

Drinking has always been a part of 'holy days' and on that particular Sunday the locals in Windleroot were intent on celebrating. Has inbreeding dulled the rural wit? We may now judge for ourselves.

Most, if not all of the regulars from The Crumpled Horn in Drake Street were assembled, an assortment of men of different size and temperament, as is fitting in rural society. A certain lubricity of eye might betray that they had been 'getting them in' since the pub had opened its doors at noon.

Kate, the landlady, kept a watchful eye on proceedings. She noted that her customers were lit but not incandescent, and some distance from staging an open riot. That morning much chaff had already been exchanged about the way the town was run. Throughout history, the common man has never wasted much breath on praising his masters. Clifford was leaning half on the bar, the rest of him propping up the wall. He saw fit to nudge Ted Weaver who was perched upon a stool next to him.

"Woss think on it all then?"

He who was addressed pondered, but not for too long.

" 'Tis all changed and nowt fer the better."

"Ah, maybe thas right … but you can't live in the past, Ted, not yere nor anywheres else."

"Oo, can't? Windleroot were a better place when old Major Tigwell were the mayor … I can tell 'ee. This Boxer bloke ain't no good."

Ernie, who invariably sat four square at the table nearest the bar, pronounced. As always, pungently.

"Townie. They never knows nowt. That Boxer 'e be from Lunnon. Comes 'ere, takes over 'alf o' Lowe Street … then they makes the bugger mayor! He'm in with that Lampet what runs the paper. That bloke! 'e bought up places 'ere cheap years ago. First one 'e 'ad was old Mrs. 'Iggins cottage so's they could put up they 'ouses on Mangle Corner."

"Woss mean? They ain't 'ouses, they's flats."

"They ain't neither, I 'ouldn't put th' old dog in one o' they."

"Put the old bitch in there though wouldn't you?"

Ernie was scandalized.

" 'ere you watch what you say, Clifford Neap. Me an' our Phyllis been married forty year come September."

Kate looked up from polishing a glass.

"Forty years! The poor woman deserves a medal for putting up with you that long. Listen to you! Going on all the time."

"I only goes on in yere."

"Well … aren't we lucky then?"

Ted had been reflecting the more.

" 'nother thing 'bout that Boxer … 'e do go around lookin' like Jesus…"

Kate paused in her polishing. With her strictly Chapel views, such a remark was not a whisker away from blasphemy.

"That's enough of that, Ted."

" 'Tis true, I tell 'ee. 'E do look like 'n, with his beard and sandals 'n' all that. An 'e do look like 'e be wearing 'is pyjamas most days, if you sees 'n."

"Well, that's up to him then, but I'll not have the Good Lord's name taken in vain in my front bar."

Clifford grinned.

"You'm 'll catch it. Get struck down by a bolt o' lightnin' from 'eaven you will, Ted."

Kate resumed her polishing.

"Catch it from me too, Ted Weaver."

Clifford laughed into his pint pot, but Ted was determined to have his say.

"What about his missus then? So big, she do look like she bin and sat on a air pump up the garridge fer a week."

A gale of laughter met this sally.

"I sees 'er up the Chapel ground and I thought 'twas somebody put up a marquee fer a party."

Ernie piped up, as always, pungently.

"You seen the state of that place up Badcorn they do live in? Halfway 'tween a pig 'ouse and a slurry pit."

Clifford looked arch.

"Ah, an I tell 'ee what. They say 'e and his missus, they do smoke that funny stuff all the time. The wacko tobacco. Knows how I do 'ear about that?"

"Go on then … 'ow?"

"Jimmy Whippet from down Blowse got paid to put an extra

chimbley in for 'em ... take all that there smoke away."

They were off laughing again. Clifford nudged Ted once more.

"You been in that shop o' Boxer's?"

"No, I ain't. Woss the bloomin' place called?"

"I dunno 'Pig in 'is pyjamas' er summat..."

"Thas 'ee. Boxer isself! 'Eem a pig in 'is pyjamas, an she'm the nightmares 'es always 'avin'!"

So merry were they that fresh pints of Old Todge and flagons of cider simply had to be ordered up. Kate put the brimming glasses on the bar and dropped the proffered coins in the till with a mellifluous tinkle. Clifford took a goodly swig from his mug and leant a shade more heavily against the wall. His features were beginning to resemble a Jack o' Lantern.

If the crash that came from the middle of the town had not been so loud, they might not have heard it, what with their squiffy state. But this was like the Hammer of Thor.

"Yere! What be that?"

In the rush for the door, furniture went flying and not a little liquor was spilt. They stood outside The Crumpled Horn to gaze stupefied at the cloud of dust that rose from beyond the horse trough.

"Th' old chapel's bloody fell down!"

And it had too.

Rivet, unaware of all that was transpiring at that moment in the town, belched profusely for the third time. His loud bark came as the result of consuming an entire Melton Mowbray pie, two scotch eggs and several pickled onions at luncheon. Rivet would have pleaded an acute state of anxiety as the cause of this thunderous eructation. An appointment to meet the 'Essex Boys', as Rivet now referred to them, had been made for this very afternoon, and he was showing signs of a distinct nervousness.

Squiddle was to accompany him to the meeting and her insistence on Zeep being also of the party was another reason for his trepidation. The dynamic between the trio had from the beginning been precarious and, since the incident in the stock room, it had been as finely balanced as the legendary angels upon a pin head.

Squiddle's current habit of wearing a deerstalker at all times of the day and night also troubled Rivet. A certain amount of eccentricity was almost *de rigeur* in Windleroot, but Squiddle had overstepped the bounds of decorum. The habit of displaying this headgear during council meetings had been remarked upon by some of the more conservative members. She had also taken to wearing the hat in Paganorama, with the flaps hanging loose, so that she resembled a St. Bernard snuffling about in search of lost mountaineers. The insistent snapping that did service for speech for Squiddle, cut through the air.

"Tell me again, why exactly are we meeting this riff-raff?"

Once more, Rivet explained patiently what he considered to be his consummate tactics in this campaign.

"It's all very simple. I want Paganorama to have the monopoly in Windleroot. That's a good way of describing it now I think about it. I played that game when I was a kid … you put everybody else out of business … so they haven't even got the ackers to put a house up on The Old Kent Road."

Squiddle was not prepared to assign any credence to this allegory, her view was more pragmatic.

"And you really think everybody is just going to stand there and let you take over the town?"

"Not a question of *letting* me, darling. They won't have any choice in the matter. I'll be the only retailer in town, and they'll have to get my permission to even operate as a business."

"This sounds like the worst kind of fantasy, Rivet. You've not been taking magic mushrooms again have you?"

"No, sweetheart, I have not. Not since the last time … that was when I saw Fanny Jangle floating over the top of the Nob."

Rivet recalled the episode. This monstrous medium, a local fixture, was always arrayed in a caftan that sported butterflies, purple moons and silver stars in its design. In Rivet's hallucinatory state she had seemed to sprout wings and fly, resembling a barrage balloon that had escaped its moorings. Squiddle was dismissive of this female as all her supposed rivals in Windleroot.

"Fat cow."

Rivet thought momentarily about pots and kettles, but held his peace.

"I was poking about in the cellars of the Town Hall … "

Squiddle's mirthless laugh interrupted him once more.

"More likely you were poking some tart in the cellars, you randy old goat."

Putting this witty sally in abeyance, Rivet continued with his tale.

"I know that somewhere down there is an old charter from 1831 that entitles the mayor to close down any business that, I quote '…cometh to offend ye morality upheld by God and ye king, to the detriment of ye people' etcetera etcetera."

"And you think this is still on the statute book?"

"Definitely, I had Dibley Wedge the solicitor check it."

"Well, I've never been impressed, with anything Wedge says. Whenever we've tried to sue anybody he always advises against it."

"That's because we've never had any spare money, darling, and I don't fancy losing this place in solicitors' fees particularly because of your personal vendettas against almost everybody else in this town. I have to see these people every day you know."

Rivet immediately regretted this show of asperity. The hue of Squiddle's features had shifted from pasty to pink. Rivet had touched a raw nerve and he knew it. His wife was celebrated for having fallen out with most of the inhabitants in Windleroot at some time or another. Her tone went from cool to icy in a quick jiffy.

"What else is in your grand plan, Rivet?"

"The paper's on our side."

"*The Windleroot Chronicle*?"

"Fingers Lampet will put anything in his editorial that we ask him to."

Squiddle snorted.

"He's just an old soak. Who pays any attention to the nonsense he writes? It's like reading bad science-fiction novels."

"The old brigade still respect him, dear, and we need the support of the Town Council. That is if we're going to do anything legally."

"I thought your idea was to get things done *illegally*."

Rivet, about to reply, was cut short by a cacophony of sound coming from his mobile phone. He squinted at the number display.

"Hello, Fingers, we were just talking about you."

Squiddle glanced at Rivet. Whatever he heard next had more than a passing affect.

"What? When? Christ! I'll get over there right now!"

Rivet jumped out of the kitchen chair with more animation than he had displayed in several years. He stared at Squiddle helplessly.

"Why have you suddenly got a face like a pregnant weasel, Rivet? What's going on?"

"The bloody chapel's fallen down."

"Shit!"

A nano-second later Squiddle was looking suspiciously at her spouse.

"Are your new chums anything to do with this?

"I'm not sure. I hope not."

"Are you sure you don't know if they're mixed up in it?"

"No, I don't know. I mean, yes, I am sure I don't know."

Abandoning Squiddle to this flurry of flustered contradictions, Rivet rushed out of the door.

"I'll be back as soon as I can! Call me on the mobile! Pick up Zeep! Get over to the Cee and Pee as soon as you can!"

"Don't get pissed before we come!"

"Not much time for that, these blokes are supposed to be there at three."

The Chapel of St. Swego had been in ruins since before the Dissolution of the Monasteries. Further destruction that came about then had somehow exposed the crypt, supposedly the resting place of the venerated saint. He was renowned for worshipping the stars, considering their light to be the reflection of the holy word. It was always said that if ever his tomb was exposed to the eyes of the profane, ill fortune would be the lot of the world.

'If light be brought upon ye tombe,
Followeth shall be thy doome'

This ripe kind of superstition, given added authority by being deeply carved in rude script upon the stonework, was tofu and drink to the mystical legions of Windleroot. Already a crowd of miscellaneous devotees had encircled the pile of stones and crumbling mortar clasping hands and chanting some mumbled mantra. Rivet, hurrying from Gallows Square where he had left the Volvo, surveyed this melancholy tableau with mixed feelings. Despite his inborn cynicism, he felt a certain remorse which quickly turned to apprehension when he glanced at his watch and realised the hour had come – or nearly. He hurried through the door of the Chuff and Peacock, sorely in need of some restorative.

Rivet calculated that he had time for a couple before Squiddle, Zeep and the Essex Boys would appear. Accordingly, he marched up to the bar and ordered a pint of Moondipper and a double scotch. No sooner had he taken his first sip than he felt an insistent presence at his elbow. Beans, in his usual manner, had noiselessly sidled up to him – a move which made Rivet start involuntarily. He gave Rivet a look that mixed curiosity and contempt in equal measure.

"Alright, Mr. Boxer?"

"You must be Beans."

"S'right."

Rivet offered his hand, a gesture which was pointedly ignored.

"It's not three yet is it? I was just having a quick one."

Beans' eyes were expressionless.

"Right."

Rivet nervously reached for his wallet.

"Have a drink?"

"Nah."

Rivet was thoroughly put out, the more so when Rover and Goldie made their entrance. They might well have been a pair of desperadoes out of the Old West. Constantly looking to right and left, as if expecting any minute to be ambushed, they took up a position either side of Beans. They said nothing to Rivet, just stared out into the room. The word 'thugs' embedded itself on Rivet's forebrain and would not go away.

The unfortunate mayor continued to gulp at his drink, while only too aware that Beans was watching him closely. The hands on the clock behind the bar moved remorselessly towards the hour. Rivet could stand the silence no longer. He began to blurt out his thoughts, not to the company, but to the world at large.

"Just waiting for my wife and my personal assistant…"

The words seemed to echo in his head, tumbling over themselves to land in a meaningless heap. Three o'clock. Right on cue, Squiddle and Zeep came through the door. If Rivet had imagined that Squiddle would modify her appearance for the occasion he had made a gross error.

The tartan trews were the most grotesque part of the outfit, the mauve tank top a close second. The leopard-skin bikini top was mercifully hidden from view. A pair of pink wellingtons and a football scarf completed her ensemble, while a sombrero provided the *pièce de resistance* at the top end. In comparison, Zeep's costume appeared almost tasteful – the usual graveyard garb, numerous shiny pendants, and a pair of lethally-pointed boots.

The reaction of the Essex Boys would have been difficult to predict. Bursting into peals of raucous laughter might have been one option, but it had not occurred to them. Instead, they behaved as if the spectacle before them did not exist. Introductions, if they could be described as such, were exchanged, and in some confusion the two parties moved to occupy a table by the window. Rover and Goldie took to staring steadfastly at the passers-by in Lowe Street. Beans, who had purposely sat down opposite Rivet, wasted no time in getting to the heart of the matter.

"My employer, Mr. Snipe has certain business interests in this town. We're finkin' you might be able to help us aht wiv any *nee-go-shee-ay-shuns* … what might be needed that is."

Rivet had difficulty in decoding all this, so he was at a disadvantage. Normally in company he was disingenuous to the point of being almost invisible; now he found himself at a loss. He began to act like an adolescent surprised in some solitary pleasure. Totally intimidated by the situation, and as a result imbibing more beer than was good for him, his tongue began to wag like a perspiring puppy.

"Right. That's what I thought. Your gaffer and I could get together … work out some sort of arrangement … um … obviously beneficial to us both. Being in my position … managing one of the major commercial outlets in the town … and … um … occupying the most senior position in the community of Windleroot … I obviously do have quite a lot of influence. People tend to come to me when…"

Beans cut him short.

"And wajoo want aht of all this, then?"

Rivet was about to answer when proceedings came to a sudden halt. He had suddenly and noisily broken wind. The origins of this raucous honk that had echoed around the bar were unmistakable. Rivet's tactic was to stare in a shocked way at Zeep, who although totally innocent of any hint of flatulence, blushed the colour of a ripe tomato. Rover was swift in his own response.

"Oi … who cut the cheese then?"

Squiddle had gradually been growing more irate. She was not used to being ignored, and had no intention of being upstaged by a mere fart. Opening her scarlet lips wide, and with a voice like the whine of a dentist's drill, she laid it on the line.

"As my husband is too drunk or too stupid to say anything sensible I'll tell you exactly what the score is. We want *Paganorama* not to be one of the also-ran places in Windleroot, but the *only* establishment selling the sort of stuff that goes well here. If you and your *friends* can convince the opposition to pack up trading that's great, in return we'll help your boss to get what he wants. That's the deal."

Zeep then mumbled her support. Beans regarded them both for a brief moment then turned to Rivet.

"You wanna train your bitches to keep to heel, mate."

The effect on Squiddle was like a blow. Before Rivet could stop her, she leapt to her feet, her eyes incandescent with rage.

"Don't talk about me like that, you common lout!" She indicated Zeep with a furious sweep of her hand. "Beware! We are the daughters of Hecate, dark goddesses of the night. If you want a pretty nasty curse put on you, you're going the right way about it, sunshine."

Beans met the eyes beneath the sombrero and immediately concluded he was in the company of a lunatic. He stood up and leaned over the table towards Rivet. His words were as friendly as the gleam upon a switchblade.

"Right. I get the picture now ... what's goin' on rahnd 'ere. When I get back I'll tell my boss all abaht it."

Rivet was speechless with horror, and could only watch helplessly as Beans and his gang swiftly left the bar. His pallor resembled the Cliffs of Dover. Stumbling to his feet, he abandoned his half-full mug of beer and led the two women out of the Chuff and Peacock. Outside, the crowd around St. Oswego's tomb were still in evidence, though their numbers had already markedly thinned. A morbid air lingered over the scene. After some deliberation, Zeep stepped across the street and joined their ranks.

Rivet began to walk back to the car while Squiddle went off in the opposite direction to retrieve her bicycle. In Gallows Square, Rivet was astonished to be approached by Rover. He was leaning on the bonnet of the Volvo, in an insolent fashion.

" 'ullo again Mr. Boxer ... "

Rivet looked around, fully expecting the rest of the gang to leap out of the shadows intent on doing him some harm.

"Yes? What do you want?"

"I was wonderin' ... "

The grin turned to a leer which almost split Rover's face in half, like a ripe peach.

" ... this sorta place. Gotta be a bit of the old funny gear abaht ... bitta nice blow ... "

Rivet hesitated. He was torn in two, rather like Rover's features. On the one hand he did not want to admit selling illegal drugs, but the idea of any cash deal was always attractive. Particularly on a Sunday afternoon, when any deal was a bonus.

"Possible I might be able to do something for you. You after this gear right away?"

"That'd be good, don't wanna keep the uvvers waitin' too long do I? Wouldn't be fair … know what I mean, like?"

Rivet quickly made up his mind.

"How much d'you want?"

"Coupla ton?"

Rivets eyes almost leapt out of his face.

"What?"

Rover quickly understood the exact nature of the misunderstanding. He chortled for an instant.

"I mean coupla hundred squid's worf don't I."

Rivet looking eminently relieved. Almost immediately, stoner and satyr could be seen entering Paganorama by the rear door to conclude the transaction.

As he had anticipated, Squiddle began grumbling as soon as Rivet returned to Badcorn.

"…ignored Zeep and me, as if we were part of the furniture … only talked to you … what good are scum like that to us … or anybody come to that?"

Even Rivet's irresponsible optimism plus the wad of notes from Rover were not enough to provide a bulwark against any further assaults from his wife. Making some excuse about having left the Volvo's headlights on, he went out into the yard.

"I'll be back in a minute."

But he wasn't. In a daze Rivet wandered into the orchard. Helplessly he looked up at the sky, as if he might find some sign of reassurance there, but he was to be disappointed. Heavy squalls of rain were poised over the Nob ready to hurtle in the direction of Badcorn. The wind began to howl menacingly. Rivet, even more despondent than a moment ago, leaned against the trunk of a medlar tree. It had born no fruit for decades. He remained there, motionless until it was almost too dark to see. After he had become so wet and cold he could bear it no longer, he trudged slowly back to the house. Rivet noticed that some more slates had fallen from the roof. His world was ever more collapsing around him.

X

Windleroot was permanently a wasps' nest of rumour and scandal. Gobbets of gossip continually dripped from the awnings of the establishments in Lowe Street. An innocent remark made at the top end became a slanderous accusation by the time it arrived at the horse trough at the bottom. Making the most trivial observation about anyone in the town was like playing hopscotch in a minefield.

The Chuff and Peacock was the hub of Windleroot society, which did not really amount to a great deal. The tavern where Rivet and his cronies held court of an evening was, on this occasion, about to be graced by the presence of Mrs. Boxer as well as her husband. They entered as if the main attraction on some royal tour.

Rivet, as always, resembled an extra in some biblical epic, while Squiddle continued with her extremely successful campaign to offend the eye of everyone around her. Bustle, bonnet and boob-tube were all grist to her sartorial mill, and her current costume might have been a collage made with pages torn from an encyclopedia of fashion.

It had never been her overriding concern to be colour-coordinated, and the vermilion of her polka dot blouse shrieked at the tangerine plus-fours, while both were bullied into submission by the purple shawl about her shoulders. The whole ensemble was topped and tailed with a flying hat and a pair of motorcycle boots.

Rivet sported an inane grin as he walked into the bar. His jocular spirits had been revived by further discussions with Wedge the solicitor. It appeared that the Windleroot charter which Rivet had earlier purloined from the vaults in the Town Hall was of more significance than they had both realised. It seemed that, as long as Rivet remained in office, his ruling on the suitability of any business conducted in Windleroot was unassailable. He was now in a position to dictate any terms he liked to the other shopkeepers in the town.

Rivet was delirious with the notion that he had the power to oust his competitors in Lowe Street. On informing Squiddle of these developments, she had grudgingly congratulated him. Rivet's ego had become inflated almost to bursting point, and he began talking big almost as soon as he had ordered drinks for himself and Squiddle.

"When other Windlefarians tell me they're not making a go of things I simply can't get my head around the idea. We're doing absolutely fine at the moment ... extremely good turnover I have to admit ... *and* showing a pretty good profit at the end of every day. The other thing I can tell you is that there are going to be big changes in Lowe Street too ... some of us who can't cut it in business ... and I name no names ... are going to have to shape up or ship out."

Nearly all of those ranged about the bar had heard this sort of banana oil before – *ad infinitum*. No one was really listening apart from the greasy trio that made up Rivet's regular cronies – Archie Stark, Stu Leyton, and Wyevale Pearson. In their company, Rivet had a tendency to really let rip, becoming ever louder and more boastful by the minute.

"I'll tell anybody ... I'll admit it ... Squid and I came to Windleroot on the understanding that we were both determined we were going to make a go out of any business we set up. You can't knock our place ... Paganorama ... no one can ... we started it ... and making a go of it is exactly what we've done. Frankly I wouldn't mind taking on another outlet ... even two or three more. Lowe Street needs shaking up ... and the way we're going I think we might have ... not just a very good year ... but the best we've ever had. It just shows that you *can* mix the material and the spiritual ... and very successfully ... doesn't it?"

It was meant as a jest even though it was not a very good one. At any other time might well have floated up to the ceiling with the rest of the hot air and been quickly forgotten. On this occasion, the remark had the effect of incensing one particular customer in the bar.

Standing next to a character who had so many nose rings and studs attached to his face he looked like an animated Meccano set, was Ted Weaver. Thrown out of the Crumpled Horn by Kate for a minor misdemeanour, he was in a prickly mood. Ted had little time for the Boxer brigade and had reached the stage of drunkenness when any kind of wit is just too subtle for the brain to take on board. The human scrapyard moved off, and Ted was left with an unimpeded view of Rivet. He was still looking pleased with himself after just delivering his *bon mot*. Ted took exception to his smug demeanour – big time.

"You'm about as spiritual as a bleedin' wheelie-bin, mate."

Rivet stopped smirking and did a double-take. He stared momentarily in Ted's direction. When he had recovered himself, his tone was brusque and sneering.

"Excuse me, I didn't think you were included in our conversation."

Ordinarily Ted might have brushed off this snobbish put down, but as he was as far from being sober as an elephant is from a flea, he was not to be squashed that easily. He fought back – not with a rapier wit, more with the broadsword.

"What makes I mad about you, ye fat turd, is that you don't belong yere and nobody do want thee. Cos you'm the mayor you thinks you do run the whole flippin' town. Why don't you just piss off back where you come from … wherever that is … not that anyone bleedin' cares…"

Even for one with a hide like a rhino, Rivet was pained. He was not unaware of local feeling towards him, and Ted had hit a raw nerve. He bristled, and was about to respond with his own brand of invective when Squiddle, as was her wont, intruded into the proceedings.

She advanced on Ted, presumably to administer some sort of rebuke either verbal or even physical. At some point her trailing shawl caught around her ankle. She might well have landed flat on the floor had she not fallen into Ted's unwilling embrace. As she tripped, most of the Chilean Merlot in her glass was thrown back into in her face. When the purple stain mingled with the polka dot blouse it made another interesting contribution to her colourful outfit. Realising she was held in the arms of a man who had just insulted her husband, she gave a performance as ham as Wiltshire.

"How dare you attempt to assault me, you pervert. Rape! Rivet! Police!"

Squiddle disengaged her sodden torso, helped on her way with a shove from Ted.

"Rape? I wouldn't poke you with a squeegee mop … you gurt … ugly trout."

At this, Rivet completely lost his composure and began to roar at Ted, while stabbing the air with a judicial finger.

"I know who you are … you're that bloody little odd job man … the one who lives in Spanner Street. Listen, chum, when I've finished with you, there won't even be a job shovelling shit in this town for you. Have you any idea of the position I hold in this community … in Windleroot … who I am?"

Ted needed no prompting.

"How about the biggest wanker in the West?"

Rivet turned ashen with rage and began to wave his fists, like a windmill on speed. The unfolding drama was now impossible to ignore, and the rest of the clientele were delighted by such an impromptu cabaret. Apart from Rivet's toadies, most of the company in the Chuff and Peacock shared the view of the mayor held in the Crumpled Horn. The sight of Rivet being pilloried appealed to their rural sadism. Rivet continued to splutter, conjuring up further lurid imprecations by the minute.

"You wait, I'll ruin you ... see if I don't."

Squiddle began to screech like a lift that was stuck between two floors.

"We'll put it out on Windleroot Radio too..."

From a corner of the bar came a clear voice.

"Nobody do listen to that! You gotta be the only one who do!"

A crescendo of laughter greeted this and Ted, as if acknowledging the crowd, rose to his feet. If his intention was to assault Rivet, the spirit may have been willing but the flesh was definitely not up to the job. Ted would not have connected with any target even if it was twenty-feet wide. He had reached a state where he did not know for certain whether he was in Buenos Aries or Balham. Perhaps with a view to orientating himself to his current location, he staggered out of the door, the dusk swallowing him up.

The effect of all this on Squiddle was as if thunder clouds had gathered about her. Her features were coal-black with rage and revenge was centre stage in her mind. She was now determined to exact the most terrible retribution on any or all in Windleroot who dared to speak ill of her or, by implication, Rivet. No one in a radius of twenty miles from the town would now ever be safe from her ire. She was already rehearsing ancient spells and new imprecations in a brain now as toxic as Chernobyl. Destiny then set in motion a chain of events, one with far-reaching consequences, for at the same time another equally vicious mind decided to aid Squiddle in her unholy schemes.

Some twenty years ago the Law Society had not looked too favourably upon the professional conduct of Rupert Charles St. John-Pemberthy. A habit of regarding his clients' funds as his own had led to his undoing, and he had been 'struck off'. An amount of embarrassment and a narrowly avoided appearance in court followed. After a period in the wilderness it was inevitable that such an incisive and erudite mind would not lie fallow for too long. Sure enough St. John-Pemberthy had set himself up in business as a legal consultant. He was attached, albeit unofficially, to a very respectable and old-established law firm in the centre of Bath. The connection was not advertised and never admitted outright, but it was an open secret in legal circles.

Shortly after the junket in the Paradise Relax, the New York attorney – Sibe Schwab – had announced his retirement. Said to be for reasons of health, it may have been prompted by too enthusiastic a participation in the 'entertainment' provided by Beans. St. John-Pemberthy was thus left holding the baby, and a fractious infant it had turned out to be. Vargle Snipe was not an easy client. Yet, as St. John-Pemberthy often reminded himself, money has no pedigree – and expenses must be met. A conference with Snipe was never any sinecure, and after one of these sessions St. John-Pemberthy always felt he had earned not only his fee, but a large scotch.

On this occasion a meeting had been convened in Westminster. Colin Sopwith had engaged a rather grand room that he ordinarily used for entertaining foreign dignitaries. St. John-Pemberthy did not particularly warm to the diminutive diplomat. The only advantage to his being present was that he might provide some ballast during the inevitably fractious proceedings that lay ahead.

It had been a benign September, and gentle sunshine played through the windows set high above the Victorian Gothic panelling. But no matter how richly did the amber rays glow, they did little to sweeten the temper of Vargle Snipe. He had immediately made it clear that on this occasion, as on others, any point of view other than his own would not be to his liking.

"Why ain't this moving faster than what it is? Just tell me that and I'll be a happy man. The money's sorted … the developer bloke's up there every day in his 'elicopter … but what do I get? Nuffink. What's the problem? That's what I want to know."

The other two exchanged a brief glance. Sopwith looked in silent appeal at St. John-Pemberthy. It was as if they had drawn lots for who would speak first, and Sopwith was left clasping the short straw. A man who relied on oiling the wheels, he began the necessary lubrication with alacrity.

"Everything *is* going extremely well … actually. It's just that certain … er … negotiations are taking a little longer than expected."

Snipe continued to stare silently at the carpet. The same that grandees and ambassadors had paced in times long gone when diplomacy and tact were the niceties of the hour. These things Snipe would not have known, nor would he have cared. The carefully weighed word, the balanced epithet, they were not part of his jagged, dangerous world.

"That's exactly what I mean, innit. Why is this happening? Someone's not listening. Like that little geezer that Beans had a talkin' wiv ... he had to listen ... eventually. I want this sorted. Right now."

Above the mantle was hung a portrait of William Pitt the Younger. His refined features appeared to look down upon Vargle Snipe with an expression of mild bewilderment. He glared at Britain's youngest prime minister and Pitt returned his gaze with a studied aloofness. A man who has weathered the French Revolution might well consider Snipe and his kind to be very small beer indeed.

"I think our little problem can be solved reasonably easily – that is if my own researches prove to be correct."

St. John-Pemberthy spoke in that brisk way that he did, the result of an expensive education combined with the aplomb of a natural actor. At his words Snipe, interested despite himself, wheeled round like a cheap top.

"Researches? What you on about?"

St. John-Pemberthy continued. The same measured tones.

"As you may remember ... I mentioned certain documents that were essential to secure the properties in Windleroot that we wished to purchase. Those who have the authority to release these documents ... among other papers even more pertinent to our cause ... are, for some reason, digging their heels in. They do not seem inclined to comply with my repeated requests for access. I have therefore come to the conclusion that someone ... somehow ... has got wind of our plans."

Snipe began to get heated once more.

"Grassin' us up? It ain't possible."

"I regret to say that these things are always possible. Prior knowledge accounts for how nearly everything pans out these days. It is a fact of modern life ... and I'm sure Colin will bear me out, moving as he does in government circles ... renowned for their ... uh ... leaky ways."

Sopwith nodded vigorously.

"But ... I rather think it makes little difference how – or even how much – the good burghers of Windleroot ... or anyone else ... actually *knows*. But, as I read it ... they have become entrenched ... displaying rather reactionary views to change of any sort ... particularly anything as radical as our present scheme."

Snipe put his hands on his hips, in a gesture that could have appeared fey in anyone else.

"Right, I think I clocked all that. So, where do we go from here then?"

St. John-Pemberthy paused, as a duellist might before delivering a telling thrust.

"It seems that the mayor of the town – a rather exotic figure, with the unlikely name of Rivet Boxer – known to you, I think…"

Snipe interrupted.

"Yeh, right. I sent Beans down there to see what his game is. Finks he's one very sharp geezer I'm told. Tried to call the shots n' all. I ain't 'avin that. Anyway … what you got lined up for him then?"

"Just this … I am reliably informed he might be amenable to obtaining the papers we require. I plan to see this gentleman as soon as possible and broach the idea with him. He naturally has access to the vaults where these papers are and has apparently already … uh … borrowed certain other documents for his own ends. I learned this from a colleague *in situ* … so to speak."

St. John-Pemberthy paused once more, this time even more tellingly.

"I have to insist that what I am about to say must remain strictly between these four walls. Although I am prepared to arrange these matters … as I cannot see any other way forward at present … I prefer not to be in possession of these papers. I do not wish to arouse the displeasure of Her Majesty's Minions of the Law a second time … if you take my point."

Snipe did, and nodded. Secretly much relieved at this turn of events, he assumed a kindlier tone.

"He can bring 'em round to me … no problem. Take that as sorted then. Tell me what's happening as soon as you can."

"Of course. One other thing … if you don't mind me saying so…"

Snipe automatically tensed.

"What's that then?"

"I think we should still be wise to tread a little carefully here … and not underestimate the people in a place like Windleroot. There is quite a sense of *community* there. It is a strange mix. The old guard still hold sway but the other element … the uh, pop festival lot … and their outlook on life is the coming thing you know … they would not appreciate our rather mercantile approach … as they would see it … Just a thought…"

Snipe had no time for what he considered to be idle musings. Ignoring the lawyer's strictures he snapped out a question.

"What d'you know about a bloke called Standley-Strange? I got 'is name in me head. He's got to be one of your lot wiv a 'andle like that."

St. John-Pemberthy's large shoulders, the same that had once supported the varsity pack at Cambridge, and felled many an opposition forward, rose and lowered in a passive shrug.

"Doesn't ring any bells, I'm afraid."

The eyes of Snipe owned a hint of menace.

"…something to do with that Windleroot place, and 'im trying to mix it there … I'll get Beans on it … I want to know what his game is."

It was noticed by all the company that the light in the chamber had appreciatively lessened. The roar of the wind could be distinctly heard in the small courtyard outside and the trees there were suddenly bent nearly double. Sharp gusts, slapping against the window panes, made those within start. Snipe, particularly, had his own reasons to be more than usually fearful of the natural world.

St. John-Pemberthy was the first to break the silence. With some deliberation he took up his hat and umbrella, bade farewell to Snipe, and strode towards the door. Like a small dog, Sopwith was suddenly at his heels. They left together. Vargle Snipe took once more to exchanging glances with William Pitt before he too quit the room.

The very storm that had caused no little consternation in the east of the kingdom was later visible over the hills that surrounded Windleroot. Clouds tumbled over each other as if intent on fleeing from the searing glow that could be seen upon the horizon. The darkest kind of magic was brewing in the abyss, ready to erupt with venomous intent.

Vargle Snipe had suddenly taken a deep interest in occult matters. On his return from Windleroot, Beans had made certain observations concerning Squiddle and Zeep. To his surprise, these had strangely interested Snipe. He became convinced that other powers, rather than mere physical force, could be employed to implement his plans. That he knew little of these things did nothing to deter him. Snipe had found that a few questions asked of the right people, and at the right moment, invariably yielded satisfactory results.

XI

To the unsurpassed delight of the entire kingdom, the Indian Summer continued well into late October. The national news revealed that some cricket clubs had added post-season matches to their fixture list. As is the way of any aberration, it did not last. A week away from Halloween, the days took to being capricious, one moment casting a warm countenance upon all the world, the next a chill frown. Nature was anxious at the coming of the changing season, even though her beauty would be just as radiant during Autumn days. Come the Winter she would be as a haggard widow, her skin laid bare to the elements, bones exposed to wind and storm alike. Like a sudden scythe came the coldness and overnight the less Keatsian aspects of Autumn were set to give no quarter.

A chill wind harried the citizenry of London. Vargle Snipe in one of his hideouts, a flatlet above a kebab-house in Notting Hill, shivered continually. Even the heat from the lethally boiling radiator in the room gave him no warmth. He kept glancing at his watch, wishing that time would move faster and he could abandon this bolt-hole for another. Yet wait he must.

His mobile phone lay on the table in front of him. Every few seconds he willed it to ring. Snipe needed information, sadly not the sort he could get in a hurry. Try as he might, he could not force the pace – not a situation he was used to nor one he welcomed. The minutes dragged themselves along, grudgingly becoming hours as the day passed. With the coming of evening the room became dim, but Snipe did not think of bringing any light to his present world. It suited his present mood to exist in a world of deepening shadows.

The forces of chaos and destruction are a necessary part of creation. Kali has as much right to strut his stuff as Vishnu. If all is hunky-dory in the universe, yin and yang are neatly balanced – like a kumquat on the end of a bicycle pump. In this room, the scales were tipped – in the direction of hell. A darkness, one that grew more intense by the minute, was gathering about Vargle Snipe. It had sensed a refuge in the cold cavern of his heart. His thoughts, like those of Faust, began to turn away from all things that were of heaven made.

Rivet, and the rest of the cast in this grim pantomime, were too absorbed in their own performance to quit the stage. They clamoured about the pasteboard gate believing that once it was opened all they desired would be bestowed upon them. Snipe also feverishly sought the key that would allow him access within. His soul, always in torment, was now harried by an angel so dark that Snipe could offer no resistance. He was about to be led down into a grim world, one of devils and dunghills.

At last the call! That which he lusted after had been found. Even at the news no warmth came to him, Snipe only shivered once more. A man who never wore an overcoat, he pulled on a pair of leather gloves and left the room behind. Gratified by the success of any scheme he embarked upon, he was still acutely aware that he had ventured into unfamiliar territory. Unwittingly, Snipe had set in motion a succession of events that would eventually lead to his own destruction. And if he had known this, would he have paused to reconsider? It is unlikely. Snipe was not a fool but he certainly rushed in, often to tread where no self-respecting angel would venture even a tiny tootsie.

A more mundane darkness met him as he stepped into the street and made his way to the Festinog Arms in Kensington. There he had arranged to meet Beans, who on receiving his summons had been obliged to force his way across central London in heavy traffic. Snipe edged his way into the plush and plastic emporium to find Beans already there, a glass of some colourless liquid before him. Snipe ordered some equally innocuous drink and sat down with it. Beans noticed that he was unnaturally pale, as if the greater part of his vitality had been drained from him. Snipe did not speak for some time, seemingly unaware that anyone was seated opposite him.

"I want you to get down to Windleroot again."

Beans tried hard not to react, but gave himself away when one of his hands gripped the edge of the table. Snipe noticed, and his voice when he spoke again was breathless – a mere rasp, desperation shaping the tone.

"Urgent this is."

Beans nodded perfunctorily.

"Them two women you was talking about …"

"Yeh?"

Snipe chose to ignore the venom in his voice.

"What you make of 'em then?"

Beans spluttered out a reply, fitful like a damp sparkler.

"They're all nutters them Windleroot lot. That Boxer, 'e's a cry-baby and she's a total head case, the uvver one's nuffink really. I fink they'll do whatever we want. But … "

Snipe looked alarmed. "What?"

"… they're up to summink else down there, Mr. Snipe … I dunno what it is. 'S a right old dump that place … can't get me 'ead round it. 'ippies and all that … dressed up like they was at some sorta party. Summink fell dahn just before we got there last time … an old castle I fink … and they're all out there rahnd it cryin' their eyes aht an' all that. Dooney-loonies all of 'em."

Snipe appeared to concur with all that was said.

"None of them ain't gonna be no use when all this is up and running next year. Somehow we've gotta make sure they don't get yappy rahnd the place."

Beans did not hesitate.

" 'ave a word! That's the fing to do, Mr.Snipe. Put the frighteners on 'em. Slap 'em about if they get arsey…"

Snipe held up a warning hand.

"Don't go there, son. I got special people that I get in for that sort of fing if it's wanted."

Beans realized he had stepped out of line.

"Yeh. Course."

Snipe was silent – long enough to make an impression.

"Don't worry about it, son. I appreciate you're lookin' out for the firm, that's good."

"Ta."

The pause was brief this time.

"Listen … someone I want you to find aht abaht … geezer called Standley-Strange. He lives over in that West Country as well … Barstowe … got a posh house in Clinton … that's the nobby bit of the town. Snoop abaht a bit see what you can find."

"I'll sort that out straight away, Mr. Snipe."

Snipe softened a degree or two.

"I know you will, son. I can trust you … you're a good boy."

Beans knew from experience that as soon as the compliments started coming the meeting was over. But Snipe suddenly, and unusually, went on to confide in him.

"Fings gotta be 'andled right dahn in that Windleroot place, that's all. Lot 'appenin' in a lotta different places right now. I gotta bit on me plate. You understand that doncha?"

Had Beans known it Snipe was reaching out to him, but only as a drowning man would reach out to one who was also going down for the third time. In only a matter of months the deeps would claim them both.

"I'll sort everyfink out, Mr. Snipe."

Beans stood up.

"Right. Nice."

Snipe stayed where he was, wondering. He wanted to dismiss from his mind certain things he did not understand, but he did not succeed.

In the hamlet of East Buttwell the stillness of September had become the storms of October. Damp leaves congregated around the front door of Trumpton's cottage like urchins on a Victorian street corner. Feeling peckish, our septuagenarian survivor had just lobbed a piece of plum cake onto a platter. The phone rang; he cursed. Even before Trumpton picked up the receiver he sensed there was trouble.

A lifetime of dealing with strangers and the strange had given him a certain instinct about these things. From the instant he heard the Essex boy accent he didn't like it.

"I got the right number for Trumpton's Books ?"

Morley deliberately spaced out his words as if he was playing a game of Scrabble in the air.

"Indeed you have. How can I help you, sir?"

"I'm told you got some books there abaht spells 'n' all that?"

Silently, Trumpton took a deep breath.

"It would help if you were a little more specific. I get a lot of enquiries for Fergie Pooper's *Cream of Crystal Channelling*. She really has cornered the market if you like that sort of thing ... bigger than the *Barstowe* Channel, eh? So what exactly were we looking for, sir, that is in the metaphysical ... paranormal or occult line ... "

Vargle Snipe was once more out of his depth, not quite drowning but with more than a tendency to flounder.

"Well ... I dunno really ... I fought you'd know."

Trumpton was prepared to be patient, but only until he became the opposite.

"We have here on the shelves in that section a rather *comprehensive* collection, sir."

Snipe wasn't listening.

" 'ang on, I fahnd the bit o' paper I wanted ... 'Black Road of the Cress ... '"

Trumpton twitched a trifle – a phenomenon you don't very often come across these days.

"*The Black Road of the Crescent Moon*. Was that the book you were looking for, sir?"

"Yeh … That's right. You got it there?"

Trumpton paused, this time not for effect – he was thinking hard, very hard.

"A rare volume. As it happens I do have a copy. Not something I get asked for very often except by the specialist collector. What may I ask is your interest in the book?"

Snipe wasn't used to answering questions, he always preferred to ask them himself.

"Nuffink to do wiv … Nah, I mean yeh, I'm an … uh … uh … expert in these fings."

"Really?"

Whatever tone Trumpton had employed, it would have made a perfect counterpoint in any symphony of sarcasm.

"Look, you gonna sell me it or what? I'm a busy man."

"That makes two of us, sir."

" 'ow much?"

Trumpton paused.

"Just a moment. If you'll excuse me, I'll have to look that up."

Ordinarily he enjoyed a spot of haggling, but on this occasion he had little or no respect for his adversary. He held the phone on his lap for as long as it took to eat a mouthful of plum cake. Snipe had got ratty by then, it never took much.

"You still there?"

"Absolutely, sir."

"Well?"

"Seven hundred and fifty pounds, sir."

"What?"

Trumpton was as cool as a bed of that well-known salad article.

"Seven hundred and fifty. I won't charge you any VAT."

Snipe snorted savagely. Alliteratively, even.

"You gotta be jokin'. For a bleedin' book?"

"An extremely rare book, sir."

"Like rockin' 'orse shit I reckon. Alright, I'll 'ave it."

Trumpton quickly switched to his matter-of-fact voice.

"And where would you wish the book to be dispatched, sir?"

Snipe muttered. He was on the edge – balanced very precariously.

"Yeh, well, it's like this … I wannit delivered somewhere … personal courier, that kind of fing."

"Really, sir? And where would you like the book to go?"

"Dahn that Windleroot place in the sticks … "

Trumpton twitched a second time, a repeat of the previous trifle routine.

"Windleroot, sir? I see … most certainly. Now let me just jot down the address, when I've done that we'll discuss how you intend to pay."

At the same time as Trumpton was concluding his business, Dick Symes was studying the silhouettes of the houses opposite. Through his drawing room window he watched the gables of the roofs as they became dark right-angles against the pale translucent sky. The peal of the phone put an end to his reverie.

"Mr. Symes? Morley Trumpton here."

Dick sensed no friendly chat was approaching. More like the cavalry coming over the hill.

"Everything all right?"

"I don't actually recall an occasion when I could ever truly say that was the state of things in my life. The continually persisting enigma of existence constantly stands in the way of my gaining anything like a sublime state."

"I see."

"I'm glad you do. It is my fate to encounter on occasions the scrotted and soiled scrolls wherein some choose to harvest the poisoned crop that is our darkest past. I don't suppose you've ever heard of a volume with the winning title of *The Black Road of the Crescent Moon*?"

"Sounds like a vinyl epic by some dodgy folk-rock band."

"Not a bad try … it's actually a grimoire … or rather a bowdlerized version of the original work …"

"What's a grimoire?"

"I thought you'd never ask, my dear boy. It's a spell book … like the sort of thing you'd find in a fairy story perhaps. All medieval magic was founded upon spells for demons, the evoking of … "

"But wait … why did they do that?"

"These elementals, and various other existences, were called upon by the sorcerer to do his bidding … or so he fervently hoped. The 'dishonourable tradition of wizardry' as Hector always used to call it. Not the sort of occultism he practised ... of course ... but he had some sympathy with his predecessors because it was the only magic they knew back then. The Church had driven the old ways so far underground is it any wonder these chaps made a pact with the infernal powers? The Church confiscated vast amounts of the sort of stuff I'm talking about ... the Vatican library is stuffed full of it. Some of the juicier volumes are residing under the Pope's bed ... no doubt as we speak."

Dick was suddenly very curious about this grimoire, obsessively so. "What's in it?"

Trumpton could hear the insistence in the voice and, as well as being surprised, heeded the warning.

"The usual stuff these things are filled with ... rituals for getting pots of gold ... voluptuous maidens to serve you ... and numerous ways of causing ill-fortune to your neighbours."

"I see."

"Not too nice really."

Dick, for a moment that stretched out far too long, knew the hold that the grimoire could have upon any soul. The power it promised was one that came accompanied by the greatest temptation, one that few would be able to resist. How could they? The twisted soul of the grimoire knew the secrets of all, the desires that were closest to their hearts. A voice, so convincing, so reasonable would persuade them to follow a path that appeared to promise all that they could ever wish for. It was no wonder that over the centuries it had claimed so many victims, left by the wayside of that glittering path, broken in spirit – damned for all eternity.

Without even having it before him, Dick could still see clearly the writhing shapes of the glyphs upon its pages. That image disappeared to be replaced by a more animated scene. A city – London or even Paris, a place of narrow streets, with timber houses leaning precariously towards one another. He saw barefoot urchins running through puddles, thieves and cripples mingling with merchants and priests, and amongst it all an occasional knight on horseback. A peculiar stench was in Dick's nostrils, one of decay and death. An eternal emptiness echoed there, one he unconsciously prayed to be vanquished.

"Hello ... hello ... you still there?"

"Sorry, I was miles away."

"I'm not surprised. Did your sojourn in the unknown answer all your questions?"

The face in the mirror above Dick's desk belonged to someone who had recently been hunted by mad wolfhounds.

"Yes, yes."

Trumpton dispelled the twilight zone.

"Right, now here's the skinny, as they say in Seattle ... or so I'm told, having never been there. We have to accept ... or go completely potty in the process ... that Hector is still around and having some influence on you. Call it a ghost ... whatever you want ... but I'm certain his spirit is still here. That's got to be the reason why you felt, at that moment, you were actually him."

Revelations came to Dick as quickly as if he was cosmic channel surfing. Now he was convinced that it had to be Standley-Strange that he had met on that day in 1967. It couldn't possibly have been anyone else. With an effort he tuned in once more to what Trumpton was saying.

"But, why me? I didn't know anything about this magic stuff until I moved in here ... and I feel I don't anything about it now ... except of course when he kind of takes over ... "

"True, on one level, but there is something else to consider. That is, whether you and Hector have been together before ... you know ... in a different time ... previous life ... reincarnation and all that ... "

"Oh ... no. I'm not into all that stuff."

"I'm not actually a great fan of the past lives bit myself. Everybody wants to be Cleopatra, Saint Germaine or Richard the Lionheart. They won't settle for being a road sweeper in Bombay, or an Eskimo who can't catch any fish. Stop me if I'm waffling ... "

Dick was suddenly aware of the power of magic, specifically of the Standley-Strange variety, all around him. He felt about as safe as a goldfish in a cats' home.

"No, go on."

"We've got to face it; Hector wants us to finish off whatever it was he started. He doesn't want us stand idly by and let Windleroot ... the very place that was so dear to the old boy ... be taken over by vampires, gangsters and all the other riff-raff."

"But how do we know that's all happening? How did he know?"

Trumpton was almost pleading, not to Dick, but to any deities that might happen to be eavesdropping on the conversation and offer some solid assistance.

"I'm sure Hector would have wanted you to go into the enemy camp ... a sort of Wooden Horse job ... "

"How do you mean?"

"One of those gangster types has just bought the grimoire from me."

"What!"

"I know, it sounds odd. Somehow he's in cahoots with Rivet ... the mayor ... but more sinister is his wanting to get the grimoire to the ghastly Squiddle, *toutsuite*."

Dick closed his eyes. A pulsating blackness, its beat an infernal rhythm, filled his head. It was a sound he never wished to hear again, in this world or any other.

"From what you've told me I can see this Rivet getting mixed up in dodgy stuff. Who's this Squiddle?"

Dick could hear the old boy wheezing a bit but he was determined to get off the launch pad.

"His missus ... she wants to cook up some foul hell broth with it."

"Why?"

"Revenge of some sort? Just plain vindictive?"

"Okay. Go on ... "

"I reckon our gangster pals believe that the more flak flying about in Windleroot the easier it will be for the mob to take over the place. Then they can ruin it with their ghastly schemes whatever they might be. That grimoire will be right up Squiddle's street ... she'll lap it up ... as the feline does the best cream."

"But what does she really want?"

"One thing and one thing only ... *power*. It's always the same with her sort ... they don't care how they do it or what happens when they do. I've had them in the shop all the time for years. They get some kind of unholy rush of elemental energy and that's enough for them ... until the next time. Punks in black leather jackets listening to heavy metal while reciting the Lords Prayer backwards is kindergarten stuff compared to what she's up to ... very nasty indeed ... I'm sure of it."

"But why give her the actual means to do all this? Isn't that just a bit ... dangerous?"

Trumpton didn't miss a beat.

"Absolutely ... I agree ... but it's all simple psychology. Hector would have approved, I know he would. Squiddle is bound to go too far. Give her enough dynamite and a big box of matches and she'll blow the whole bloody lot of them up. Presto! We've saved the day."

"You think it's as easy as that?"

Dick was convinced not one jot. Trumpton sensed this and pressed onward – just like the Light Brigade.

"It works like this … if you summon up enough darkness the balance eventually gets restored … the whole place then gets flooded with light. Yin and Yang … all that. What we're doing is just helping everything along."

Dick thought that believing that the Earth was flat made more sense.

"Listen … desperate times calls for desperate measures. We've got to do *something*. Hector used to say 'Nature abhors a vacuum, but I abhor it more.'"

Dick thought that was one of those lines that sounds really impressive until you think about it. Bob Dylan played that game, but at least he admitted it later on – sort of.

"But what if it all goes wrong?"

"That's the risk we've got to take."

Dick's mouth felt drier than a budgie's cage in Death Valley. He somehow felt this was not just crunch time, but snap, crackle and pop as well.

"But why am I playing the part of Little Jack Horner?"

Trumpton chuckled, wheezily, of course.

"Aha, a historical reference, very good."

"I liked History at school, the past is another country so they say. One that's easier to deal with than … "

"Right now?"

"I just don't believe any of this is happening … "

Trumpton was brisk.

"Well, it is, chum, whether you like it or not. Dick Symes, you are required upon the Astral Plane as the emissary of Hector Standley-Strange … late of this parish. If that sounds like complete twot, so be it. Now, what say you, sirrah?"

It might have been the mention of Standley-Strange that changed Dick's mind. A few seconds ago he was ready to run for cover, but if he knew Standley-Strange was there with him it might just be all right. Nothing could harm him if the old wizard was there. Then he would be protected by magic … it was a good feeling. Others must have felt it before … heroes, adventurers, men of yore … and he would be one of them. Why not?

"Okay I'll do it."

Trumpton might have been applauding – the sound of one hand clapping. Nothing too mystical there, the other one was holding the phone.

"Good man. Right, now I'm round your way in Clinton tomorrow. I've got an appointment with Philip Pye-Decker in The Whippet pub at twelve. I'll drop this thing in after that shall I? About half-one?"

"Fine, but just one more thing … did Hector ever get married?"

"Not that I know of … 'Betrothed to the Goddess and her handmaidens' he told me once."

"What did he mean by that?"

"No idea. Bye."

Dick felt as if he had been jumped by a mugger with a sock full of wet sand. If he had been a drinking man, he would have ordered up a Humphrey Bogart-style scotch – 'no ice no water'. Having his ear bent by Trumpton *and* agreeing to run this extraordinary errand was quite enough to let loose the grizzly bears of big-time stress. Constantly hanging out with the shade of Standley-Strange was altogether something else as well. Dick thought the late owner was probably hanging around in the hall right at this moment, waiting for the morning post to arrive. Just because it was the middle of the evening made no difference, ghosts worked on a different time scale.

The night brought its own reflections, as always. The thoughts he encountered in the small hours got bigger and bigger through the night. Most of them were about the topic of the moment – magic. The difference between the real thing and the Squiddle stuff seemed to be as limestone and lymeswold. Most people would consider the Windleroot variety as being the real thing – glamorous, scary and in 3D. Those kind of dabblers and dunces wanted miracles, SFX and sexy sensations – just like they got on cable TV.

Standley-Strange was a true practitioner of magic because he was a great artist and a craftsman. Modesty, wisdom and being a real gent were all in there too. It seemed to Dick that rarely did the true magician choose his calling, it was chosen for him – and often reluctantly did he follow the call. Magic was an honourable profession, and like any noble path, beset with temptations and hardship.

Dick felt that he was being transported to that realm where magic ruled, benign and majestic at the same time. Such power could only emanate from the Heavens above. It had its manifestation on the Earth but that was the only time it left its invisible domain.

A vision came to Dick of a king lying upon his tomb, sword clasped to his chest, the blade a symbol of his life – his very being. His brow was firm, an even line for a mouth – features that told of duty done, authority exercised with prudence. Lying in repose, the gods satisfied, the debt paid in full. Dick looked upon that king and knew it was an aspect of Standley-Strange, the one who had the authority to lead Dick beyond the veil. Dick would follow him willingly, even though he knew it meant that he would enter the kingdom of death. He would see for himself all that resided in that place of awe!

Behold! The pale rider came, his steed moving in a rhythm so slow that each footfall was suspended in eternity. Lit by a bleached sun, one never rising or setting, Death looked upon the world. What did *he* see through the hollows in the eyeless skull? What was it like for him, to be in such a place, one of eternal silence? Garlands and streamers fluttered, and eventually fell, from the black armour that Death wore. They trailed in the dust and ashes of the way, a road the hooves of his steed never touched.

Dick felt no fear, and was somewhat amazed that he did not. But how could he feel anything but respect, even affection, for a figure of such majestic beauty? Every mortal would at some moment in their existence yearn for his breath upon them. When they sought ultimate peace, the deliverance that Death always promised would be bestowed upon them. Death never reneged on the promise that he had given to man.

Standley-Strange had taken him by the hand and shown him the land beyond the horizon. This was the most hidden element of magic, the part that resided there, in the deeps of the underworld. It was where the old gods ruled, those who had come before time, even before creation itself. Dick knew he would come upon other things in the days to come, many he would not wish to see, but with the strength that Standley-Strange could give him he would win through.

Dick was certain he heard the old magician's voice at Dawn.

Much you do not know about the one who is you.

The room was filled with blazing points of amber light, coming together to become an orb. The light filled the air and, it seemed to Dick, he was part of that light. Then the chimes of the university clock reminded him that today Trumpton would deliver the grimoire, the sign that the play had begun. Dick predicted that a bit later on a lot of smelly stuff would hit the fan.

XII

The stained glass in the doors of the Chiswick Flyover Inn were art-nouveau, providing some relief from the otherwise tasteless interior. In the twenty-first century the English Pub had finally gone into hiding. It was not going to be coaxed out into the open with promises of Wide-Screen Sports and access to wi-fi.

Vargle Snipe was perched on a vinyl-covered bench near the door. He inched back a leather glove, glanced at his watch and thought about his coming meeting with Atherton Hook. Snipe had no desire to hear of JCBs and concrete laying, the universal language of developers and their ilk. Instinct told him that Hook had something important to confide.

The dapper, red-faced figure duly appeared. He was only a few minutes late for their appointment, enough to irritate Snipe – that and his obvious eagerness to impress. After perfunctory greetings, Hook went to the bar to return with a large brandy. He slid his diminutive frame into a seat at right-angles to the pub table, allowing him a view of both Snipe and the interior of the bar.

"You know this place?"

Hook was airily evasive. Laying claim to such an oxymoron was quite a feat in itself.

"Occasionally pop in … one of my regular contractors is in Fulham."

Snipe showed little interest.

"Right. So, what you been havin' a butchers at, up there in your little twirlybird?"

Hook looked smug and conspiratorial – he was good at multi-tasking.

"Something very interesting around Windleroot…"

"Yeh? What?"

"Place called Marvell, where they have the Pillstown Festival every year … you know that rock music thing … some farmer bloke owns all the land … bloke called Buttle … Grainey Buttle. Not sure we shouldn't extend our plans to include his place…"

Snipe looked more suspicious than enthusiastic, Hook did not notice.

"How's that work then?"

Hook took a sip of brandy, pulling in his cheeks like a horn player about to begin a solo.

"It could be a satellite town for Windleroot ... few thousand more units in there ... no problem. Link road to our new complex ... Bob's your uncle."

Snipe didn't want to be anyone's nephew.

"But why should this Buttle bloke want to give up his Festival fing? Gotta be more than a few bob in that sorta lark ain't there?"

Hook tried arch – a new look for him.

"There's always been objections to the festival right from when they started it. Now it's Health and Safety ... environmental issues ... and the residents generally getting pissed off about being invaded by thousands of kids every year in the summer. It's nearly got the chop two or three times ... only needs a bit of pressure..."

Snipe's tone was dry as the best sherry, but laced with menace.

"What sort of pressure?"

"I'm told there's someone in Windleroot who might set the ball rolling."

"Who's that then?"

"The mayor ... Rivet Boxer, I think it is..."

Snipe struck, quicker than the asp that did for Cleopatra.

"How d'you know about him?"

Hook looked less assured than he had a few seconds before.

"...um, dinner party with St. John-Pemberthy ... you know ... the lawyer chap ... we were chatting ... Boxer's name came up ... that's all ... nothing really."

Snipe's voice went up the scale, somewhere near a semi-tone.

"Leave it out! You know what I always say? Do one fing at a time. Makes sense dunnit? We got enough to sort out already wivout gettin' more involved. Know what I mean?"

"Certainly, I see what you mean ... but the potential there is incredible ... it would be a sound investment...kill two birds with one stone ... while everything's lined up on site ... "

"*I said, leave it!*"

Hook, although gazing into the depths of a bottomless pit, rashly chose to continue peering over the edge.

"Surely we could just approach Buttle with an offer ... I mean ... nothing binding..."

Snipe stood up. The glass in front of Hook tottered slightly, a little brandy splashing onto the table.

"You're not listenin' are you? *I'm tellin' yuh right now.* Get off it."

Hook watched Snipe stride out of the bar. He sat sullen and silent for some time then ordered another brandy. It was time he showed everybody else who was involved in the project that he knew more about running things than Vargle Snipe ever did. His way was always the best. Hadn't that been proved and time again? He took out his mobile from a pocket of his suit and called Dewey Ringle, arranging a meeting with him for tomorrow morning. The time had come for things to be done properly, and he was sure he knew how. Hook sucked up the last drops of brandy, and left the bar.

Two days later a line of sinister silhouettes could be seen upon the hills that surrounded the Isle of Teflon. These behemoths of heavy plant in their yellow livery had been summoned by Hook, standing ready to do his bidding. Waiting – the beasts whose hellish purpose was to gouge and rip the body of the holy earth of Windleroot, waiting. Was the rape that the Goddess had foretold about to come to pass? Sanctified by commerce, none would oppose the outrage they were about to commit in the name of Mammon. Only Heaven could prevent the deeds of man upon Earth and already the gods had chosen one who was to be their trusted emissary.

After Trumpton had delivered the grimoire, Dick could not resist glancing at its pages. He could make little sense of it all, which was perhaps just as well. Returning the volume to its black velvet case, Dick looked once more upon the endless rain outside. He wondered how any birds were able to fly in it, or why they would even wish to. Deciding that the grimoire had given his brain enough metaphysical jogging, Dick decided to venture into a part of the house he had inexplicably left unexplored.

Another storey lurked above the second floor where Dick slept. This distant domain had once been the maid's quarters in Victorian times. Access was gained by a steep stair which Dick now ascended, only to find the door at the top firmly locked. He vaguely recalled being given a key by the agent – some frantic searching revealing its whereabouts. When Dick unlocked the door and saw the interior he realized he was in Standley-Strange's inner sanctum – his Temple. The detail of his surroundings was not as dramatic as the atmosphere in that hallowed space. Here was an entire world.

Originally two rooms, then converted into one, the space spanned the house from front to back. The walls were cream with a warm tinge of orange giving the effect of a transparent screen of reflected sunlight. A skylight could also add natural illumination to the space. Dick noticed the thick blinds that could be drawn across the window at night. The whole ambiance would then alter, and although the actual moon would be concealed, the lunar Goddess would cast her aura over the entire area.

Ornate brass candlesticks, of an imposing height, stood in each corner. On the walls were four hangings, one in each quarter, and corresponding to the seasons. Green for Spring, gold for Summer, crimson for Autumn and dark blue for Winter. These could be lowered to the floor as required. It seemed significant that the crimson of Autumn was in place, telling Dick that the last occasion Standley-Strange had ventured into this room was at that season.

Certain symbols were on the walls – a blue circle representing the element of Air was in the East, a red triangle for Fire in the South, a silver crescent for Water in the West, and a yellow square for Earth in the North. A black ovoid, representing the eternal spirit, was set in the ceiling.

The floor was in a black and white chequered pattern, each a foot square with a Star of David – two interlocked triangles – in the centre. To the right of this was set a two-cubed altar, and upon it a black silk cloth, a silver tassel at each corner. On top of this was set a white square, and upon that, a plain vase within which was a rose. The once red petals were dry and withered, almost turned to dust.

A small door in the South wall led into a cupboard. A long wooden case, bound at each end with luggage straps, stood there. Dick carried it into the light. A key protruded from the lock, implying that the owner had assumed he would return.

Dick's heart began to beat like a reggae groove. The key, when he turned it, made a satisfying click. At such a moment many would have gone downstairs and started on the Daily Telegraph crossword instead. Dick was obviously not one of those.

The interior of the case was divided into compartments of various sizes. One of these ran its entire length and contained a wand encased in black velvet, and a sword in its scabbard. A silver chalice and a small shield decorated with a pentagram took up two of the smaller compartments and, in yet another space, there were two books. These were both bound in tooled leather and held with a clasp.

Dick continued to look at all this, uncertain how to act. Unbidden, certain words came into his mind. '*You are permitted to touch these things.*' Needing no further invitation, Dick took up the first volume. It had the words *Magical Diary* inscribed on the cover in a neat copper-plate hand. The notes within it were written in the same concise manner. Dick opened the book at the first page and began to read.

The word 'magic' or 'magick' derives from the Greek magikos *which in turn comes from* magos*. The O.E.D. gives as its definition 'the art of influencing events, control of nature'. An older root is the Persian* magus *or* magi*, the title given to the ancient priestly caste, and celebrated in the Biblical tale of the 'Wise Men' from the East.*

On the Inner Planes absolutely any experience is possible. I have never experienced comparable happenings on the earthly plane. The awe felt during these is overwhelming. Physical laws of time and space are banished. Encounters with beings on these planes are always profound. A resonance echoes within the very essence of oneself, such an experience very unlikely to occur with such intensity anywhere else. Merely entering these planes implies that one is meant to be there. The profound meaning and relevance of any particular vision (again, such an inadequate description!) to one's soul is incredible. In terms of knowing oneself, these things happening to one are beyond price. This understanding is the same as knowing all the secrets of the universe all at once, mainly because on the inner planes all is actually one.

By developing the ability to work with the unconscious forces, balance returns to life and illusion is avoided. This knowledge is particularly important in our times when falsity has almost become a way of life.

Nothing is quite the same after the seeker has entered the Inner Worlds. It is not that I wish to dwell there constantly, I would be in error if I did! It is that the very knowing of this other existence gives strength and purpose to this life.

I feel myself to be an intrinsic part of the universe and thus there is no reason why I should not be in command of its outward form. The shadows that once threatened me have fallen back and my fear of the unknown has completely disappeared. Illusions still possess their glitter, but no longer is there the slightest chance that they will turn to gold.

October 31ˢᵗ 2011

I must continue in the great task set for me. To evoke Sekhmet the Mother of All Gods, the daughter of Ra, I have already prepared myself. Tomorrow is Samhain, the time when the Celtic nations believed the veil to be at its most thin. If I am to succeed in this evocation surely it will be at this most auspicious time? May all the deities of Ancient Egypt, and any of those other gods and goddesses I have known, spare me for this task.

Dick read the date of this entry in the diary, the read it again. Standley-Strange wasn't spared; he died the same night he had written those words. He could not complete the ritual. And no one had been in the Temple since that day. A curious feeling came over Dick. Like everything else to do with Standley-Strange, this was all meant to be! Putting aside the Diary he took up the Magical Work Book and opened it at the first page.

Which comes first the magic or the magician? I never particularly set out to be a magician; I became one as a result of where I was going with my own researches. Magic came into my life in such a powerful manner that I could ignore it no longer and out of that turmoil something positive had to emerge. That something was magic. I realized that the power of the mind was greater than anything else in this world – how one perceived the universe determined how it was. Practising magic seemed the best way to hold onto that notion.

The Magus always remain still even while the planes of existence constantly move about and around him. Wherever he desires to be, that will be where he is. His power is bestowed upon him by the Heavens above. It is given freely; the only restrictions come from the magician himself, and the Divine Will.

If true perception is to embrace all shades of meaning, and realise that truth is never absolute – then magic is the ideal medium for success. The Magus must at first labour in order to discover the gap between the worlds – Heaven and Earth. He calls upon the deities, devoting himself to praising them and possessing absolute faith in their ability to bestow power upon him. He then asks for aid in his endeavours.

I, Standley-Strange the Magus, have sworn a sacred oath that the forces that are bestowed upon me shall be used solely to bring the light of creation into this world. I shall employ these powers solely for the good of man and the universe.

Dick continued to read until the light began to be drawn from the sky by the night. Then, almost as if directed by an unseen hand, he began to make preparations for his own ritual. He was meant to continue the work of the arch-magus himself, this he knew! Time meant little, nothing at all, in these magical surroundings. Standley-Strange's original intention was still as powerful when it was first vouchsafed. Even though many months had passed, that same moment when Standley-Strange was about to begin the ceremony would be manifest once more. He, Dick Symes would evoke the goddess Sekhmet himself!

Another altar cloth, its border embroidered with the twelve signs of the zodiac, was soon found. On this Dick laid the four magical weapons. The wand, cut from a hazel branch at the waxing of the moon, was carved with sigils. The sword was drawn from its scabbard, the chalice brimmed with holy water filled from a leathern cask, and the shield (engraved with a pentacle of protection) gleamed dully. Now all were together, the elements working in divine harmony to fulfil their purpose upon the Earth. In each corner of the temple Dick placed a candle of the appropriate colour and lit each one. A rich perfume of frankincense filled the air when he ignited the charcoal in the thurible.

From its hiding place Dick extracted a cloak. Lined with crimson on one side, black on the other, he donned it, along with the Wizard's Hat. Then he stood in the East, the quarter of magic. He sounded a sharp peal upon the magical bell and his ritual began. Did he know what words he would utter, what gestures he would make? Faith, and the hand of Standley-Strange the Arch Magus, would guide him.

Dick took up his wand from the altar and raised it. He spoke the words of power he had memorized from his reading not an hour or so before. In the Direction of West a figure began to appear. It was not yet fully formed – still a vision. The magician spoke once more, his wand held aloft – commanding the figure to appear. All at once this spirit he had summoned began to advance into the Temple space approaching the point of the Star nearest to the West. Dick addressed the deity before him. For a moment he could not believe the voice was his own.

"I know ye to be Sekhmet, the lion-headed goddess, favoured daughter of Ra, whose breath created the desert. Ye who are the arbiter of justice, the one before whom all evil trembles, I humbly request that ye will enter the Temple and that thy presence may be known to the magus."

In answer a great roar filled the Temple and all at once Dick beheld this great goddess! Sekhmet told her tale, Dick hearing the words as if they were spoken aloud. She told of how the Lioness was indeed terrifying and merciless, one who slaughtered without mercy the enemies of the pharaoh. But when she was with wine she was Hathor the goddess of love, and most passionately did she embrace her partners.

What mortal other than a magician would willingly make love to a goddess, and not drown in ecstasy or be devoured by the fires of bliss? What mortal would welcome the embraces of a lioness crowned with a serpent, and survive? Only one kind of man was capable of such things – the mighty magus whose initiate stood now before the altar in the temple! Arms raised in the Ka posture, the newly ordained one willed that ultimate power came forth – no matter that it embraced the entire universe. The force that filled the Temple was nothing less than the fire of creation, the primeval spark that caused the cosmos to be. And now a terrible voice rang out, one that would try the magician's courage to the very utmost, even he who now possessed the boldest will.

"Who dares to call me? It seems that is thee who you request my aid, O mortal! Take care you do not incur my wrath also!"

The magus responded, his voice as clear as the peal of a mighty bell.

"Know ye, O Sekhmet, I am the magus. I am Merlin the Wizard and also Thoth the Ibis headed god. I am he who is the voice of Ra, as you are his daughter. Let us stand together in order to banish the darkness, and those fell creatures that would put out the sun."

And the Goddess laughed at that, and her eyes were as white flame, rushing endless fire, such as are only seen in the vaults of He who is the Eye of Heaven.

"Truly, I perceive thou art a wizard! And … you would have me believe … my equal! Either very bold, or very foolish, thou art, O mighty Magus."

Sekhmet looked upon the one who stood before her, he who had taken up the mantle of magic as if it was his right. In that moment, Dick Symes had the endless belief and eternal courage that the magician must have, that he was destined to be as a god. It was the nature of she of the lion head to embrace only the valiant – for only those like herself did Sekhmet consider to be at all worthy of her presence.

Sekhmet smiled upon the Magus, though to any who might have seen, no reassurance was in that grimace, not even the smallest part. This goddess was the force of the Sun, the beam that scorches the land. For Sekhmet may dry the very oceans if she wishes and nothing that lives can withstand such an intensity of light. Life and light are just as powerful as death, and upon such a paradox is creation founded. Sekhmet roared once more, and Dick was almost rendered deaf for ever, but he fixed his eye, unwavering, upon those terrible jaws. He waited for the answer that Sekhmet – at that moment the very voice of the universe – should give him.

"Know ye, that I *have* decided to bestow my power upon thee, wizard. I shall aid thee in they endeavours. For I know now that thou too have command over the Earth. Thou art as another, one who sought to summon me once before, and would have done so had not Anubis according to his own wisdom claimed him. This was as the greatest of all who follow the path of magic! You do well to walk in his footsteps, O Magus! Now tell me who thou art! For if thou art truly Thoth is it not ordained that the Ibis-headed god can never lie?"

And he who was the god of magic once more became the hand of magic. As Hermes holds the caduceus, Dick was presented with the sacred staff that had once belonged to Merlin. Now, the ankh that Thoth always held hovered in the air between Sekhmet and the Magus, and both fixed their gaze upon it. Then it flew into the hand of Dick Symes and he grasped it. This was the ultimate confirmation that he was at that moment the guardian of the mightiest of any symbol. He knew the greatest power that any mortal may own, equal to the Ankh the symbol of life. The voice of the Magus resounded in the Temple, as majestic as the words of the goddess had been but moments before.

"I am the Magus, I am Merlin the Wizard, and I am also Thoth the magician, the master of measure, and the scribe!"

Satisfied, Sekhmet smiled once more, then throwing back her wondrous head to emit a final roar, she withdrew. The goddess returned to the otherworld from whence she came, the domain of the gods and goddesses of Ancient Egypt, the kingdom of the oldest magic.

Dick, with an enormous effort of will, managed to complete the formalities that closed the Temple offices and return this sacred space to the Earthly plane. Still in somewhat of a trance, he gathered the magical objects and returned the case to its place. Then he left the Temple quietly and retired to the kitchen where he drank several cups of Earl Grey tea. He might even have chewed on a few biscuits. An hour after that, he went gratefully to his bed and slept deeply.

On waking, many thoughts came to Dick, almost too many. It was no use him pretending he was familiar with this kind of stuff. The brain works even when we sleep – any author will tell you that. In the next few nights Morpheus would not come to him so speedily. He threw himself about as if trying to capture sleep and subdue it, eventually falling into a kind of slumber, but one essentially troubled.

Dick reflected that Sekhmet was obviously not an entity to be taken lightly; her powers of healing only matching the power to destroy her enemies. Dick was amazed to realise that Standley-Strange must have spent most of his life engaged with such extraordinary powers as this. It was as if his spirit was within them, and they knew only too well that he had sworn a sacred oath to serve them always.

Fortune favours the bold and, like the cat, curiosity had nearly done for him. Perhaps he was saved by emulating Schrödinger's feline and being able to be in two separate states at once. One part of him was still Dick Symes; the other was now the sorcerer's apprentice. From now on everything would be different – he was privy to a great secret. Dick felt rather like some youth caught scrumping apples in a neighbour's orchard. When he went out into the world again he would have to try to look as if he had not been up to anything at all. But how would be able to tell if he had succeeded in this grand ruse?

Even knowing that the Temple existed had added another dimension to Dick's life. His reality was now that of the world of the Magus. It was reassuring to know that Clinton, the world of four-square Georgian piles and their paved walkways, still greeted him as an old friend. Striding along the Princess of Lancaster Walk, Dick adopted a dapper manner as if he were Leslie Howard or some other (probably forgotten) matinee idol. He had a spring in his step as if life was nothing but a lark. If the gods are feeling the same way, chances are it probably is.

For Dick, reality constantly hinted at new prospects. It promised new ways to keep the mundane at bay. Nothing could ever be dull from now on. In Wilde Terrace and Clementine Place, if he wanted, he could sing at the top of his voice or perform a gavotte and no one would notice. He could make clouds move in the sky, cause time to slow or speed – anything he wished. He could probably have flown over the rooftops if he had just concentrated hard enough.

How he was others about Clinton was also a revelation. He could appear to be invisible or tower above them so that they visibly shied from such a giant in their midst. Dick went so far as to be convinced he could walk down King Harry Street stark naked and no one would pay him the slightest attention. He did not attempt the experiment however; he felt that might be pushing his luck.

XIII

The great clock atop the University tower was chiming three when he left a lazy Sunday afternoon in Clinton for the bleakness of the moors. The hour of his mission to Windleroot had arrived; it was time to beard the lion in his den! In Richardson Gardens the gales of recent days had left a sea of auburn leaves beneath the lines of maple and beech. As he drove along Princess of Lancaster Walk it appeared to drift gently away towards the distant hills, as if guided by a divine hand. Windleroot was calling to him. There, he knew all would be devoid of colour, the hedgerows dripping with rain, iron-grey clouds hovering above the horizon.

Dick had known that his growing magical skills were soon to be called upon. Thus he had further prepared himself by yet more study of the *Magical Work Book*. Upon the back seat was the case that contained Standley-Strange's magical equipment. Dick had also brought the cloak, its crimson and black were the hues associated with Scorpio, the dark side of Mars. Dick was only too aware that the magic he would be required to perform would require unremitting and ruthless energy. Mercy was not to be included in this particular equation.

As he wound his way across the wetlands in the fading light, Dick was not to know that Beans and his gang were at that moment in Windleroot and cruising along Lowe Street.

Rivet, who was about to round up business for the day, was not best pleased to see another customer enter the shop. His avuncular air evaporated as soon as Dick came through the door. Rivet's rodent instinct warned him to be on his guard.

"Mr. Boxer?"

"Yes? How can I help you?"

The tone was abrupt, just a hairsbreadth from being hostile. The stranger did not seem to care one way or the other. He reached inside his coat, took something out of a pocket and handed it to Rivet.

"I'm delivering this on behalf of a Mr. Vargle Snipe. I'm not sure you've made his acquaintance … actually this is for Mrs. Boxer I've been told to say."

Rivet's eyes narrowed, ferret fashion. Dick wondered if he were going to summon Squiddle. He had some notion of how this queen of crones might look, and he was not over keen to make her acquaintance. The silence began to be almost tangible. Trumpton had specifically told Dick that he must remain in Rivet's company just long enough to make sure he held the grimoire in his hand – in order to make a physical connection with it. It was unlikely that he would dare not to pass it on to Squiddle.

From the black velvet bag he had been given Rivet pulled out the small, leather-bound volume. He turned it over in his hand, reading the title – *The Black Road of the Crescent Moon* – embossed in fading gold. Rivet stared uncomprehendingly at this for a time then opened a page at random. His eyes strayed over the arcane symbols executed in woodblock; in the uneven margins were stains that could have been dried blood. Rivet recoiled slightly at the sight, but curiosity forced him to continue his examination of the text. For all the sense it made to him, it might have been a Chinese telephone directory. He looked up, in order to make some remark to Dick, and realized he was no longer there.

Rivet stared at the place where Dick had been. The light in the shop, never bright, suddenly seemed to dim and the whole interior seemed no longer to have any solid form. He also felt unaccountably cold as if he were now part of the night outside. Rivet even had to reassure himself that he was actually there – standing in the shop. Why hadn't he asked this ghostly emissary his name?

A pair of brothel-creepers clumped down the stairs from the stockroom, making Rivet turn towards the sound. Noticing his dazed expression, Squiddle was about to make some caustic remark when her attention became fixed on the object in Rivet's hands. As if suddenly losing control of her own limbs, she grabbed the black book. Rivet knew better than to resist, and the small, black volume almost leapt into Squiddle's hands. She held it greedily, her eyes lit like hot coals. Unconcerned as to where it had come from, or how Rivet had come upon it, Squiddle was anxious to hurry away with her prize. She, the Priestess of Hecate, would shield this sacred thing from the gaze of the unworthy.

The shop door opened once more. Rivet stared, Squiddle glared. There stood Beans, an insolent look on his face. The look Squiddle gave Beans was a short head from being murderous. She almost screamed.

"What do you bloody want?"

Rivet began hopping from one foot to the other like a bilious camel, while Beans simply carried on as if Squiddle was not there. He stared fixedly at Rivet.

"Anything we oughta know about what's been 'appenin' lately, Mr. Boxer? You know we like to protect your interests as well as our own, don't you? Anybody been in here that you fought was dodgy like?"

Rivet shook his head vigorously like an old dog – an appropriate simile. Beans stared at him, the smile still in place. This tableau – the two men facing each other, and Squiddle poised at the foot of the stairs, might have continued indefinitely. A voice from another part of the shop suddenly made sure it did not.

"What about that bloke who came in here just now? The one what went off in a puff of smoke. He had some funny vibes about him … "

Emerging from behind a cabinet of Travellers' Trinkets shambled the figure of Boggy. An antique Windlefarian – a classic of its kind – the hair was long and lank, the colour and texture of a discarded shaving brush. Boggy had an equally mangy young female in tow. Beans regarded them both with equal distaste, at the same time alert to anything that might prompt his next move. Rivet desperately tried to keep things moving along, like a keen uncle at a children's party. The little darlings, he sensed, might be rapidly becoming fractious.

"What were you saying, Boggy?"

Challenging all known medical science, a few synapses in the Boggy brain were still intact.

"I saw him hanging about on the Nob in the Summer … and in Lowe Street … sussing things out he was … "

Beans' look was a piercing glare.

"What motor's he drivin'?"

As if on cue, a car drove past the window.

"That one there."

Beans was already out of the shop, seconds later giving Rover directions. Dick's car turned into Ackwater Street joining a trickle of traffic to and from the town. Beans peered into the gloom, the street lighting on this stretch of road being only minimal. Rover stared fixedly ahead.

"That the motor we're after?"

"Gotta be."

Beans concentrated.

"There he is. Turning off up that road there."

Fingerlickin Lane led up towards the Nob. Rover was acutely aware that the way was narrow and dark. Being a city boy, he was not comfortable driving along rural cart tracks. Another vehicle came down the hill, forcing him to dim the headlights so he could hardly see at all.

Dick knew perfectly well he was being followed, and began to prepare himself accordingly. If magic was being in another state of mind, then he could imagine any situation and simply make it happen. Naturally, the universe had to give its permission for this to happen, he knew that was part of the deal. The miraculous nature of anything that would occur was almost irrelevant. To consider that everything was a miracle separated the magician from other mortals.

The spirits of the land were known to be particularly potent around the Isle of Teflon, and Dick would only have to evoke the forces of earth for them to do his bidding. He made a few telling gestures in the air, at the same time visualizing the powers he wished to call upon. It did not take long for them to respond to his call. The Earth Goddess always recognizes her own, and although Dick was new to the fold he had, become part of a clan that recognised Merlin as its mentor. The arch-wizard had always claimed total dominion over mountain, river and sky.

Rover was suddenly aware that a mist had surrounded them. Within minutes it grew so thick that it was impossible to see further than the front of the car. He was forced to slow down to a walking pace. In the seat beside him Beans ranted and raved.

"Woss goin' on? Where's all this come from? Oo ever 'eard of wevver like this?"

The tail lights of the car they were following grew more and more faint, finally disappearing. Beans was now pale with rage, and with not a little fear as well.

"You'll never catch him now. We 'ad 'im nailed only a minute ago. What a bleedin' cock up!"

They crawled along various country lanes for what seemed a very long time, during which the mist grew thicker and thicker as if a grey blanket now completely enveloped them. Eventually, Rover was forced to stop.

"They don't have fog like this up in the Smoke, nowhere. Not even aht by the Isle o' Dogs."

"You'll have to turn round and get out of 'ere."

Rover stared at Beans in some disbelief.

"That ain't quite so easy. These is flippin' narrer roads, and this ain't no little motor. I could go slap right in a ditch, no problem. We'll have to go on a bit and find a gateway or summink."

"Yeh, you do that."

But to this end nothing suitable presented itself, even after what seemed like an interminable time. They were crawling along at pace that would have qualified a woodlouse for the Olympics. Tensions were as taut as a tambourine stuck in a microwave. Goldie's voice was heard from the back seat, a sound like a punctured accordion.

"'ere, woss 'appenin'? 'S like a bad dream."

"Woss the matter wiv you? You 'avin' a baby or summink?"

Goldie was almost crying.

"I don't like it, Beans. I don't know what to do next. Woss 'appenin' to me?"

Beans let rip his pent up emotions in one terrifying blast.

"You're off yore 'ead. That's woss 'appenin' to you. You're a nutter. A useless old nutter."

Goldie continued in a sing-song whine.

"I dunno what's the matter wiv me ... I don't ever feel right no more ... Me stomach's always playin' up these days. 'Get up the doc's', they say ... they don't know nuffin'. 'Stress'. Right ... stress o' putting the frighteners on blokes for firty years. They'd like that wouldn't they. 'Ave some of these pills...sort you aht...make you feel awright abaht doin it."

"Shut up!"

Goldie cringed further into the corner of the seat.

"Don't shout at me like that, Beans. I ain't done nuffink. I can't take it when you gets cross wiv me."

Goldie looked at his hands, they were shaking, and a kind of deathly cold was creeping over him such that he had never felt before. Tears were streaming down his cheeks.

"'elp me, Beans, 'elp me ... be noice..."

Beans turned round, leaping over the seat so that he was but inches from Goldie's sad old face.

"Shut up ... shut up ... 'fore I shut you up, permanent."

It was right at that moment Rover hit the wall, invisible in the ever thickening fog. The crash sent Beans tumbling and cursing onto the floor.

Dick stopped near the Nob and stepped out into a grey world. He saw nothing but a wall of stillness with the profiles of trees staring out at him. Ordinary this was not. The mist was under his control, but he knew that some other force had been evoked by some malignant meddler. Calmly, Dick drew out the cloak from the back seat of the car and donned it. Opening the magical case, he drew forth the wand. As soon as he grasped it, an amber light sprang from its tip. As a lantern attracts moths, the wand was a beacon, drawing the entity slowly but purposefully towards the Magus. What was it? Where had it come from? These were questions that flitted in and out of Dick's reason, the magical part of his mind however, acted more decisively.

There is a world of difference between an invocation and an evocation. What was about to emerge from the mist had its existence in the conscious realm, there was no doubting that when it lumbered into view. The wizard raised his wand and it halted momentarily, like an animal sniffing the air trying to detect the scent of its enemies. Dick regarded its form, almost academically, as if he were engaged upon research into various classes of demons. This one was neither human nor entirely bestial; it was something created from the darkest clay of the astral realms.

This shapeless hunk exuded an unmistakable menace. As Dick took a pace towards it, no eyes or any other features seemed to be visible in the lump of matter that was its head. His own expression was stern and set, and the creature seemed to sense this for it faltered in its advance, swaying gently. The wizard raised his wand high, and his voice, although dulled by the cloying mists, was nonetheless laden with power.

"Go back, thou demon. Return to those who sent you. There is no place for you here in this world. Go, I command you, lest I strike and you fall asunder before me."

The figure halted, unsure of what to do next, aware of a power greater than that which had given it life. Dick, aware of its doubts, strove to ensure that it would obey his command totally and utterly. He, the wizard, looked down upon the creature from the skies and saw it far below him, small and vulnerable. But this contest was far from over, it had only just begun. The shapeless mass looming before Dick was still the product of a will, cruel and terrible. Dick knew his only hope lay in convincing the creature that it did not exist. To do this he would have to overpower the will of its creator.

Dick concentrated, determined to be diverted by nothing that existed about him. The rustle of the reeds in the rhines, the shadowy profile of the car – all must fall back and withdraw from the world. Dick withdrew into his inner self and battled along pathways that he knew must lead to the epicentre of the mind that he was required to subdue. It was a terrible journey that he made in the Otherworld. Beset on all sides by wraiths and formless terrors, once or twice he nearly faltered. When he did so, the creature stirred and tried to advance once more. With a tremendous effort the wizard continued to restrain him.

Eventually Dick entered the Realm of the Souls, a place where the darkest secrets of every individual reside. Now that he had the measure of those who had brought such this unholy thing into the world, he could make one final attempt to be merciful. Even though what was before him was made of vileness, through no fault of its own had it had been created.

"Begone! I can speak no more. The powers are with me this instant, and now they call for your end. One word and they will destroy you utterly."

Unwilling, or uncomprehending, the creature did not seek to move – or was there a slight tremor of the ungainly head that hinted at contrition? It mattered little now. Composed of such dross that the universe considered it to be an outrage against the divine will, the fate of the creature was now sealed. The magus stood between Heaven and Earth, and it was he who would be the instrument of the creature's destruction.

He raised his wand and the first flashing bolts from its tip struck the creature. It began to lurch to and fro like a drunk in an alley. Stronger and more frequent were the shafts that struck it, until great rifts began to appear in the stone-like frame and it was rent and broken. Eventually it crumbled and fell into a heap of ash. Dick lowered the wand, and this dust too was borne away – taken by a sudden gust of wind across the moors. With that, the mist lifted and fled heavenward. Dick, knowing his task was complete, put wand and all away to drive into the night.

On the journey home Dick was forced to reflect on all that had happened. He knew that with Squiddle in possession of the grimoire, the thing he had grappled with was more than likely to have emanated from her twisted consciousness. Snipe too, in obtaining the evil book, had stoked the infernal flames. A great threat to the spiritual fabric of the Isle of Teflon was looming. Another evil too lurked in the shadows beyond Squiddle – those who had tried to pursue him across the moors. This was only the beginning.

The familiar sight of Clinton came into view. The sweeping crescents seemed to welcome his return as he drove past them. Their noble fabric helped him to dismiss from his mind the sinister and shocking sights he had witnessed that night.

XIV

onight all shades of magic were in the air, from grey to black and back again. It was Halloween – the bogey night of the bourgeois. By chance or design the night of Tricks'n'Treats fell on the Full Moon. With an arcane correspondence, its beams were reflected in the mirror in which Zeep was examining herself closely. She had been constantly checking and rechecking her appearance for the last hour. Dressed entirely in black, no radical departure for her, she postured and primped in front of the glass. Now she felt the very essence of *darkness* in each garment she had donned. The collection of bracelets, necklaces and brooches with which she had festooned her ample frame, shone with a ghostly incandescence.

Just lately Squiddle had encouraged her to believe she was a night spirit, a denizen of the deepest shadows. She had been very specific about the stygian fogs that should fill her mind in the hours leading up to the Mini Black Mass they were to do together. Zeep had attempted to follow Squiddle's instructions for the nightly meditations she was supposed to practise, but she had not found the exercise easy. She had always found it difficult to concentrate on *anything* for longer than a few seconds, her mind tending to flit about like a bumble bee in a garden centre.

She had once been part of a meditation group that met in the home of Willow Wanderer, a woman she had met at a pagan moot in The Wildfowler's Arms. The experience had not been a great success. On the first evening she had left early complaining of a headache, almost asphyxiated by the stench from the dozen or so cats in the house.

During another session she had fallen into a deep slumber and had inadvertently slumped against Rainbow Rod, Willow Wanderer's partner, sitting next to her on the sofa. She had woken to a frosty atmosphere caused by a revelation from one of the more mediumistic members of the group. She had asserted that while Zeep had been unconscious, Rod had been slyly fondling her ample rump.

Zeep had dutifully made herself familiar with the responses that would feature in tonight's ritual, yet she was still puzzled by the greater part of the script. Unknown to her, Squiddle had memorized whole chunks of oaths and incantations from the grimoire, adding various gabblings of her own invention. The result was a hotchpotch of diabolism and necromancy which, with a few heavy-metal CDs, would have completed the whole weird-arsed pantomime.

The doorbell to her basement flat sounded, and with an excitement almost mounting to hysteria, Zeep ran to answer it. Opening the door, she goggled at the bizarre sight that was revealed. Squiddle's deerstalker hat was festooned with enormous feathers and coloured glass balls. Her complexion, always florid, was enhanced by the addition of several layers of rouge. The scarlet bow of her lips further raised the temperature of her features to volcanic heights. She wore a scarlet t-shirt and leggings of coal-heaver's black, overlaid with luminous green pop socks disappearing into pink trainers. With increasing alarm, Zeep realized she was not only in the company of a mad sorceress, but someone with a totally lunatic dress-sense.

Squiddle was in a bad temper and was not reticent about sharing her foul mood. She had sensed that something had gone very wrong when she had summoned the golem. At one moment she had been flung on the floor before her altar and everything on it hurled across the room. She was still suffering from a painful bruise bestowed on her by a pewter chalice whirling through the air.

Worse still, she could not work out whose power had thwarted her own. Squiddle was not used to being beaten and was determined to increase her powers rather than accept defeat. If this involved low-rent sorcery with Zeep then so be it, she was not above a certain amount of occult slumming.

She was also not too pleased about performing the ritual in Zeep's basement flat, and had only agreed to do so because a sudden storm the day after her disastrous evocation had now made the lean-to uninhabitable. A deluge of water coming through the roof had swept the remains of the altar, magical implements and her magical library onto the lawn. She had found her books – a forlorn pulp – the next morning beneath the gooseberry bushes. The grimoire was unharmed, secreted as it was beneath her pillow.

Squiddle inspected the dank little cupboard that Zeep had assigned as their temple space and found it distinctly wanting. Feebly lit by candles that would have looked better on a birthday cake, she glowered disapprovingly at Zeep's arrangements. But there was nothing for it; the ritual had to be performed at exactly the hour of the Full Moon, less than twenty minutes away. Zeep, flustered, and realizing that not a single word had passed between them since Squiddle's arrival, attempted to introduce a forlorn hospitality to the proceedings.

"Would you like some tea?"

Squiddle dismissed the idea with a wave of a gloved hand.

"No time. What we need right now is some blood."

The line was delivered in Squiddle's customary flat tone, while Zeep could only dumbly gape at her. Eventually, she squeaked in enquiry.

"Sorry?"

"Wake up! I said, *we need some blood.*"

Zeep managed to respond, her voice hardly above a whisper.

"Why?"

Squiddle spoke slowly and carefully as if addressing a pre-school child.

"Zeep ... tonight we are ... amongst other magical practices ... *drawing down the Moon.*"

"Oh, yes, like the witches did."

"Do ... Zeep ... *Do*. That is what we are going to *do* tonight ... or this is all a complete waste of time ... and I'm not having that ... no way!"

She drew from what looked like a battered school satchel, an ivory handled knife. Drawing off one wrinkled glove, Squiddle tested the sharpness of the blade by pricking her finger. A tiny, crimson globule appeared. Zeep started involuntarily, prompting a sneer of contempt from Squiddle.

"Don't be such a wimp! I've been through forty-four pigeons, three cats and countless toads in the last six months. Now ... come on ... your turn."

The drawing of Zeep's blood was achieved without any major trauma and Squiddle carefully smeared this onto a bat's wing she drew from the apparently bottomless satchel. She also produced a small, black book from its depths. As soon as she saw this, Zeep could not stop her fingers moving to grasp it. Her voice was as husky as ... a husky.

"What's that?"

Squidge snatched her hand back.

"Nothing to do with you, my girl. This stuff is way beyond your angel cards and silly bags of runes. This is the real thing."

At her words Zeep assumed a shade that went a stage more pale even than her graveyard make-up. *The Real Thing?* What did this mean? Were they going to meet Beelzebub himself? Zeep shivered with anticipation but had little time to savour any spicy sensations as Squiddle was already issuing instructions.

"Now, light some of these black candles…I don't suppose you've got any incense that's any good … never mind, I've brought some of my special lumps of frankincense. That should get up a good fug … then *they* will appear."

"*They*?"

Zeep's echo reverberated off the cupboard walls.

"Dark angels … demons of the deep."

"Oh, yes … right … "

Impatiently, Squiddle handed her assistant a stuffed crow. Zeep shuddered slightly while placing the moth-eaten bird in the centre of the altar. What else did Squiddle have in the depths of that bag? To Zeep's relief, preparations seemed nearly to be complete. Squiddle took charge once more making Zeep feel as if she was back in the company of her bossy elder sister.

"You stand in the North … that's Winter and the Earth … you won't get too spaced out there."

Before the ritual proper began, Squiddle could not resist a waspish aside.

"As you've been … uh … *initiated* by Rivet… I suppose you're up to this."

Zeep blushed redly, but said nothing. Squiddle more than made up for her silence by beginning to wail manically and at a painful pitch. She then goose-stepped about the tiny temple like Eva Braun in a punk band.

Apart from topping up her powers, Squiddle's other intention during the ritual was to create as much havoc for all those who had slighted her. Giving a hard time to any who featured in her long-standing feuds was definitely on the agenda. Squiddle made enemies as often as kids make faces.

When she was not being blinded by clouds of incense, Zeep stared at Squiddle's antics. Most of the time was spent in struggling to breathe, the clouds of incense made the air so thick, it was like inhaling cotton wool. The floor seemed sticky too and at the same time shift around apparently of its own accord. Zeep wanted to cry out, to tell Squiddle to stop it all, but the words would not come. Suddenly, with the screeching of some final incomprehensible imprecations, it was all over. Zeep almost cried with relief.

They emerged into the light of the hall. Squiddle's eyes were bloodshot, as ruddy as her rouge. She looked like Lady Macbeth wondering if serial killings really did add spice to a marriage. First stuffing the stuffed crow into her satchel, Squiddle gathered the rest of her paraphernalia. Zeep hovered uncertainly in her shadow.

"Um, would you like some tea now?"

Once more Squiddle waved the gloved hand.

"No time now."

Zeep opened the door of the flat. Outside, the wind was howling like a pack of wolves. Hardly able to keep her feet, Zeep clutched at Squiddle's arm. Leering triumphantly, the sorceress made her exit, not on a broomstick, but a bicycle.

"The dark forces are with us."

Such a pungent imprecation hung in the air as Squiddle mounted her machine and pedalled away into the black heart of the tempest, the satchel flapping at her side like a broken wing. The full moon, a gigantic spotlight behind her, lit up her progress. Zeep watched the silhouetted figure disappear and then went back into the flat.

After bolting the door, Zeep went and put on her pyjamas. She drew her dressing gown around her, made a mug of Horlicks and took it with her to bed. Lying there, in the soft glow of the night-light on the dressing-table, Zeep tried to calm her racing heart. She knew she would have a headache for days after all this.

The manner of darkness that had been evoked during the ritual was not the kind that disappears when you get to the end of the tunnel. This was the kind that increases by the minute. Elsewhere, in the dark deeps, the forces that Squiddle had evoked were now seeking out the minds of their likely victims.

Perhaps the antics of Squiddle and her reluctant apprentice had sent their tenacious tentacles as far the crescents and malls of Clinton. When Dick had woken up that morning he decided he was losing it all, and that magic was all to blame. When do finely honed perceptions transform themselves into the delusions of Bedlam? What was madness? Act like a madman and you will soon construct your own padded cell.

That day great fear came upon Dick, a state of mind that would not be shown the door that easily. Waves of writhing blackness – the same terror that would soon have Windleroot in its grip, began to possess him. Dick was aware this was all part of Trumpton's master plan to set the universe back on its feet, and it was inevitable he would be the target of Squiddle's diabolic dabblings. Dick accepted all this rationally, but he was still convinced his head was about to explode into a billion tiny pieces.

Had Dick but known it, Standley-Strange had a great-uncle Perris who thought he was a magpie and took to roosting in the willow trees on his estate. That gentleman might as well have believed he was a parrot or a revolving bookcase for all the attention he got from his immediate family. They locked him in his bedroom, fed him every so often and made sure of their inheritance when he eventually died. Perhaps it was the shade of Perris who sent Dick scurrying to the temple to consult his great-nephew's Magical Workbook. In a frenzy, Dick thumbed through the pages in an effort to find some enlightenment as to his present mood.

The Watcher at the Gate or The Shadow is often encountered in the beginning of the student's studies or even during his first magical ritual. He may be terrible in appearance and instil the worst kinds of fear deep into our being. Our pain is unimaginable our despair seems endless, yet the lesson we must learn from the 'Dweller on the Threshold' is one of identifying the hubris, or spiritual pride, that lies within ourselves. We must all come to terms with the darkness within ourselves, and to deny this ultimately harmful state. We should gain comfort in knowing that when we are drawn to love, truth and beauty we are in harmony with the light. That will return, as surely as day follows night.

Dick read this through and read it again but ultimately it did not do the trick. He wished he had never got mixed up in all of this. In a frantic attempt to climb from out of the bog of chaos and regain the rock of reason, he decided to abandon magic as if it were a stray dog. Poor Dick, he decided he was cracking up, and like many when faced with the same sorry condition, grabbed at any straw that had 'help' printed on it.

Derek the postman was also the sacristan at the local Catholic Church and told Dick of the whereabouts of the local priest. Father Declan O'Duffy holed up in a bit of a hole at the very edge of Clinton. Dick discovered the prefab where he lived, squeezed uncomfortably between the church and a kebab stall. With some trepidation he rang the doorbell.

Our man of the cloth came to the door in his dressing gown. Perched on a tangle of white hair was what looked his spare biretta. He looked put out, as if the notion of a layman visiting a priest was somehow in bad taste. In modern times it might have been a relic of medievalism or even Popery, at the very least an obscene symbol of piety. Any one of these things could have made him disapprove of Dick's presence.

"What is it you'll be wantin' now?"

Dick had rehearsed his opening lines carefully.

"I wondered if I could speak with you for a few minutes, Father. I'm in the middle of some kind of spiritual crisis I think."

The response of this Man of God was not encouraging.

"*Croisis?* What can be more of a croisis than my havin' to take Confession this very mornin' and listen to a lot of eejits bletherin' about their sexual problems?"

Dick had never considered the nature of ecclesiastical duties in any detail before. He feigned surprise and concern.

"Oh."

With obvious reluctance Father O'Duffy ushered Dick into the hall and from there into a small study. The whole house seemed to reek of fish and cabbage. When the door of the study had been fastened the smell was slightly less nauseating but still evident. The priest indicated a broken sofa where Dick was to sit.

"Have ye come to talk about yer sex loife as well? Don't beat about the bush now."

Dick wondered for a fleeting second if this was some subtle jest. One glance at the purple-chinned features of his host convinced him otherwise.

"No, it wasn't that, it was more to do with … uh … the truth of things."

The priest sneered, with such emphasis that his hat fell over one eye. He did not bother to set it right again.

"Desiring the world to be in some fashion that it is not, are ye? Am Oi roight … or not? Yer stance on all this is fundamentally an error of judgment, do ye not think?"

Dick tried again.

"But surely your Church teaches that there has to be some meaning in life?"

This time the hat fell off and landed neatly in the coal scuttle.

"Meaning of loife? Of course there is not. That would be grand –

the very business – would it not? Bejaysus, what are ye thinkin' of? If the Good Lord and Our Lady wanted us to be a-thinkin' along these loines would heaven have been and created such fools as what we are? You see my point, do ye not?"

Dick was not sure he did. Reverting to the technique he had once perfected with his father, he was as the grave.

"Now, anythin' else?"

The tone was perfunctory, even threatening. Dick summoned up enough courage to ask the other question he had rehearsed.

"Do you think there are such things as flying saucers, Father?"

O'Duffy's eyes were like flint, his mouth a small *o* of disgust.

"Who is it has been fillin' yer head with such blarney, Oi moight ask? Ye'll be wantin' to know of myself concernin' the Little People next. Are ye a drunkard?"

Dick told the truth.

"I don't drink actually."

The priest rose angrily to his feet. He recovered the fallen biretta, now smeared with coke dust, and gripped it tightly in his trembling fist.

"Then ye should. Alcohol cleanses the bowels most vigorously. A little Jamerson's of an evening moight make you a better citizen … one that does not disturb the peace and quiet of the honest people of this world. Now get off with ye down the poob. This interview is at an end."

He flung open the study door. The piscine pong had become noticeably more pungent. Dick stood in the unkempt garden. The door slammed behind him, making the thin walls of the priest's dwelling shake alarmingly. As he made his way home Dick reflected briefly on Father O'Duffy's words. He had not dared to inform him that he had seen the spacecraft once more. While they had been talking in the priest's study Dick had happened to look out of the window. It was there, hovering in the sky, its silver hull majestic and mysterious.

Dick booked an appointment with a psychiatrist for the next day. His address told that his practice was not located in the fashionable part of Clinton. The premises were in Wilby Walk, a small *cul de sac* that led off the main thoroughfare. Dick noticed that rooks were massing in the tall trees that lined the pavement. He wondered if that was an omen of something or other. Chastened by his encounter with Father O'Duffy, Dick had turned to secular wisdom in the hope that would provide clarity to his confused thoughts. His hopes were to be dashed, *toutsuite* – if not quicker.

The surroundings for this new encounter were undeniably more attractive than the priest's hole. The furnishings were tastefully arranged in the room where Solly Comfit saw his clients. The ambiance was one of restrained comfort. A glistening Chesterfield took up one wall and from here it was possible to survey the neatly managed garden.

Proceedings began slowly, the topic of the weather being discussed with more intensity than Dick was normally used to.

"Cold now, I think, colder than usual for this time of year. Very much so wouldn't you agree?"

Dick was inclined to quibble slightly at this observation.

"Pleasant enough when the sun's out."

The psychiatrist peered at Dick over his half-moon glasses.

"Do you really think so?"

Dick detected an overly challenging tone. He put it down to the doctor coming from a long line of Lithuanian intellectuals. Was his great-grandfather prone to calling out opponents to fight duels? Perhaps over meteorological issues?

"Now then ... "

Dick presumed this was his cue.

"I've come to see you because really ... I suppose ... I don't know who I am right now. Maybe I haven't known that for the last forty years ... even longer maybe."

Solly wrinkled his nose – expertly, professionally.

"Do you like yourself?"

Dick tried to answer honestly; he presumed that was what he was supposed to do.

"Never thought about it really. Um, how does anyone actually tell if they do or don't?"

It was a matter of professional pride to Solly that he had had always relied upon certain techniques for his success. If his client asked him a question he simply did not answer, just stared at them with his full-on therapists' grin and waited. Most times it did not take long for the client to start feeling uncomfortable and make some remark – usually foolish. Thus did Solly keep the upper hand. Dick however was made of sterner stuff and stared right back.

"Mmmm."

"Mmmm."

Solly polished up some theoretical gem he had picked up in Zurich around 1965 at the Jungian Centre and lobbed it into the discourse.

"If we dislike somebody ... then that is generally regarded as being some aspect of ourselves that we are reflecting. The *shadow* as Jung calls it..."

Dick noticed that when the name of Old Carl was evoked, perceptible sparkles of light came into Solly's watery eyes. A benediction was probably only just round the corner.

"What about Stalin then?"

"I'm sorry ... I don't follow."

"Well ... if I met Stalin ... a man responsible for the deaths of countless millions of people ... and I said to him 'I say, Josef, I think you're rather a shit' ... Follow me so far?"

"Er ... Yes."

"...Then you're saying that indicates some questionable ... unacceptable or even *negative* aspect in my character...which ought to be expunged from my psyche. Is that it?"

"It's possible."

"Possible? Well, that simply won't do, I'm afraid. And in this instance, I would say you were talking the most total and utter twot."

The light dimmed in Solly's eyes. He tried the grin, but there wasn't enough voltage.

"We would have to look at many factors ... some relevant, others not so ... before we came to any definite conclusion ... "

Dick shifted about a bit on the old Chesterfield before reloading.

"So are opinions like dreams ... simply things that having happened in real life get turned into a dream experience? Or do we instil some degree of verisimilitude to them and thus regard them as absolutes?"

Dick could see that Solly liked this even less than he had the stuff about Stalin. But, of course, it was a question, or a brace of them. So Solly did his bit of staring intently out of the window, after a bit switching to the picture rail above Dick's head and giving that the once over. Eventually, he seemed to tire of it all and offered up a few gobbets of wisdom of his own.

"Interpretations are always subject to the references the mind constructs as to their intrinsic qualities ... "

Dick interrupted rather sharply, his tone similar to the high C on a trumpet.

"So what's that all about? I mean it's all symbolic isn't it, surely? I'm surprised you don't see it that way … Your mate Jung was heavily into archetypes wasn't he? And while we're onto him … he was pretty cool about flying saucers am I right?"

Dick couldn't help noticing how much Solly was slumped in his chair. His legs were sticking out into the room to the point where there might be a serious danger of him *invading someone else's space.* He droned on.

"We can never be certain that the literal … as indeed the metaphorical … can be satisfactorily attached … attached … dream … not sure … sure…"

Dick, all ready to do a spot of talking back, realised Solly was burbling … slurring his words to the point of being incoherent. He didn't think he had been on the old *kvass*, which was not particularly potent anyway. Dick concluded this was simply the time he took his afternoon nap. His eyelids drooped even more heavily and a minute or two later he was snoring, none too gently either.

After a short interval, Dick, taking care not to wake the slumbering shrink, slipped through the open French windows and out of the garden gate. Dick's conscience was clear; such a crappy performance didn't deserve a cheque.

Once more Dick found himself retracing his steps to Richardson Gardens. What had been achieved? He concluded that a pair of his fellow creatures, who were authorised by society to set the cosmic records straight for others, were totally inept. If a flying pterodactyl had been introduced to either situation, Solly would have sat there waffling about *schadenfreude* or some such and Father O'Duffy would have put it down to the DTs. Both of them had such a tight-arsed view of the world!

Dick concluded that if this was the best that psychology or the saints could offer then he was better off facing the fast bowling himself. He hadn't lost his wicket or his wits yet, so he would stick it out till the end of the innings. Dismissing any further sporting analogies that might occur to him, he reflected that if he saw things that nobody else did then so be it. Perhaps that was merely a bonus to being on the planet. Colourful fizzings and loud reports in the near distance reminded him it was Guy Fawkes Night. He would purchase a large rocket and set it off in the garden to celebrate his triumphant return to the world – or at least his version of it.

XV

Half way through December, and 'without so much as a by your leave', the snow came. First came swirling veils of white, then tiny flakes like fairy sugar. Within hours the world looked so very different, all that before had seemed so ordinary was now profound. In Clinton, window sills were edged with cotton wool, branches brushed with an impressionist hand. A low sun put delicate shadow in the ruts and grooves from scores of footsteps.

Out on the moors near Windleroot, nature wore a harder face. Trees made dark sculpted shapes, a spectral presence beside the rhines. Those who work the land fail spectacularly to see any romance in a winter wonderland. Farmers are perfectly happy with snow on a Christmas card, but prefer not to be digging buried sheep out of the stuff.

One with such a view was Grainey Buttle, out on his morning round while all the time mildly cursing to himself. Preoccupied with thoughts of cows and cow cake, he had climbed off his tractor to open the gate into the home field. Encountering strangers on such a day was not to be expected, and he swung round sharply at the sound of an unfamiliar voice.

"Hullo, Grainey."

The gate swung to under its own weight and closed with a clatter. Buttle turned in the direction of the voice hailing him. A spanking new Barbour, Burberry scarf, Hunter boots and buff-coloured corduroys along with a tweed cap completed the fashion plate of this off-the-peg countryman. Atherton Hook advanced with outstretched hand, one which Buttle took somewhat grudgingly.

"Met you in Thurles not long ago ... Atherton ... Atherton Hook."

This was not too long a shot, and Buttle did not feel he could deny such an encounter with any real confidence. About his business, he met a lot of people, many of whom he could not say he would ever recognize again.

"How are things, Grainey?"

Buttle let his shoulders sag in the way that those who are constantly doing physical work tend to do. The muscles relaxed gratefully.

"Oh, not so bad. Things get done eventually."

Hook took advantage of the other's easy smile, even returning it with a cheap version of his own.

"I expect they do. How was the Pillstown Festival this year? Lot of work involved there I expect…"

"Went very well all things considered. I've never wanted it to get too successful or then it starts to be a big hassle. I'm getting too old for that kind of thing."

At that Hook beamed so much he almost melted the snow around him. He was leaning on the gatepost in the way that he imagined rural folk would do, even chewing a blade of grass to add verisimilitude. He adopted a reflective tone, one hoary with age-old wisdom.

"Well, Grainey … I expect some days you find yourself thinking … I'd like to give it all up and retire … "

Buttle was still cheery.

"Don't know about that … I quite like to see folks enjoying themselves…"

"Come on … be honest … if there was some way you could give it up all up tomorrow you would … wouldn't you?"

Buttle detected something in the voice he thought didn't like too much. A chat was one thing, but he had work to do. When another figure emerged from behind a hedge, he was even less pleased. If he had been wary of Hook, he took an immediate dislike to this latest addition to the party. Kitted out in the same pseudo-rural style, Dowie Ringle trotted up like a scavenging lurcher.

"Hello, hello. Bit parky, eh? Be nicer in the pub by a roaring fire with a pint in front of you, wouldn't it?"

Noticing Buttle's rigid features, Hook quickly stepped in.

"My partner Dowie Ringle. Used to be in this game, didn't you, Dowie? Kept a few sheep yourself at one time…"

"Oh … God yes … near Ebbw Vale it was. Got out of all that as quick as I could … no money in farming is there now…"

The valley falsetto grated on Buttle's ears, and sensing this, Hook moved in for the kill.

"Thing is, Grainey, we're the ones who can make your dream to retire come true, as it happens. The people I work for would like to make you an offer for your property."

Buttle stared.

"An offer … for my place?"

Hook, in his usual ebullient manner, threw caution – not just to the winds – but into the furthest corners of the cosmos. He looked about him, his tone patronizing, dismissive.

"Right … an offer for this place and what I'm going to suggest is that we all go somewhere a bit more inviting … your place or the pub p'raps and talk this one through. At the end of it all I can only promise that you will be very pleased … probably grateful that I popped over here this morning and put this to you. We're talking about an offer you won't be able to refuse."

Buttle set his hands on his hips. He was now seriously angry.

"Yes, I bloody well can refuse, and I just did. What a cheek! Coming here and trying it on! Now get off my property the pair of you … before I put the bull on you."

It would have been obvious even to the bull that Buttle meant what he said. But Hook was the sort who was inclined to be persistent.

"Grainey, surely you can see … I mean … anyone could understand that…"

Buttle was now shouting, and very loudly.

"All I can see is a pair of buggering trespassers on my land … now get off out of it … right now."

He swung into the cab of the tractor, and thrust the machine into gear. Hook and Ringle leapt aside as Buttle deliberately sent its front wheels in their direction. The pair sprinted to the safety of their 4x4 and shot off across the field. Slipping and sliding across the snow, only when the image of the predatory tractor dwindled to nothing in his wing mirror did Hook slow down. Swinging through an open gateway, they gained the main road which eventually led to the motorway.

On their return to London, the sizzle of tyres echoed against the piles of grey slush on the hard shoulder. Hook was thinking hard. With no intention of abandoning his plans to take over the Windleroot project, he still had a card or two to play. One was the Jack of Spades – Beans – who he called on his mobile. Hook needed another ally, and he had surmised correctly that Snipe was no longer part of his world either. Beans confided his misgivings.

"Don't get me wrong, Mr. 'Ook. I fink a lotta Mr. Snipe, always 'ave … but he's been under a lotta pressure lately annee? When that 'appens you just gotta *deleegate* ain'tcha? Somebody gotta make the 'xecutive decisions. I know this *partickular* situation inside out and backwards … so I fink thas me ennit … gotta be."

Hook had agreed enthusiastically and they agreed to meet as soon as he and Ringle drove into London. Undermining the current regime was his aim, then he would be back where he deserved to be – at the top. The call over, a note of triumph sounded through his whole being, and he turned to Ringle with a cheesy grin. Atherton Hook would usher in a new era, and those who were prepared to follow him would know the golden city, a place where riches would flow like sweet water.

The thaw had begun, and in Hammersmith the roofs of the houses looked as if they were dusted with chalk like a schoolmaster's trousers. The melting snow was rapidly turning to the colour of milk chocolate, the traffic swirling along in a brownish tide as Beans parked outside Nero's Café in the Chiswick High Road. Hook and Ringle arrived a few minutes later.

At the counter Hook bought a cup of tea and a doughnut for each of them. He set down these offerings on the formica-topped table as if they were a sacrifice to some deity known only to those assembled. Ringle sat in silence, his Barbour, wrapped tightly around him. Hook, though only having the slimmest of acquaintance with Beans, was at his most sanguine. Beans' slow descent into the twilight zone of the psychopath had begun. Hook was not to know this, he simply assumed that Beans' habit of nodding his head rhythmically at intervals was a sign that he was acquiescing to everything proposed. Without warning he launched into a delirious soliloquy, strangling his vowels more horribly than did Richard III the Princes in the Tower.

"I been double straight wiv Mister Snipe all dahn the line, and it ain't got me nowhere. Know wot I mean? Last fing 'e tells me is get after this geezer Standley-Strange in Clinton … that's the toff's part dahn in Barstowe. I get askin' abaht 'im right? Guess what? He's brown bread innee … a bleedin' stiff. What's that all about? 'E shoulda known that. Then we goes off anuvver toime to Windleroot. 'Keep an eye on fings,' Mister Snipe sez … You know wot? I hates that place … nutters everywhere. Me and the lads we takes off after annuvver geezer, summink to do wiv this dead geezer. That all went very … very … wrong I can tell yuh. That Mr. Snipe … well … I reckon 'e's lost the plot good and proper."

Ringle had been following all this closely and was aware that lurking in Beans' singular character was a seam of pure Puritanism that had never been mined. He proceeded to fuel this strange sectarianism by painting a graphic portrait of decadence in Windleroot. Ringle took particular pains to stress that the Pillstown Festival was an orgy of depravity. Beans appeared to be wrestling with the paradox of his gangland persona and a newly-acquired evangelism.

"We gotta show all them wurzels dahn there they gotta lissen ... right? One of them toe rags down there done me wrong 'n' all ... wiv a bitta business ... that gotta be sorted 'n' all. Me and the lads ... we got a jooty to teach 'em wos goin' on."

Ringle was only too ready to applaud Beans' mission – in strident Chapel tones.

"You got it, my friend. You get down there and show them what's what ... make that sheep-shagger who runs that filthy festival pay for his sins."

The intensity of Beans' righteousness could be assessed by the rhythm of the pulsations at the back of his neck. His eyes had a haze like the light that lingers when a TV screen is switched off, and he began to mutter through his teeth.

"I don't like it...I don't like it..."

Thoughts dash back and forth in his head, like a searchlight glinting on razor wire. Hook speculated that the seeds of anarchy had been sown, and ironically, like Snipe, he believed that chaos would bring forth its own rewards.

"You let me know how things are going ... with your ... um ... campaign. I can see a bright future for you and your lads with us."

Hook even went so far as to pat Beans on the shoulder. That gesture was about as sensible as diving into a tank full of piranha fish, but Hook somehow got away with it. The three of them went out into the street and stood beneath the awning of the café. Water dripped onto the pavement in front of them making an arch that led into the unknown.

"Hello, Morley, how's tricks?"

"You actually find me a touch tiddley, old chap. I felt in need of restoring my flagging spirits with the old sauce. You don't imbibe yourself?"

"No, never have."

"I thought not. You sensitive types never do. Hector was the same. I on the other hand most certainly *do* ... and always in my own company. I look at it this way ... if I get pie-eyed ... then there's only me I have to deal with. If I was in a pub I'd probably be surrounded by a score of shaven-headed oiks … then I'd have to argue the toss with 'em."

Dick didn't quite follow this but said he did anyway.

"I see what you mean."

"Do you? Most people think I'm a misanthropist of absolutely unbelievable proportions."

Dick could sense that Trumpton was fast approaching the land of the garrulous, thus he pitched his bid.

"I've been up in the attic here, the place where Hector did his magic."

Trumpton's response was guarded.

"Tell me … there weren't any *books* up there I don't suppose?"

"Afraid not … apart from his own magical stuff he'd written … "

Trumpton was quietly serious.

"Promise me you'll hang on to that … "

"I certainly will."

Trumpton began to plough another furrow.

"So … you had the dubious delight of meeting Mr. and Mrs. Boxer the other day … and you handed over the mysterious package … as they say in all the best detective stories?"

"I did … but managed to push off before she appeared … "

"Wise move … though if you'd hung around you'd have made an acquaintance with a genuine vampire … "

"Really?"

"She probably doesn't know she is … but I found out she has Slavic ancestry. Not an indictment in itself I hasten to add … but such practices come naturally to those races. She is a worshipper of Hecate during the dark moons … and probably sees herself as Empusa as well … "

"Who?"

"Some say Empusa was the daughter of Medusa … a right little beauty with the charming habit of seducing young men and then feasting upon their blood."

"Gosh!"

"I reckon that Squiddle may well have been mixed up in that Highgate Vampire business in the Seventies."

"But does she go about the place putting curses on everybody? Maybe that was why I thought I was going off my trolley last week …"

"She probably does cast spells quite regularly. Anybody annoys her … out with the black candles and the sacrifices. Don't take it personally is my advice. Anyway … I'm sure the Great Magus … that's you by the way … can cope with anything she or anybody else can chuck at you. I thought you were being a bit too coy about your own powers right from the start."

"I didn't really know I had any."

"'Cometh the hour, cometh the man', old boy."

"Looks like I may have to do it all again at some stage … "

"Well … don't get anxious about things … that's my second helping of wisdom. Remember thoughts aren't necessarily your property. They probably have nothing to do with you at all."

Dick – dare we say it? – thought about this.

"Where do they come from then?"

"Most of them from some mental landfill I reckon. You've got to remember that for most people how they see the world is a matter of agreeing with everybody else. I can see why that happens to humans … I mean it's just for the sake of convenience … we call an umbrella stand just that. If half the people started referring to it as a toast rack that would confuse things rather."

Dick let Trumpton waffle on unhindered.

"We no longer believe in gods and angels because we think it's smart not to … it doesn't mean they aren't there. When I was a kid I saw a ghost in the dorm … I know I did … at my boarding school. Foolishly, as it turned out, I told someone else and he sneaked to the head. I was curtly informed that there were no ghosts at St. Newbolts or anywhere else. Suddenly I was made worldly and wise. I humbly acquiesced with authority … less trouble all round … but I never ever doubted that I had seen the spook."

Dick agreed. After his experiences of the last fortnight he had decided the mentality of the world was dangerous, not his own.

"In ancient times, no one would have thought very much of all this magic stuff … simply part of a day's work. They believed man has the power over everything that happens to him … or appears to happen, let us say. What we see … how we feel … how others perceive us … we have the power to change anything and everything … if only we believe it. That was the thing about Hector, he believed in himself all his life … right up until the moment he popped off, bless him. All his life, nobody ever told him what to think … he made up his own mind. Not many people like that … perfect magician material. To coerce the magus is like trying to force the hand of God … simply can't be done."

Dick pictured Trumpton at that very moment – affectionately. He had his head on his shoulder, looking remarkably like a heron.

"And talking of mortality, old chum … if a life is a week … for me right now it's Sunday afternoon."

With a terrible clarity, Dick heard the words and knew they were true.

What Trumpton said next would serve as his epitaph.

"Whose side am I on? I know there no sides … only angles."

XVI

2013

Pulling a Christmas cracker alone is not only a melancholy procedure, it is almost impossible to achieve successfully. Dick had spent many a Yuletide on his own yet this year his situation seemed particularly forlorn. From the dining room window he could see a robin sheltering from the icy wind. Winter being a time of reflection, it was perhaps inevitable that Dick would start thinking about Janice.

What had happened on that afternoon in 1963? The greatest pop group of all time providing a fanfare for the most amazing kiss in the history of osculation … that's what it was. Dick wondered and went on wondering. Who was she? Where was she? For all Dick knew Janice could be living in Australia or Alaska, and have done for thirty years. Was she born in Windleroot, or was she in a coach party on a day trip from Blackburn? Did that explain why she hurried away? Not to miss the bus? Dick certainly did. And why did he never go back to try and find her?

It had all happened nearly fifty years ago too, so 2013 was some sort of anniversary. If Dick had been a drinking man he might have reached for the bottle. As it was, he sluiced down a little spring water. The robin still fluttered in a chilly way round the garden. Once or twice they regarded each other with a kind of mutual sympathy.

The way Rivet treated Zeep, his employee, would have made a Victorian mill owner seem like Santa Claus. He was more Scrooge-like than Scrooge himself, declining to hand over even the most meagre Christmas bonus. Regularly for the last five years he had also sacked her on Christmas Eve. He did this so that in the New Year he could sadistically enjoy the spectacle of her begging to be reinstated. This he was always prepared to do, but with the proviso that she received slightly less in wages than that of the previous year. This Christmas she had been even more penniless than usual, and when dismissed, even hinted to Rivet that her favours might be exchanged for hard currency. The porcine satyr was greatly tempted, but his lust was somewhat dampened when he remembered the trouble that the previous liaison had brought about.

In the Boxer household the Festivities were being celebrated in a surreal Gothic style. Squiddle's demented mother and her equally crazed Aunt Dot had arrived unannounced early on Christmas morning. It was soon apparent that not only did they expect to be fed, but endlessly entertained. As would be expected, Rivet had amassed a larderful of festive fayre, but resented sharing even so much as a brussel sprout with his in-laws. The guests then extended their visit, their presence at Badcorn lasting way into the New Year. If he considered that Squiddle displayed insane tendencies, her family would have qualified for the padded cell. After a week or more of this unrelieved agony Rivet thought he too had lost his wits.

Even with their eventual departure, Rivet's composure did not return. He took to waking, terrified and bathed in sweat, in the small hours, his mind whirling like a razor-edged frisbee. Many a night he could be found – torch in hand – patrolling his property looking for intruders. Once he disturbed an amorous badger, that was all. Neither did his waking hours bring any respite to his jangled nerves. In the opening months of the year business was slack, expenses correspondingly heavy.

Rivet spent his days in a wearisome limbo. If he spent too much time at Badcorn he incurred the wrath of Squiddle, and hiding in the stock room at the Paganorama simply made him depressed. On one of those dreary days, when it never seemed never to cease from raining, Rivet took a call from St. John-Pemberthy.

The lawyer suggested a lunch appointment and Rivet, almost pathetically grateful, agreed to the meeting. St. John-Pemberthy was careful not to reveal any details, but hinted that certain monetary advantages might result from the encounter. It was agreed that they have lunch at the Beetlerush Hotel outside Windleroot, an establishment renowned for its generous helpings of roast beef.

St. John-Pemberthy was used to assessing the worth, or otherwise, of those he encountered. Over the years he had honed these intuitive skills, dealing as he did with those who upheld the law, and others – as a good proportion of his clients – who sought to circumvent it. The Cambridge years had sharpened his wit, and his shrewd mind speedily grasped the implications of any matter, legal or otherwise.

Observing Rivet in the car park of the Beetlerush Hotel, the lawyer instantly had the measure of the figure with the lugubrious grin that loped towards the lobby – a man of straw. Perfunctory greetings being exchanged, St. John-Pemberthy led Rivet into the bar and ordered sherry for both of them. The *maitre d'hotel* handed out menus the size of a school atlas, and they took to studying the fayre in silence. The wine list had also been temptingly placed on the bar and Rivet hoped that, in due course, it would be given a thorough examination by his host. He had no doubt that St. John-Pemberthy would be footing the bill, part of the reward for the services he could provide. As yet he did not know what they were. Mid-sherry his host shot a question at him.

"Do you know this place very well?"

"Oh yes, I come here quite a bit."

With any new acquaintance Rivet always invented things, it was a habit he found impossible to break. He had lied to the world almost from the moment he had gained the power of speech. The lawyer was immediately aware of Rivet's mendacity and was determined to glean what sport he could from it. Not too much, just enough to make what could be a tedious occasion into something a little more entertaining.

"Really. What do you recommend then?"

Caught on the hop, Rivet made a thoughtless reply.

"I always find the ... er ... fish is extremely good."

"Is it now? So you're having that, while I tuck into the roast beef?"

Rivet realized he had made a false move. With some slight embarrassment he ordered the same for himself. His guard down, Rivet accepted another schooner of sherry before they were summoned to their table. When they were seated, St. John-Pemberthy looked about him in an avuncular fashion. He almost beamed upon Rivet, as if he were a favourite uncle taking his schoolboy relation out for an afternoon treat.

"And how well do you know Mr. Snipe?"

"Er ... I don't. I've only met those oppos of his..."

"Ah ... yes. *Beans* and the rest ... quite a rum collection of characters don't you think?"

"I suppose so."

St. John Pemberthy noted his discomfort.

"Not quite like us ... eh?"

"No, certainly not ... I should say."

St. John Pemberthy's smile grew even wider. Rather like a cat eying a mouse, Rivet thought. Although he was always pleased to be eating and drinking at someone else's expense, he began to feel that it was his benefactor who distinctly had the advantage.

"Mr. Snipe, on the other hand, is quite an accomplished man … in business circles that is. I don't think there's very much doubt that all his schemes will come to fruition in due course, but there is a little difficulty that has come up."

"Oh?"

"Nothing that can't be got over I'm sure … particularly considering your somewhat exalted position in Windleroot society … and your expertise."

Rivet was totally confused at this, not sure of he was being a fool of or not. He chose to force a laugh out of some odd corner of himself, the resulting sound resembling an air-raid siren. His host looked away for an instant then fixed Rivet with an incisive look.

"Mr. Snipe is interested in obtaining certain documents…"

"Oh, ah … yes?"

"…that he understands are in the vaults in the Town Hall. Now you being the mayor of Windleroot…"

"Yes."

"… and having a certain authority … you might possibly have access to these, perhaps…?"

The effects of the two schooners of sherry had conspired to make Rivet garrulous.

"I do know what you mean. I've seen quite a lot of interesting things in those vaults … for instance …

St. John-Pemberthy raised a gently restraining hand.

"If you don't mind … can we keep to the matter in question?"

Proceedings were temporarily halted by the arrival of the starter: boar's head pâté, reeking of port wine. St. John-Pemberthy had ordered a fine claret to accompany this delicacy. After sampling the vintage and assuring the waiter of its excellence, he got down to the real business in hand, that of attending to Rivet's glass, and making sure it was continuously filled. After disposing of a few gobbets of pâté, Rivet once more took up his side of the conversation.

"What exactly are these documents?"

St. John-Pemberthy assumed a diplomatic air.

"I think it's probably better all round if you don't know the details of the actual contents. Just the file numbers will be enough to readily identify them."

St. John-Pemberthy opened the ever-present briefcase that was resting on the chair next to him. He took out a single sheet of paper on which was printed a list of numbers, which he handed to Rivet.

"I think you'll see that's all pretty straightforward. The most important files are the first four … as you can see those numbers are printed in bold type. The other two would be useful but are not essential."

Rivet examined the paper. He had by now quaffed two large glasses of wine and, while not exactly swimming before his eyes, the numbers in front of him seemed to be a little fuzzy at the edges. He studied them once more and was about to pocket the sheet when St. John-Pemberthy, who had been closely watching his every move, retrieved the paper.

"Just jot them down on the back of your hand will you … then memorise them. We don't want anything *incriminating* left around, do we?"

He produced a fountain-pen, and with a little encouragement, Rivet succeeded in this task. At this juncture, the boar being dealt with, it was the turn of the cow. A trolley arrived with a side of beef, the waiter liberally heaping Rivet's plate so high with meat and vegetables that there was hardly room for any Yorkshire pudding and gravy. Rivet, wasting no time, anointed the whole with horseradish sauce, and set to. The claret being disposed of, he hardly noticed that the wine in his glass was now a very full Burgundy.

At this stage, neither vintage nor grape would have made the slightest difference to Rivet. The amount consumed was his only consideration. Oblivious to everything except what was on his plate, Rivet stuffed and stuffed. St. John-Pemberthy only encouraged him.

"Marvellous to see a chap tuck in like you're doing. Sure you won't have any more of this wonderful beef? I'll call them over if you like … Roast potatoes? No? No? Pudding to come later, of course, good idea to leave a little room for that, eh?"

And Rivet, his mouth full of sprouts and fat, gravy dripping down his chin – the very picture of gluttony – shouted back cheerfully.

"Expect I'll manage somehow."

Emerging from a vinous haze, Rivet found St. John-Pemberthy studying a point in the far corner of the room. His gaze immediately returned to Rivet, who started involuntarily.

"And so … how soon can you get those files to Mr. Snipe?"

With some difficulty Rivet attempted to collect his thoughts.

"In a couple of days. I can't just waltz into the vaults without some good reason for being there. They do operate some sort of security system … if you can call it that."

St. John-Pemberthy looked impassive.

"Shall we say next Wednesday?

Rivet repeated the word as if it was a mantra.

"Wednesday?"

A leather bound dairy appeared and was consulted.

"Wednesday. The twenty-fourth, I believe. Noon. You will have to take them to London for delivery. You have no objection to doing that?"

"Well, no, I suppose not."

"My client would like to examine the files, see that they're all present and correct, so to speak."

"Hof coursh."

Rivet, realizing too late he had slurred his words, recovered enough to ask the question he knew he ought to ask.

"How mush…"

St. John-Pemberthy was impassive.

"Two thousand pounds."

"Yesh…"

"In cash … of course … on delivery. That alright with you?"

Rivet nodded. He was vainly attempting to stop his eyes spinning. To add to his distress, the room had also adopted a tendency to do so. The grin of St. John-Pemberthy was now like the Cheshire Cat, floating some way above the table.

"Are you alright?"

"Mmmphh."

"Jolly good. Now then, how about a bit of spotted dick and custard?"

Dick had vowed to hone his magical skills for a time when they might be required once more. To this end he undertook to perform a daily routine in the Temple. He lit candles and incense, studied and meditated upon each page of the magical work-book, and solemnly made his oblations to the deities of Ancient Egypt.

Dick was unaware that while engaged upon all this he was being studiously observed from the Twenty-Seventh dimension. Fantuk was tuning in to the mental and physical form that made up the being known as Dick Symes. He was also employing technology that would have made Einstein's moustache dive off his upper lip in sheer disbelief.

The gap in scientific knowhow between Earth and the Twenty-Seventh Dimension was awesome. For anyone on Earth to attain the kind of intellectual understanding owned by the Xogs, the physical equivalent would be like leaping across the Grand Canyon. The difference was not just that they owned spacecraft; the Xogs were advanced in every aspect of logical perception. They had mastery over existence, down to the smallest atom, by simply analyzing the potential of every existing proton and electron in the universe.

Right now Zavrod was examining an image of Dick sitting in a full lotus position in the Temple, a turquoise pendant encircling his neck. His eyes were closed and a blissful expression encompassed his features. Dick was perfecting the art of shape-shifting, an ancient shamanic practice.

First he became a hawk, flapping lazily in the space above himself. Then, as the bird alighted on the floor, it became a wolf, to be transformed into a rat, then finally a bee. The buzzing insect then disappeared through the open skylight.

"What is he doing?"

"Meditating."

"I thought that was doing something obscene with … "

"You're thinking of another word beginning with 'M'."

"Oh."

Fantuk continued to observe. The stillness of Dick's body seemed to affect the space around him, considerably reducing the natural molecular activity in the air. By scanning Dick's brain the Xog could see that the functions of several different areas had merged. The result was a width and intensity of mental focus that was quite astonishing. The more Fantuk had studied Dick, the more he had been impressed by his cerebral potential. He was certainly a unique earthling!

Fantuk altered the settings on the screen so that he could see a virtual representation of the future. Once the exclusive domain of oracles and soothsayers, such an ability had been commonplace in the Twenty-Seventh Dimension for many millennia. Fantuk reprogrammed the function so that he was able to see various events that would occur in Windleroot in a few months time.

The screen dissolved and a graphic image of Windleroot Nob and the surrounding area came into view. At first glance the immediate future for the Isle of Teflon did not look good. Its spiritual essence was about to be attacked, resulting in appalling damage to its physical form. The first sacred site to suffer would be the Dallas Well, whose founts and pools were fed by aqueous convulsions beneath the Nob. The courses would dry up, and no matter how much its sacred springs were coaxed by healers and Reiki masters, it would not yield even the tiniest globule of holy water.

The magnificent Nob would split from top to bottom and collapse. In some horror Fantuk watched the images appearing on the screen. First a livid gash appeared in the side of the mound and the very clay from which it was composed was laid bare. The tower that had once stood so proud and erect upon its summit collapsed and was no more, a jagged stump all that remained. Dark clouds gathered over the ruins and an air of desolation held sway. Fantuk was visibly shocked. His neurons racing, he vowed to provide Dick with the means to alter destiny somewhat.

"It seems there is a crisis about to overtake Windleroot. Although we cannot entirely prevent that happening I think Mister Symes should be helped to restore the situation to something approaching normal."

Zavrod was non-plussed, double-minussed even.

"Really? How do you intend to go about that?"

"We shall adapt and strengthen his mental processes so that he is able to manifest any image that appears in his brain. That's exactly the goal of this 'magical training' anyway as I've just been watching. We can improve that … about ten thousand per cent."

And so it was that when Dick ended his latest meditation he could feel a new power surging through that part of him that was his higher self. He began to read, and the words of Standley-Strange's book glowed in his heart.

Thoughts tend to collect in their respective medium – that of Air. The symbol of this restless element is the Sword. An incisive weapon, it frees the perceptions from cloying emotion. Justice is not subject to any consideration of feelings, and it is said that revenge is 'rough justice'.

Dick took this to mean that he must be ruthless in severing the poisonous tendrils that were choking Windleroot. The Goddess who was the spirit of that place must be released from her travail and once more be at peace.

XVII

The Town Hall did not, as one could have expected, proudly dominate the town of Windleroot, but cringed in a courtyard off Lowe Street. In Elizabethan times the Courthouse had stood next to it, a gallows nearby for the summary dispatching of offenders. Rivet felt like a condemned man as he made his way down the stone steps to a door below the building. He had deliberately chosen the early evening to enter the vaults and make his assault on the strong box within.

The box was quickly found and Rivet, unlocking it with the key he had surreptitiously obtained, was already congratulating himself on how easy all this was going to be. His triumph was short-lived. The documents he needed were inside a stout metal case that lay secreted within. Rivet cursed the zealous official who had realised the value of its contents. There was only one thing to be done – return to Badcorn and fetch appropriate tools.

Returning an hour later he informed the sedentary caretaker that he had not concluded his business in the vault and would require some further time there. The man grumbled terribly, muttering about 'irregular', and more worrying, 'overtime'. After some swift talking, Rivet persuaded him that he could be safely left *in situ*. Hastily gathering his safe-cracking equipment from the back of the Volvo, Rivet returned to the vault and squared up to the strong-box.

It was unfortunate that an emergency meeting of some junior sub-committee had, that very evening, been convened in the room directly above the vault. Believing that he was alone, and without any possibility of being overheard, Rivet had attacked the recalcitrant lock with great violence. A misdirected blow with a crowbar had caught him neatly on an exposed knuckle and his resulting oaths were loud and vehement. The members of the committee, their debate interrupted by blasphemous bellowing directly beneath their feet, were at first puzzled, then thoroughly alarmed. It was decided to abandon the meeting and investigate the origin of these sinister sounds without delay.

An extraordinary sight was revealed to these councillors as they entered the vault. The mayor of Windleroot was engaged in what appeared to be petty, if not grand, larceny. They gazed incredulously upon the figure of Rivet, in his shirt sleeves and sweating profusely, his bloodied hands holding the classic tools of the burglar's trade. Rivet stared at the interlopers, but could not conceal the guilt embedded in his features. In a terrible silence both parties regarded each other for some moments. At last, Rivet spoke, in a high-pitched squawk, as far from his usual self-satisfied tones as it was possible to get.

"Having a bit of trouble finding what I wanted down here ... had to force the lid ... bit harder than I thought ... quite annoying ... think I'll leave it for the moment ... probably not what I'm really after anyway."

Various expressions of disbelief greeted this speech, ones that intensified by the moment. Rivet matter-of-factly gathered up his tools and threw them into the carrier bag he had provided for the purpose. Roughly pulling on his jacket, he made for the door. So astonished were the assembled party that not one of them felt able to address him. Any comment on the mayor's intentions or behaviour seemed quite beyond them all. As he mounted the steps, Rivet, regaining his usual imperious manner to some slight degree, called to them over his shoulder.

"Put the lights out when you go will you. I've finished down here for the night."

In a surreal coda they listened to Rivet's footsteps echoing through the courtyard and out into Lowe Street. As the sound finally died away, those who had witnessed these extraordinary events suddenly recovered their wits. The chairman of the present committee took it upon himself to report all they had seen to the town clerk that very night. He in his turn decided that the Town Council must act quickly, and at an emergency meeting the next morning, Rivet Boxer was relieved of his mayoral post. The reason given for his dismissal was recorded in the minutes as, 'conduct unbecoming mayoral duties, possibly caused by overwork or mental instability'.

When Rivet was back sitting in the front seat of his car, his heart was pounding so much he thought it would burst through his rib cage. A total state of panic fought with a desire for alcohol in some quantity. The Volvo lurched into the night. Even with all his reckless optimism, Rivet knew that this time he was in big trouble. Neither was it of the kind he could bullshit his way out of too easily.

He drove aimlessly, never once considering that he could return to Badcorn. The prospect of facing an inquisition from Squiddle threw him deeper into despair. Feeling the comforting lump of his wallet in the inside pocket of his jacket gave him some relief. He set course for an obscure hamlet on the very edge of the moors. None would recognize him in the Elfplod Inn at Bunhill.

He was obliged to leave the pub at closing time. He had drunkenly pleaded with the landlord for permission to sleep in a corner of the bar, but this request had been curtly refused. Rivet had then spent a hellish night in the car park, curled round the steering wheel of his car. He had enjoyed little sleep, and as soon as it was light went in search of refreshment – tea was essential, breakfast a close second. Creeping into the town of Windleroot by the back roads, he waited in a side street until half-past eight, the time when the Huckleberry Café opened for business.

Peering through the window to ensure that he did not recognize any of the clientèle, Rivet sidled up to the counter and ordered the largest breakfast it was possible to assemble in the shortest possible time. He settled himself at a table as far as possible from the door, and hid behind a copy of *The Sun*. Before long a plate the size of a bicycle wheel was set down in front of him. On it was ranged a collection of anything that would possibly submit to being fried. On a side plate was arranged a mountain of buttered toast and some cutlery wrapped in a gaudy paper napkin. Rivet grabbed the sauce bottle and liberally doused everything in sight, so that a brown tide flowed to the edges of the plate. Whatever elixir it was left an acid tang in the air, one that stung the nostrils.

Rivet was about to shovel a tomato and a hill of beans onto his fork when the mobile phone in his pocket warbled loudly. He rarely responded to its summons, on the principle that most communications spelled trouble. Befuddled by lack of sleep and everything else, he answered it.

"That you, Rivet? Grainey Buttle here. You might know this already … word usually gets around in Windleroot like some deadly bloody virus … we've had the place trashed. They really had a go … fencing set on fire … the decahedron ruined … lot of other festival stuff damaged … This is real arson … vandalism … you name it … and it's not the local yobs either … this is organised … vicious…"

Rivet lapsed into his pompous manner almost immediately.

"Well I'm sorry to hear all this. At the last town council meeting I said I wanted a stronger police presence round here and…"

Buttle interrupted him, coldly and insistently.

"I'm sure you did, Rivet, in your best mayoral style. Now you listen to what I'm going to say and bloody carefully too. Some toe rag came round here threatening me just before this all happened … and what's more he's some crony of yours. You were seen hanging about with him and his mates in the Cee and Pee the day the Old Chapel came down…"

"What!"

"That's not all either. Some other spivs came here during the bad weather … Ringle … Hook … I think they were called. Names ring any bells? I'm sure they're part of this cartel I've got wind of … the one that wants to turn Windleroot … *and my place* … into a cross between a council estate and a bloody theme park."

Rivet's grip on the phone tightened so much that it almost shot out of his hand. Buttle continued to bend his ear, and with mounting horror Rivet heard more than he could possibly want to hear about himself – ever.

"I don't know anything about … "

"I'm sure you do … you must … and what worries me, Rivet … and it should certainly worry you too … is that if you're as mixed up in all this as I believe you are, then I'm going to have to go to the law. And why not, I ask myself? You're as bent as a bloody fish hook. I wouldn't trust you to tell me the right time … never have … you bloody stinker."

Rivet, fork in the air after spearing a chip, paused – a pair of scarlet lips pouting. He proceeded to suck in so much breath he could easily have swelled up and exploded. Assuming an air of outraged dignity he recovered enough to offer some sort of riposte.

"I don't know what you're talking about … and I'd be very careful if I were you … chucking accusations like that around, Grainey. You be careful I don't have Dibley Wedge my solicitor get in touch with you…"

Buttle was in no mood for this sort of blag and said so.

"Bollocks to bloody Wedge! You're the one who's going to end up in court, Rivet, you and your dodgy mates. It's a wonder you never have before. *And* I know you've been dealing dope out of that shop of yours … a little bird told me the law are onto that too. Apparently you ripped off one of your gangster mates for some stuff and he sang like a canary about you, anonymously of course. So I should watch it very carefully if I were you. "

Rivet screeched in mock anger.

"You can't talk to me like that … *I'm the mayor of Windleroot!*"

"Yeah, and I'm Buffy the Vampire Slayer. Just be warned, Rivet! And I'll say what I just said again … because you've got your head stuck so far up your arse you need to be told it twice. If I think you're involved in this business at my place then you're for it. I'll make sure they chuck the bloody book at you."

Any impassioned riposte was forestalled by Buttle ringing off. The last of the fried egg turned to ashes in Rivet's mouth and he let his knife and fork clatter on to his plate. The sudden crash made an old hippie at the next table nearly jump out of his loons. Mechanically, Rivet pushed his chair back and rose from the table. Equally robotically he walked out of the café, seeing nothing, feeling even less. The gig was up. It was all over. He had blown it … with the Council, Snipe, Beans and now this Buttle business … it was all too much.

Rivet returned to his car in a trance, and drove without plan or purpose back to the moors. He knew not where he was going and he didn't care. He just wanted to get away, anywhere where the voices could not follow him. They were in his head – harsh, accusing, condemning, there would be no escaping from them now. As he drove along tears began to roll down Rivet's pasty cheeks. They soon became a salty torrent, one so endless he could hardly see.

St. John-Pemberthy was a man who generally knew not only which way the wind was blowing, but also when it was ruffling his *sangfroid*. Hints, dropped rather heavily in his direction recently, had confirmed his impression that all was not well in the Snipe camp. He was aware that Rivet's efforts to obtain the documents had failed. Such an outcome he could have predicted almost as soon as he had entrusted the mayor with the commission. The cost of the lunch at the Beetlerush Hotel he had appended to the account already forwarded to Snipe.

He was even more convinced of an impending *dénouement* with the unannounced arrival of Colin Sopwith at the door of his office. Few knew of the whereabouts of these premises – in an anonymous village on the outskirts of Barstowe – and St. John-Pemberthy never encouraged callers. The lawyer reflected that Sopwith running him to ground, although irritating, was a tribute to the other's tenacity. The badger is renowned for such a quality and his visitor seemed to bear a distinct resemblance to that nocturnal creature. St. John-Pemberthy had decided the visit should be brief and, with this in mind, did not offer Sopwith a seat.

"I hope certain *rumours* about our project have not dissuaded you from your usual diligence regarding Mr. Snipe's affairs ... "

St. John-Pemberthy paused before replying. He was wearing a lime green shirt of rather startling brightness. Sopwith reflected that women often sported such a bright plumage when celebrating the end of a painful affair.

"Mr. Snipe?"

It was as if St. John-Pemberthy was endeavouring to recall the name of some forgotten celebrity of silent films.

"Mr. Snipe was enquiring why he had not heard from you for some time ..."

Again, there was a marked interval before St. John-Pemberthy responded. His great height combined with the sharply-pointed side-whiskers that he was inclined to sport, gave him the look of an ibis.

"I decided some days ago to sever all connections with Mr. Snipe. I've already written to him enclosing my final account. Perhaps you, as his cohort, might be good enough to ensure that it is promptly settled?"

Sopwith was somewhat taken aback but, remembering the tenacity that had been assigned to him in a previous paragraph, rallied marvellously.

"Isn't that a little presumptuous ... premature even?"

St. John-Pemberthy was not to be drawn.

"Call it what you like ... I'm giving this whole development business the brazen hoof."

Sopwith could not disguise the alarm in his voice.

"Really?"

"Yes, really. I keep my ear to the ground, Colin ... and daily I hear more and more disturbing things about Mr. Snipe and his carryings-on. In my profession one often steps in a little *ordure* ... par for the course ... but I'm not prepared to wade up to my knees in it."

"I didn't realise you felt like this. If only you could have had a word with me I'm sure..."

St. John-Pemberthy was too old a hand not to recognise flannel when it was being applied.

"C'mon, Colin, this is all rather coming apart at the edges isn't it? It has been for some time. Hook and Snipe have apparently fallen out, and from what I've heard the money-lenders have all got cold feet ... and as for this Beans character and what he gets up to ... let's face it, it's a total shambles."

"I'm sure things can be patched up, it's extraordinary what one can do to remedy a situation."

St. John-Pemberthy picked up his briefcase and set it down on the desk.

"Not in this case I don't think. You may have other views on the matter ... but that is entirely up to you."

Sopwith recognised this as indicating the interview was over. Desperately, he tried clutching at straws. He seemed to have drawn the short one on several occasions lately.

"But surely you can't just abandon Snipe to the wolves..."

It was an unconscious metaphor, and a ghost of a smile flickered across St. John-Pemberthy's features.

"Mention of the *lupine* seems particularly apposite, Colin. What are they up to, eh? Snipe and his grisly bunch of gangsters! Thuggishness, conspiracy, fraud, criminal damage ... I could go on. It all sounds like the Kray twins again ... "

"Snipe always seemed to me as if he was ... "

St. John Pemberthy had heard enough.

"Frankly, Colin if I don't get my fee that's probably a minor inconvenience compared to being mixed up in this ghastly farrago any longer. Now ... if you'll excuse me I've got to go and see a client ... a rather more respectable one than those who we've been discussing just now."

St. John-Pemberthy opened the door. Sopwith found himself being ushered outside, into the moderate bustle of a village street. He stood on the pavement, straightening his tie with an awkward, mechanical gesture.

"Well ... um ... bye then."

"Cheerio, Colin ... best of luck. Might bump into you one day ... you never know."

Sopwith felt, as perhaps did the Fuehrer *circa* 1945, that all was not going exactly according to plan. In his own life he had been party to many a crisis. When things went wrong it was always the same. One domino toppled over and invariably took the others with it. The Windleroot scheme was now just a pie in the sky, and someone was about to get it full in the face, hopefully not him. Returning to his car he sat and listened to a snatch of Mozart on the radio. The tinkling harpsichord spoke of a soothing, civilized world, one well away from that occupied by Vargle Snipe. Sopwith eased his car along rural roads, his mind trying to fit pieces of a jigsaw into a puzzle that he should never have begun to solve. The parting of the ways would not be easy. He alternated between fiddling with his tie and the radio dial.

XVIII

Occasionally in the small hours, Zeep would recall her sexual shenanigans with Rivet. The memory rarely evoked any erotic impulse, usually quite the opposite. The aftermath had been so traumatic that she still found it difficult to look either Rivet, or Squiddle, directly in the eye, especially when she was anywhere near the stockroom.

When she returned from another dreary day at Paganorama the salacious recollection returned. One particular detail came to the fore of her mind; during the encounter something had fallen about her ankle – apart from her underwear that was. Zeep had been puzzling where her ankle chain might be. It was solid silver and had been given to her by a former boyfriend, the only half-decent gesture he had ever made in her direction. The thought of the silver chain began to obsess her. She would search the stockroom and find it.

Few people were about in Lowe Street as Zeep put her key in the lock of the shop door and eased it open. Even more of a Stygian murk hung about the interior and she was surprised by a pair gnome heads suspended from the ceiling, particularly as one of them so closely resembled Boggy.

Zeep began to climb the stairs to the stock room and was immediately assailed with a great wave of unaccustomed heat. The shop being infamous for its sub-zero temperatures, this was definitely odd. She groped for the light switch on the wall. The stock room, when it was illuminated, revealed an unexpected sight.

A gas heater was blasting forth redly, giving out a hellish light to the tableau before her. Rivet was slumped over his desk, a half-empty bottle of brandy at his elbow. This might have implied he was in a drunken stupor if the heap of pink and green capsules had not told a different story. More alarming, was that Rivet seemed to have ransacked the poisonous herbs box. Packets of henbane, deadly nightshade, hellebore, ragwort, yew and wormwood lay torn open and scattered about on the floor. Zeep did not need to see any more, the situation was clear – Rivet, for whatever reason, had decided to top himself.

A glance at the bluish countenance, and livid eye sockets indicated that he had slipped into a coma. Zeep held back the scream she was about to let loose, picked up the telephone on the desk, and summoned the emergency services.

Another soul was also troubled, but for more mundane reasons. Rover, having not heard from Beans or Goldie for some weeks, decided he would find out what was going on. He was in low spirits and even a joint the size of a baseball bat had not restored his usual jack-the-lad demeanour. A speedy drive to Potters bar brought him to the warehouse, which betrayed an even more abandoned air than usual, but Rover was on his guard. As he got out of his car, a figure came out of the warehouse and loaded something into the back of an unmarked van. Rover, recognizing the loose limbed Derek, hailed him.

"Alright, mate? Woss' appenin' 'ere then?"

Derek shrugged his shoulders.

"S'all over, mate."

"Wajoo mean?"

"'es aht of it innee … that Beans."

Rover needed no further prompting; the reference was obviously to Beans.

"I ain't 'eard from him for weeks. Packin' up 'ere is 'e?"

"Right. I ain't 'sposed to tell yuh, but y'know…"

Derek grinned rodent-like. Rover flashed a mini-smile in return. Honour amongst thieves.

"Wajoo make of 'im these days then?"

"Beans? Total nutter. Shot away, mate. I'll tell yuh … get aht of all this, mate. It ain't 'appenin' no more. 'is boss 'as blown it … 'n' all. I know that. 'E was coppin' the rent for this, but 'e ain't no more. People talk don't they? Specially in my manor. The word's aht, mate."

Rover shifted his eyes from ground to sky – a way of showing he was thinking.

"Yeh?"

Derek indicated the building behind him with a jerk of his thumb.

"Nuffink in there no more except a coupla bent motors … an a bitta doobie…"

"Doobie?"

"Hey … you're into that encha?"

Rover was careful.

"Might be, why?"

172

Derek got confidential.

"Way I 'eard it was this. Beans been buyin' gear from some geezer in the sticks. Right aht in wurzleland … Wimblerod or summink … "

Rover was all ears, he looked like a corn field.

"Yeh?"

"Anyway, he rips him off. The geezer in uh … "

"Windleroot?"

"Right … that's where it was. He give 'im a loada duff gear. Beans was a bit upset abaht that. Wanted to sort him aht … big time. His boss, Mr. Snipe … wasn't 'avin' it though."

"Yeh? And it's 'ere … this duff stuff?"

"Right. Wanna have a butchers?"

"Why not?"

The plastic bag when opened revealed a sorry sight. Rover stared amazed at what looked like a mixture of silage and Christmas tree needles. It was true. Rivet had sold Beans bum dope. Why? The gear *he* had bought from him had been dynamite stuff … and why was Beans dealing dope anyway? That wasn't his style, he was much too uptight.

"It don't even look like skunkweed, or anythin' else. You're right. That Beans he's gone bonkers, right Mum and Dad."

"Told yuh. Watchin' too many of them stoopid gangster films abaht 'ard men 'n' all that … on the telly."

"Yeh, Right. Okay, see yuh."

Rover drove back to the M25, all the time considering his options. Little did he know that Fate had decided upon one of them already. Beans was about to contact him – for just one more job.

Like the poet who always sings wondrously of her, Mother Nature cares little for the affairs of man. Yet she could not help but leave her beauty everywhere to remind the world that the Earth was her domain. The sun, appearing after early morning rain, was seemingly making amends for its earlier absence. Clouds, in shades of grey – slate and charcoal – still hovered. The cut stalks of last year's wheat bristled in the fudge-coloured earth.

On the window sills outside the Crumpled Horn the rain had left silver pearls of moisture among the flower pots. Within, the talk was mostly of Rivet. Rumours – current and old hat – filled the air.

"Bugger tried to do away with hisself they say…"

"Ambylance took'n away…"

"Gonna be alright though I've 'eard…"

"Old Nick looks arter 'is own…"

"They sacked'n as mayor…"

"Caught'n pinchin' stuff…"

Ted and Clifford were more informed than the rest.

" 'E were tryin' to get 'old of some dokkyment from way back in 'istory. One that said the mayor could do what 'e liked in the town …"

"That ain't never right?"

"Now 'e ain't the mayor no more it don't mean nothin' …"

"Just as well."

"Wonder 'oo we'll 'ave next?"

"Nobody can't be no worse than 'e."

"Ah, you wants to be careful sayin' things like that, Ted."

"But what do 'ee make on it all then?"

"Well … these be funny old times an' that be true."

An air of foreboding stalked the narrow alleys of the ancient town. The fear that had stalked these cobbled ways centuries before – a time when kings were cruel and officials corrupt – had returned to blight its citizenry. With it came a wicked vengeance, in the shape of Squiddle's curse. A strange and terrible form that evil growth would take when it flourished.

It was fortunate for all that no one was in the building when it collapsed. The Crumpled Horn, the ancient tavern that had served as a coaching inn in times gone by suffered the same fate as the Old Chapel. A heap of rubble and beer engines was all that remained. Kate, returning from visiting her sister in Oaksharp, wept copious tears when she saw the ruin of all she held dear. The locals were philosophical and offered their sympathies. With that rural pragmatism that characterizes country society, they sloped off to The Wildfowlers in Bellend Lane for their pints of Todge.

On hearing of the destruction, Squiddle was beside herself with a glee. Her forays into necromancy had now ensured that she tottered at the very edge of the Pit. In the coming days her eyes would glow with an infernal brightness as the demons below became more and more familiar to her. Even imps of the lowest rank agreed that she was hotwired and heading for hell and it was only a matter of time before she cascaded into the depths.

Although Rivet recovered quickly from his ordeal, his troubles were far from over. As the Duke of Wellington succinctly observed, 'life is one damn thing after another.' Even the Iron Duke himself would have been hard-pressed to suggest a plan of campaign for Rivet, as Fate hurled one brickbat after another at him. At the very moment he decided to put his affairs in some sort of order, disaster struck once more, and this time with even greater vengeance.

He was not best pleased to be woken in the small hours by a furious knocking at the front door. In the moments before, he had been much involved in a highly erotic dream. When he got out of bed to respond to the nocturnal summons, his arousal was still so evident that he might have qualified for a pogoing competition.

Stumbling down the unlit stairs he groped his way to the front door and shot back the bolt. The entire police force of the county appeared to be assembled in serried ranks in the yard. Beneath his voluminous night-shirt, Rivet's heart began to pound thunderously, and he almost leapt into the air, such was the extreme of his paranoia. Before him were a dozen police cars, each with a purple light ponderously revolving on its roof. The crackle of radio static and incessant electronic beeps heightened the Star Wars ambiance. A voice came out of the darkness.

"Mr. Boxer?"

"Yes, that's me."

"Sergeant Stone, sir. Good evening."

"Good evening to you. What d'you want?"

"You are the owner of Paganorama in Lowe Street?"

"Yes ... of course I am ... what about it?"

"Can I ask you, sir ... when you were last on the premises?"

"Some time ago actually ... I've not been terribly well you see ... "

"Sorry to hear that, sir."

Rivet suddenly panicked.

"Why? What about it? What's happened?"

"I'm afraid to inform you, sir, there's been a rather serious accident..."

Rivet's voice took on the hollowness that had become a regular feature of late – one preceding doom.

"Accident?"

"A fire, sir … the emergency services were called … not very promptly it seems…"

As Rivet stared into the darkness, his features were eerily lit by the moon, sidling out from behind a cloud. The dull cadences of officialdom continued.

"As far as we understand it, sir, the fire has been contained as much as possible…"

A volley of squawks from some device attached to his uniform interrupted Sgt. Stone, before ambushing another piece of equipment somewhere else.

"…fortunately it has not spread to any of the adjacent properties which appear to be relatively undamaged. Your own premises however seems to be totally…"

Rivet experienced a cocktail of emotions. Although he was horrified at the thought of the shop being no more, he was also secretly relieved. If his extra-curricular career as a drug dealer was under surveillance, any evidence against him had now literally gone up in smoke.

Further reflections were brought to an end when a figure broke through the solid lines of constabulary. Zeep, with difficulty keeping a tight lid on her hysteria, began to give her own account of the conflagration to Rivet. Her delivery did not have the laconic air of Sergeant Stone.

"Rivet … everything's gone … even the broomsticks and the goddess statues … all the incense … the crystals have melted … oh … it's all so horrible…"

Overcome with grief, she collapsed into the arms of Rivet. At that moment a terrifying vision came into view, eclipsing even Zeep's histrionics. Framed by the open door of the farmhouse the figure of Squiddle appeared. Flanked by innumerable hounds yelping loudly, the scene resembled a hell hag and her diabolic attendants from a Hammer Horror movie.

Clad in a fluorescent negligée of more than shocking pink, her breasts, resembling a pair of enormous poached eggs, were quite visible. Her hair, crowned with the ubiquitous flying helmet, stuck up in the air like a bale of barbed wire. Wrapped about her waist was what looked like a plastic snake, and on her feet were a pair of Rivet's brogues. Even the most hardened veterans of the force could only stare in wonderment.

Squiddle, when told of the destruction of Paganorama, seemed to take this more calmly than she did the sight of Zeep apparently nestling in her husband's arms. Putting two and two together and making at least twenty-seven, she began to screech imprecations in all directions.

"You've done this you foul trollop! You were sneaking about in the shop when you found Rivet! Now you go and set fire to the place! You seduce my only love … break my heart … and ruin our lives!"

Zeep could only stare in horror, before falling to the ground in a dead faint. Squiddle, her negligée now stretched so tight that her nipples were like cocktail sausages, stood over the prostrate body of Zeep and pointed accusingly at her.

"Whore … pyromaniac … nymphomaniac…"

Recovering himself, and recalling that he had a responsibility to keep the peace, Sergeant Stone moved towards Squiddle with the intention of restraining her, at least verbally.

"Madam, I think there's been some mistake…"

Squiddle turned to him like some vengeful Valkyrie.

"Arrest this filthy baggage! Handcuff her! Put her in chains! Throw her into the deepest dungeons! She must stand trial…"

Rivet gawped first at his wife, and then the terrified figure of Zeep now conscious and cowering at his feet. The panoply of the law clustered about, impotent and in disarray. High above, the moon retreated behind another cloud not willing to witness yet another mortal's descent into madness.

XIX

Wargle Snipe had taken to scurrying about London faster than a new kid on a pizza delivery bicycle. His paranoia in overdrive, he was desperately searching for somewhere to hide and finally decided to go to ground in the Wembley house. Bought cheaply in the 1970s, Snipe rarely went there, and over the years it had acquired a surreal ambiance. The décor remaining the same as the day it had been built, it was suspended in its own time-warp. The ground floor rooms were never opened, Snipe keeping an office of sorts in what would have once been the master-bedroom.

If he ever slept there, Snipe chose a box room that overlooked the garden. The permanently-drawn curtains concealed the apprentice jungle that thrived outside the window. The neighbours were only too aware of the state of the garden and sensed the owner's sinister reputation. The man generated high octane nastiness – they kept out of his way.

Once again Snipe read the letter, before throwing it aside. So, St. John-Pemberthy had jumped ship. Who was there left now? The grapevine had informed him of Beans' renegade tactics and he had taken steps to remove himself as far as possible from all of that. It seemed nothing could be salvaged from the wreckage of his schemes. Or could there?

When Sopwith rang the bell, he might have been the bearer of good tidings. Herod suggesting he was a founder member of the NSPCC would have been a better bet.

"Ringle was arrested yesterday."

Snipe's eyes took on an additional feverish light.

"Hook's mate? What's he been up to then?"

" 'Conspiracy to incite or cause criminal damage' ... I'm told."

"What's that all about?"

"Somehow it's come out that it was actually him that set up all that business that Beans and his lot got up to."

"What business?"

"The idea to make Buttle – the bloke that owns the Festival land near Windleroot – sell out to Hook."

Snipe's pupils were like acetylene torches.

"I told 'im ... I told 'im ... I said leave it alone ..."

Sopwith felt he must get to the bitter end.

"It seems Ringle got them to vandalise Buttle's property. It all then seemed to go to their heads. Now the police think Beans burnt down Rivet's shop. That could very well be true … Beans apparently got swindled in some drug deal with him … "

"I know, he told me. Leave it alone … I told 'im too … "

" … so now I hear he's kidnapped Mr. and Mrs. Boxer…"

Snipe's nostrils began to dilate and somehow flex at the same time, in a way that Sopwith found quite alarming.

"I don't believe this is all 'appenin'."

"I'm rather afraid it is."

"So, what about 'Ook? Where's he now?"

"Hiding in Weybridge … praying he's not going to be picked up too. The police are bound to question him."

Snipe stared in front of him, seeing – like Squiddle – the Pit below him. He gripped the edge of the desk tightly as if he feared slipping into oblivion at any moment.

"Why didn't anybody tell me about all this? That 'Ook … 'e tried to do it his way didn't he? 'E naffed off … like everybody else has…"

Sopwith moistened dry lips.

"It all started when Hook found out Plattel Rhomber had withdrawn their investment…"

Snipe came out from behind his desk. He paced the room, snorting at intervals like a wild boar loose in the Siberian wastes.

"What went wrong there then? I fought I had that Pumnik where I wanted him."

"It wasn't him who made the decision…"

Sopwith saw the rage was no longer there. The fire had gone out, the voice alone remaining – empty and unreal.

"Who was it then?"

"Top management … several on the Board were rabbis…"

"What you on about?"

Sopwith took a deep breath and closed his eyes, somehow finding the stamina to report one more defeat. It was like the fall of the Third Reich … Snipe in his bunker … the cornered Fuehrer.

"They were informed by somebody or other that you were personally involved in … um … occult practices. Being orthodox … very orthodox in fact … they didn't approve. So much so that…"

Snipe's expression was fixed, his body motionless. It was a tremendous effort for him to even open his mouth.

"Did you tell Pumnik about … about … what I was doing ?"

Sopwith was genuinely affronted.

"No … I certainly did not. How could I? I didn't know, for goodness sake. You certainly never mentioned you were mixed up in anything like that to me."

'Mixed up'. The words hung in the air, redolent of things unmentionable, unsavoury. An oily blackness seemed to creep into the room, blotting out the May sun that moments before had been flooding through the windows bringing light … redemption. Snipe jerked himself back into something resembling reality.

"What about Izal and 'is lot. We give 'im enough crumpet to get togevver anuvver Dagenham Girl Pipers."

Sopwith impatiently waved away the metaphor; he had heard enough of them already. The solid reality was enough to deal with; the situation was getting more precarious by the minute. Like St. John-Pemberthy, Sopwith wanted to escape, the quicker the better. He began to gabble – words frothing from between his lips.

"That was always going to be difficult … trying to put Dubai and Wall Street together as it were. Particularly with the recent unfortunate happenings in the Middle East … hopefully that may all simmer down in the next few weeks … but I don't think that's going to help our cause at all. Izal has as good as said that he's looking to put his oil money elsewhere … so there it is."

Vargle Snipe was breathing heavily. He kept clutching at the desk, as if believing it could prevent reality slipping away from him. The questions he was asking were directed at nobody, which was just as well as nobody was listening.

"Why's this 'appening? What have I done ? I fought this was going to be a doddle. It ain't me that's cocked it all up."

Sopwith attempted a different tactic, pouring oil on waters that were not just troubled, more a budding tsunami.

"There is another potential investor…"

"Yeh? 'Oos that?"

"An Indian gentleman from Bombay. Mr. Balichow. Big in the Bollywood side of things I understand."

Snipe closed his eyes, whether in prayer or pain was not altogether apparent.

"No."

"No?"

"I can't 'andle it no more. I gotta get away. I need a rest … an 'oliday."

He opened his eyes once more. To Sopwith it was not a reassuring sight. Madness could clearly be seen orbiting in the orbs.

"Perhaps that might be best. Have a break … relax … restore the tissues…"

Snipe brusquely dismissed this bedside manner.

"You don't want nuffink to do wiv this eiver do you?"

The two faced each other across a wasteland of broken dreams. The junior minister in his slightly shabby suit, and the barrow-boy from the Mile End Road.

"I must admit, I can see little future in…"

The thuggish menace returned for a brief moment.

" 'Oppit."

Sopwith was hopping already – from one foot to the other in his anguish. Seeing his way now clear, he rushed down the stairs into the relative sanctuary of Wembley.

For Snipe the writing was not only on the wall, it was like a Banksy mural. The phone rang, insistently – impossible to ignore.

"Mr. Snipe? Vargle Snipe I believe?"

"Oozat?"

"My name is Standley-Strange, Mr. Snipe. I don't think we've ever actually met … at least not in this plane … but no doubt destiny will ensure we meet in another place."

Snipe felt he was about to be claimed by the quicksand rapidly surrounding him.

"I dunno what you're on abaht. Wajoo want?"

The voice of Standley-Strange was almost laconic.

"The game is up, Snipe. Your scheme to make Windleroot yours went badly wrong, didn't it? In Rome all worshipped Cloacina the goddess of the sewers … their main drain was known as *Cloacina Maxima*. To stare into the pit is to risk being drawn into it, don't you think? Some even get to like the stench …"

Snipe looked as if he was sucking hard on a litter tray.

"It woz you messed me abaht dincha? You woz the bloke I never got 'old of … you and 'im wot they chased in the fog … I'll get the bofe of you."

"Pshaw."

"Wozzat?"

"*Pshaw* – a combination of letters that emulates the sound total contempt would make if it could. I bid you farewell, Snipe … *from another place.*"

It was those last three words that tipped Vargle Snipe over the edge. Down, down he went into the fathomless depths! The man who believed he could do deals with the powers of darkness! He who persuaded others to create monsters believing they too would be subject to his will! O foolish man! None may command demons except the Devil himself!

The great scheme was over, like the passing of a child's tantrum – and all around were the discarded toys of his ambitions. He had failed in his bid to gain that which might have quenched his unending thirst for power. Now he had become as a thing of paper – insubstantial and no different from the false coin that had once brought ruin to Windleroot.

The last of the police cars had left. A more despondent scene than that being played out in the kitchen at Badcorn would have been hard to imagine. Even Dickens himself would have been hard pressed to depict such a creepy cameo. Rivet was hunched up in a corner by the stove, nursing a mug of tea, while Zeep did the same in the window seat. Squiddle sat upright at the table, a tangible aura of rage and suspicion all about her. She had gone some way towards accepting that Zeep could not be held responsible, for either burning down Paganorama or ruining her marriage.

Rivet was now the object of her displeasure, and with some justification. Insisting that he fetch the insurance documents relating to the shop, Rivet had procrastinated, without actually refusing to look for them. To Squiddle this was a sure sign that he was involved in some subterfuge. When – after blood-curdling threats of violence – the papers were finally produced, Squiddle's suspicions were proved correct.

From the outset only the most miniscule premium had ever been paid to the insurance company, and the payments had lapsed. Making any successful claim was extremely doubtful. Squiddle was not slow in expressing her opinion of Rivet's cheese-paring and incompetence. Zeep covered her ears as Squiddle's ranting filled the kitchen.

As the first signs of morning light through the kitchen window made patterns on the opposite wall, she continued to give full rein to her acid tongue. This only ceased at the sound of a sharp knocking on the front door. Rivet, glad to escape for a moment from his wife's harangues, went to answer the summons. He flung the door open wide, fully expecting to see the return of the rozzers, but it was not to be.

The stuff of nightmares – in blu-ray and the director's cut – was revealed. Exuding more menace than Motorhead live at Earls Court, there stood another power trio – Beans, Rover and Goldie. Rivet could only stare in disbelief, the power of speech entirely deserting him.

XX

Dick emerged from the Temple. His time of devotions at the Chapel Perilous was over, now he must ride out in search of the Grail. He knew that there would be more to this particular Quest than starring in Tennyson's epic. The tale of Sir Dick Symes would only be discovered in an unknown future, one penned by scholars reading between the lines.

The months he had spent upon the astral heights in the company of the deities were his preparation for the task that lay ahead. He had been making substantial deposits in the Metaphysical Banks in the Otherworld. Now he must withdraw all his funds and spend, spend, spend.

Leaving the Temple, he took only the hat, cloak, and staff. Standley-Strange's box of tricks he left behind, and for good reason. Dick knew that all the power he would need to fight the good fight resided in his soul. The spirit of Standley-Strange, the guidance and the wisdom he had given would be with him – that he did not doubt. All the rest was simply trappings, occult or otherwise. He was the scribe of his own epic, one he had written during his days of prayer and meditation.

Thus, he prepared to leave Clinton, packing the car with earthly bounty to sustain him – cheese and ham rolls, and a flask of tea. Such things took his mind off the enormity of what he was about to do. He knew also that the wrath of heaven would be upon him if he failed. Probably the wrath of the world too, failure having always been a cardinal sin in earthly eyes.

Yet he strode out from Clinton in stout boots and with a firm step. He felt free – the greatest power – for in freedom there is always choice. Dick was aware that a figure in an orange and purple hat, with a gold doublet and silver velvet boots, was gamboling along beside him, occasionally pulling faces. The Fool is always present at moments like this, to stop us being too serious and keep things in some sort of perspective.

Dick set course for Windleroot knowing that his first mission was to save his enemies. Talk about turning the other cheek! He had been woken in the early hours by the sound of the telephone and when he had answered its summons there was no answer. A message had been left however, and Dick immediately recognised the voice of Morley Trumpton.

Much awaits for you in Windleroot. Before that you must rescue Squiddle and Zeep ... Rivet too ... in a field near the Nob ... hurry ...

Dick had driven to Windleroot and, on this occasion *he* was the King of the Road, no one else. Although dawn was some hours away, all was lit as he flew across the moors in his chariot of intent, the fire of courage giving him all speed. The Isle of Teflon was ahead of him, Windleroot Nob a pale shadow as if uncertain of its fate.

Arriving at the foot of the slope, Dick leapt from his car and dived through a gap in the hedge like a greased gazelle. Ahead of him across the field was a vile spectacle. The sight of the prostrate forms of the two women, limbs akimbo, half-naked and staked out upon the grass was made more horrific by the sight of a makeshift cross nearby. It cast a terrible shadow, this mock crucifixion – with Rivet the victim.

It was a tableau created by the blackest of minds, and Beans had threatened and cajoled the reluctant Rover and Goldie to do his bidding. The two screaming women had been overpowered, while Rivet, already in a catatonic state from his recent ordeal, had offered little resistance. Their terrible task completed, Beans and the gang had gathered their neuroses around them like a soiled blanket, and driven away.

Rivet, who had mercifully been tied to the timbers rather than nailed, was the first to receive Dick's succour. He had fainted, and his body was a dead weight as Dick set about freeing him. The most difficult task was to ensure that Rivet did not tumble to his doom. Once on solid ground he could only stare glassily at his rescuer, his face the colour of uncooked dough.

After she had been freed, Squiddle's most immediate concern was to retrieve the flying hat from where it lay, discarded in a hedge. She pressed it upon her head and adjusted it to a jaunty angle. With this gesture, something of her usual ebullience returned. Zeep was content to sob quietly, grateful to be spared from any further indignities.

Dick watched the two women making their way down the slope, Rivet stumbling behind them. The inglorious, shambling parade personified Rivet's ambitions. All had ended with a whimper. The only bang he had enjoyed was with Zeep some months earlier.

Dick started off towards the summit of the Nob ready to play his part in the restoring of Windleroot to its former glory. Climbing the path he noticed, concealed in the grass, a small black book. Squiddle had obviously dropped it while struggling with Beans and his companions. *The Black Road of the Crescent Moon* slipped easily into Dick's pocket. Like Frodo's ring, he knew it must be destroyed for ever. Dick looked up at Windleroot Nob. In its present condition, dark and stricken, it could have been Mount Doom.

No one else was on the summit of the Nob when the flying saucer landed. The same silver craft, shiny and sleek – like a California girl – glided onto the grass. Fantuk and Zavrod greeted Dick, and he did the old flipper grasping bit. Fantuk recalled old and more recent times as if they were no different from each other, which to him they were not.

"So the world didn't end in 2012? No sign of any apocalypse anywhere … Did you really believe all that?"

"I'm not sure what I believe anymore … "

Fantuk was jokey-o.

"I make one simple rule. Never believe anything until you've seen it in another dimension."

As inevitably as night follows day, Zavrod embarked on a list of complaints about Earth.

"I don't mind your fellow earthlings believing we are responsible for making crop circles … as if we hadn't got anything better do … but that lunatic who writes books saying that the Royal Family of England – whoever they may be – are really Xogs in disguise, that's a bit much. They'll be saying we're responsible for all these ridiculous terrorist things you have next. We never let our own people watch news reports from here you know … far too depressing … "

Dick made no comment, he noticed that Fantuk didn't either.

"Have you still got the Cuboid?"

"The what?"

"Look in your pocket."

As soon as his fingers closed over the familiar shape, Dick recalled a great many things. The pink was still the same shade as he remembered too.

"Thanks."

"I think you may need that … "

The three stood together and looked out across the unending

landscape of the moors. A slim disc below the Eastern horizon announced the dawn. Dick was aware that the time for farewells had come. He knew he would never see Fantuk and Zavrod again. Xogs never die – they just go into another corner of the cosmos. At the foot of the Nob the crowds were beginning to gather. The hour had come! Zavrod looked at Dick.

"It seems the tribes are gathering. They have come to see the wizard work his magic."

Dick did not hear the usual cynicism in Zavrod's voice, he was amazed. Fantuk then turned to him.

"God be with you."

"*You mean that?*"

"More than anything I've ever said. I know He will be too."

"With a capital letter?"

Fantuk nodded. Flippers were offered, and the two Xogs made to walk towards their ship. Dick could hardly bring himself to watch the take off but he was glad he did. The sight of the gold of morning flashing on the silver fish made him gasp in awe. Then the two Xogs were gone – into the deepest oceans of space and Dick was alone. He saw the traces of the Beltane fires, the pile of grey ash conjuring visions of the celebrants and the dancing flames. Next, the voice he had been waiting for came to him.

Now the hour is thine. Have I taught thee well? Only as well as any lesson of magic may be given. Its wisdom lies in the heart and yours has been pure and always willing to receive all knowledge. Remember, the gods are there to serve you. You have created them once more, merely by acknowledging their presence. Now go! The universe is with you. You will succeed in all you do and in ways greater than even you can know …

Dick adjusted his hat and grasped the staff. His cloak billowed out around him. Now the world would see the magus, and just how much the power of magic was capable of creating.

All Windleroot seemed to be massed about the Nob. The entire mound was ringed many times with all kinds of folks. From fortune-tellers to farm-hands, they had gathered in the lanes and in the fields. Some inner voice had prompted their witnessing of the spectacle that was about to be enacted before them. Their mood was a mixture of the curious and the festive. The air was still, as if the Earth knew that a drama was about to begin.

When the Magus appeared in his glorious cloak and holding his mighty staff before him, they cheered and cheered. No dime-store Gandalf he, but the real McCoy – a Master of Magic and proud of his calling. He was Dick Symes, his father's son – and now he was the man who would open the batting for England. Would he hit the winning six off the last ball of the innings, as happens in every schoolboy yarn? And do not tales such as these keep alive the great myths that have been told since the world began?

Dick's soul freed itself from its physical shell and he flew over the Nob, seeing all there was to see. As he swooped low, the head of every dandelion was as a tiny sun. There were tens of thousands of them, each one owning the power of that heavenly orb. The magus could feel the might of creation in the ageless land about him. That force was around him and within him. There was not one part of him that was not totally connected to the eternal unchanging Earth. This planet may be indifferent to the whims and struggles of man, but the Goddess has faith that the king and the wizard will bless and preserve her kingdom.

In the sky above Dick, all did not appear to be quite so much in harmony. Ominous clouds had begun to gather, the leaden shroud that had hung in the heavens since the destruction of the Nob. Their coming was a warning. Great chasms in the earth began to appear among the ruins of the tower. From these gaping rents rose a blackness that filled the air, mingling with the clouds that had sped across the skies to meet it.

The force that had been unleashed against the Isle of Teflon was now made manifest – in all its chaos and vengeful fury. Twisting this way and that, with no intent but to cause havoc, it resembled an angry winged beast. Dick was only too aware that he could be annihilated in a moment and after that the monster would turn upon the people of Windleroot, to destroy them also.

He stood, a lone figure upon the mound, all eyes upon him. In the hearts of the people they willed him to survive the onslaught they knew he was about to face. All their hopes rested upon him. The figure in hat and cloak who stood upon the tallest peak in that sacred land was its guardian, and hopefully its saviour.

Defiantly did he raise his staff to the skies and for but one moment the darkness trembled, knowing that it was in the presence of the great light of magic. From the mouths of the serpents carved upon the head of that mighty wand, lightning crackled. Tongues of flame reached out to grasp the sinister clouds, as a hound might seize its quarry. Now they halted in their charge and for a moment the light of the sun appeared once more in the sky.

Dick's voice rang out and those watching below heard the words as if they were the pure chime of bells, a peal that gladdened and strengthened the hearts of all.

I am of the gods, and the gods are the land, and I am as the land

Thus were summoned the old gods! Let the forces of darkness unleash whatever they might, the ancients would be ever undaunted! To this end Dick struck hard the heel of his staff upon the ground. The blow resonated throughout the deepest caverns in the underworld, and all the spirits below the earth responded to his call. The old magic had been summoned! The gods responded to its music once more! They would walk in the heavens for another time, and those who would stand against them might tremble at their coming! To lead them Dick called upon the spirit of the greatest wizard and seer, he who was once the Arch-Magus of Albion.

Merlin! He who hailed from the secret kingdom of Atlantis, the wizard who owned the power to fly, walk upon water, and to become as any creature, even as the very rocks and trees stood by him. They exchanged a bow of greeting, but Merlin knew there was more to be done than exchange pleasantries. Without a moment's hesitation, he gathered together the deities from beyond the edge of time and led them to victory. He commanded them to breathe upon the dark clouds. The mighty winds they created drove back the black and threatening vapours into the void. Merlin himself dealt with the demons below, casting down the trolls and gnomes whose agency had caused the Earth to be riven. The great wizard hurled them back into the pits from where they had sprung, sealing them forever in a tomb of rock.

To the crowd this was all a bit heavy duty. Like listening to Wagner, reading Dostoevsky, and eating charcoal biscuits all at the same time. A few faces in the crowd looked fearful, a woman screamed, and a few children pleaded to be taken home. The modern world complained too easily. No more would the people kneel at the feet of the sorcerer, mumbling in prayer, imploring him to use his powers to alleviate their cruel fate.

Up above them the light seemed to grow brighter, mocking the dreary fogs that had sought to obscure the happy gleam of the morning. Dick was aware of another power, its presence impossible to ignore, making the very air vibrate in a shower and shimmer of gold. Sekhmet! The lioness burst from the heart of the sun, and none could look upon her swirling mane. The blazing locks flowed behind her as she set the crowned disc on high. To the wonder and delight of all those below amber light and turquoise skies returned.

Dick knew that something else was needed to bring back the sweet spirit of joy to the Isle of Teflon. Merlin, in the company of the ancient host, had fulfilled his task battling with forces as great as themselves. Now Dick was determined that another brand of magic would make its debut. He would throw open the lid of the toy box and let a child's enchantment come forth – glittering and sweet. Let ribbons fall, stars shine, poppers pop and tweeters tweet!

He reached in his pocket and pulled out the Cuboid. The time had come for it to perform its greatest tricks! Never had its pinkness seemed so pink – a rich rose, with a touch of strawberry, the prancing jester. The child who danced naked in front of the parade was freed. Gossamer would float about the wings of the fairy queen, and the king would be merry. Leaving his throne, he would hold his ermine aloft and dance with all abandon among his courtiers.

When Dick held up the Cuboid, countless rainbows flew from it till the heavens were all filled with a kaleidoscope of colours. The crowds responded with laughter and applause, and Dick felt as if he were floating in the air above them. Random words entered his brain as if they were playing hooky from a Thesaurus, determined to misbehave and grab at all kinds of unsuitable relationships. They formed into a chorus line, did jigs and somersaults and generally let their hair down. Prompted by these Lords and Ladies of Misrule, Dick began to randomly recite …

Dominoes, walnuts, goggles and Prussia
Thunderbolt, lobsters, varlets and blusher
Ulysses Bradshaw draws Partick Thistle
Hellebore petticoats gammon and whistle.

As soon as he began, a sound like basketballs bouncing in a belfry started up. Dick knew it was God laughing. The thought of *Him* actually being amused by things *he* said was almost too much for

Dick. His brain exploded into a wild world of whirling wisecracks. And he improvised the more ...

Gabardine, marbles, oysters in bars,
Chinchiminey strumpets, circuses in jars
Trumpets and trifles fandangos and quince
Electrical chutney semaphore prince.

God, the power of all powers, smiled upon Dick and everything beneath the firmament. The more He did so, the more the lexicon looped and the notions became more nimble.

Gooseberry crumpet – jiggle my jugs
Amorous marshmallows – fellatio mugs
Burgundy marrows and old Harry Worth
Peculiar ockers and kangers from Perth.

God laughed again and again, and the sound was the sweetest ever heard – a rushing, sparkling stream in a land forever golden. Then it boomed low among majestic mountains and the magus saw all. He looked upon the face of God and it was as the Sun. All creation He held in the palm of His hand and with a gentle breath he gave it everlasting life.

Forgiveness, friendship and best of all *love*, were all back in the charts. Love – total accepting all – had the brightest aura. Transcending space and time, the kingdom of love is all eternity and, its C.V. approved, it turned the power full up. Miracles suddenly happened, all over the Isle of Teflon, quicker than toothpaste when you squish the tube on the bathroom floor.

First up, the stricken tower was restored. Like a movie film running backwards then freezing on the final frame. Once again the mound was covered in a sea of emerald grass. Resolute and glowing, it stood as a sentinel once more – its power and pride restored. The tower appeared to bow to Dick, acknowledging that the wizard had restored its stony self.

Magnificent and beauteous was the Isle of Teflon once more. The Sun obligingly painted a corona of gold and crimson about and beyond its unseen shores. It lay in all its glory upon an eternal ocean. All who were gathered there and had seen these great things come to pass began to cheer and to rejoice, and many openly wept.

On Ackwater Street, rejoicing could also be heard in the gardens of the Dallas Well. After the Nob had been restored the sacred waters had responded with at first a shy spurt, and then a great joyous gushing. All took this as a sign that joy had returned to the Isle of Teflon. The owners of the Dallas Well celebrated by hurling their 'Closed until further notice' signs into Deadshed Lane, and plugging the tills back in. An announcement on Windleroot Radio that season tickets were back on sale was heard within minutes.

Most extraordinary of all, the Old Chapel was restored to its original design. No longer a ruin, but resplendent in its Gothic glory. By some supernatural power, some of its key stones – purloined in Elizabethan times – flew through the air from miles away and assumed their original position. St. Swego must have been doing the hokey-cokey up in Heaven.

The Crumpled Horn, freed from its curse, righted itself too. Every brick and slate, every detail from Ted's seat to the Todge pumps was restored in all its glory – if not a greater glory. It was the talk of the town among drinking men – the great majority in Windleroot – and the bar was nightly stuffed from bench to bar stool. Kate beamed on all – even Ted occasionally.

The celebrations continued up and around the Nob. Chaps slapped each other on the back, women hugged, some did both. Now was the time to dance, and dance they did – with an abandon not seen since days of yore. To the accompaniment of the squeezebox and the fiddle, they jigged and jumped and jived and some did the jitterbug.

For hours the whole of the Nob, from top to bottom, was covered in whirling twirling figures. Those at the summit, kept their feet while others were content to slide down the slopes until they collapsed laughing upon the grass. It was a magnificent celebration of life and the ale and cider flowed, and all became merrier and merrier. Smiles and laughter, something not seen for many a month, returned to every face.

And among this party parade went striding the soul of Standley-Strange, and he danced with them. Though they could not actually behold him, his spirit – and its lively steps – encouraged them to move the more. Around and around they went in an endless rhythm. Wives and lovers, maidens and men, all danced in a way they never had before and probably never would again. Standley-Strange the master magician leapt into the air, not once but many times, knowing that neither earth nor sky had ever held him. He danced and he did dance – the spirit of the man who had saved the world – along with his well-chosen protégé – Dick Symes.

XXI

Dick was not cavorting among the merry throng. He stood atop the now deserted mound, quietly contemplating a vision, one of which he was a part. He was in another summer, one long gone. Once again a girl danced to a song, one now heard only on Classic Oldies radio stations.

"Hello, Janice."

"Dick! … um, Richard."

She laughed when she said that. Dick was glad she did because it was how he remembered her. He had waited long enough to hear that sound, one that went straight to his heart and stayed there. Her smile too had helped him to keep the faith for all these years. She was still beautiful, as he would have expected, the wonder he felt when he was near her had not changed.

Dick wasn't sure if there was anything beneath his feet that could be called *solid earth*. At any moment he was going to float gently away and end up goodness knows where. But that wasn't going to happen because of what happened next, something Dick had rather hoped would. Janice moved closer to him and put her arms about his neck just as she had done once before, and as someone else had also done …

Across the velvet lawn, carrying her parasol, came Philomena. Captain Strange waited for her. Quite why she did it she never knew, but she let go of the parasol and put her arms about his neck. The Captain, quite deliberately, kissed her. For Philomena, that kiss was more wondrous than anything she had ever known and quite, quite unexpected. As they looked in each other's eyes something strange and very extraordinary occurred. The falling parasol did not ever reach the ground but flew into the air, slowly turning over and over against the perfect sky.

It was a long kiss. Never before had two people devoted so much time to pressing their lips softly together. In the history of osculation, it probably qualified for some kind of record. Dick knew it had been worth waiting half-a-century to experience that kiss. Neither did he regret one little bit any of those months, years or even decades in between their last meeting. To feel like he did now he would have cheerfully waited another fifty years, though he would have preferred not to.

He knew that all was well, perfect even. But, being a bloke meant having all the angst that goes with that. Dick had to say things and ask questions.

"I thought you might be with someone else … "

"I was, but I'm not now."

Dick wondered if she had parted from someone just to be with him – which just shows how even a magician can be a total dipstick.

"He died suddenly, not very long ago."

"Oh, I'm sorry."

She put her arms around him again, it seemed very right when she did that.

"It didn't really matter in some ways. It sounds awful, but he wasn't the right one for me either. None of them were. All I really wanted was someone to love me … like I knew you did. And you weren't there, so … "

Dick felt the odd explanation might be relevant here.

"I didn't know where to find you."

Janice smiled, a secret smile, one she often exchanged with angels.

"You wouldn't have found me anyway. It wasn't the right time for us."

"No, I suppose not."

Janice looked out from where they were standing, at some particular point in the sky. Dick suspected she could see something he couldn't, a lot more probably. That way she had of looking he had first marvelled at all those years ago came back to him. He was glad he could still recognise it.

"When Christopher died I realised there must be some reason for that to happen. Then I knew it was because I was going to see you again."

She said it all so matter-of-factly, that was the way women dealt with things. Right now it was all Dick could do not to fall over. When Janice looked at him again her eyes seemed to be all that he could see. The rest of the world may as well never have existed.

"I love you so much."

The words slowly and softly tumbled into Dick's brain and took root, instantly becoming a small forest – the most beautiful place in the world.

"I love you too."

They kissed some more, it seemed the right thing to do.

"I always have loved you ... since the first time I saw you and we sat right here."

The bench was still there after all this time. A blue plaque ought to have been put on it by now.

"I wonder why ... "

"I didn't say it then? Because I knew I had to go through all sorts of things first ... before we could be together. I didn't know when we would be back together again ... but I knew eventually it would happen. I remembered all the funny stuff we said to each other ... for years and years. I never forgot that."

Dick couldn't recall saying very much at all. 1963 was part of history now, but he didn't give the game away. He knew he desperately wanted to tell Janice all sorts of things, maybe about fifty years worth. She was Juliet to his Romeo and he would write plays about her, poems, films, books, songs ... anything. Mainly he wanted to say things that he had never said to anybody else, ever.

"I want to tell you about ... "

She smiled, and he stopped right there.

"I know you do ... and we've got the rest of our lives to share all these things. All the time in the world ... now we're together at last."

An idea whizzed into Dick's head faster than a Ferrari in the fast lane.

"Does that mean you'll come and live with me?"

"Of course, my darling. Right away if you want me to."

Dick was on automatic pilot.

"Yes ... I do. My house is in Clinton ... um ... I'll hope you'll like it."

"I'm sure I will. But ... "

Dick looked worried.

"What?"

"You'll have to tell me where it is ... "

Janice was examining his appearance. Dick still had his cloak and hat on, and was holding the staff with serpents entwined around it.

"You're a magician aren't you?"

"Well spotted! I hope that's okay with you ... I mean ... I'll give up all that kind of thing if you want ... "

Janice laughed again, a sound like the ocean caressing the shore.

"You can be anything you want. I don't want to change you ... I like you the way you are ... I always did."

She kissed him again. Dick knew she was about to go off and do something. A tiny sliver of doubt pricked his heart – a flashback of something that had happened all those years ago.

"Where are you going?"

"Don't you worry one little bit, my darling. I'm not going to run away ever again."

"Oh … good."

"I just have to go and start packing."

Dick knew that it would take Janice a day or more to collect together even her essential bits and pieces. In one way he was relieved, as he knew he had one more mission to accomplish. That morning when he had felt in his pocket the Cuboid was gone. Did it matter? It had served its purpose, and now seemed somewhat irrelevant to his life, which was now filled with something even greater than pink playthings. In the same pocket he had come across Morley Trumpton's card. Finding this prompted Dick to embark on a journey.

Leaving the city behind, he drove through a brace or two of small towns until he gained the B-road to Withy Binder. On one of the hillsides near Gibbon's Ketch (known for its ancient stone circle) a gaggle of hippies were harvesting hallucinogenic mushrooms. When Dick waved cheerily, one or two of them stared vacantly back at him.

In East Buttwell he quickly found Trumpton's cottage, lying at the end of a modest terrace. As Dick would have predicted, the garden was wild and overgrown with a small patch of lawn among it. A short path led to the front door which opened easily when he pushed it. Carefully stepping over the pile of mail that lay on the mat, Dick went in to the front room.

Dick called Trumpton's name several times, but he instinctively knew there would be no response. Death had claimed him, of that Dick was certain. The Grim Reaper is impossible to ignore – he leaves his mark. Subtle it maybe, but always noticeable, an overpowering sense of absence – and with no chance of return.

The walls, hung with pictures, looked down upon the glorious clutter – antiques, handsome furniture, the paraphernalia of a comfortable life, and everywhere – books, books and more books. Dick could see Trumpton humming to himself as he took up a paper, or plunged his hand into a bag of toffees on a stool by the desk. Through an open door could be seen the kitchen table where Trumpton nightly enjoyed his supper, the indelible mark where his mug of ale once stood.

A shiny new volume, apparently discarded on the sofa, caught Dick's eye. A piece of writing paper doing duty as a bookmark revealed some scribbled notes. They gave Dick warning of what to expect from the contents of the book.

Dolores dished dirt on brother – finishing her biography/exposé of Hector before she died – Hector – charlatan – magical career based on Dennis Wheatley, Charles Williams etc ...

Dick, looking around, decided to sit in the sagging armchair by the window – obviously Trumpton's favourite place. He opened the book at random and began to read. The passage turned out to be one of the milder excerpts from what appeared to be the epic denunciation of her brother by Dolores Standley-Strange.

An uncle told me that when Hector was a boy he was always living in a world of make-believe. It was a tragedy for his family that he never did become what we all had hoped for – a rational thinking adult. I regret to say that much of the blame for his disordered view of life must lie with my mother. She greatly indulged, rather than condemning as any responsible parent should have done, his unhealthy appetite for the supernatural. If only my poor dear brother had followed the teachings of my own, and my husband's faith! On many occasions my husband Keith tried in vain to reason with Hector and persuade him to follow our faith in the Truth as it is written in our founder's wise words. Instead Hector thought he knew better and spurned all of Keith's entreaties to take the True Way. Tragically, he preferred to follow in the footsteps of the cloven hoof of Satan.

Dick read on, but only enough to convince himself that if Dolores' intention was to posthumously destroy her brother's reputation she had certainly done a first-rate job. Naturally the blurb on the cover of the book hotly denied any such motive, trumpeting all sorts of cant about 'the truth must be known' and similar twot. From what Dick could see, after page five any pretence at being a genuine biographical account went right out of the window. A hatchet job, one that was never buried, apart from in Standley-Strange's flesh, Dolores seemed to delight in detecting evil intent in every move her brother made. In her eyes, if he enjoyed his breakfast, or took a hot bath, that would be proof of unrepentant debauchery. Standley-Strange emerged from her account with a reputation somewhere between Pontius Pilate and Al Capone.

To his surprise Dick realised how little any of what had been written affected him. What did it matter if this woman saw Standley-Strange as a total and utter charlatan or worse? If he had honed his character, polished its gloss until he had made it his own, where was the sin in that?

Dick escaped from the pneumatic embrace of the armchair and made for the door. As he did so he remembered what he had come to do – jettison the grimoire. Perhaps that was just a fake as well, another piece of artifice? Dick laid it next to Dolores' book – two volumes equally as vicious as each other in their own way.

Although it was still light outside, the evening shadows had begun to gather in the cottage. As he went through the gate, Dick was aware of someone in the lane. Thinking about it, it did seem extraordinary that no one had seen him go into the cottage or ask him what he was about. The ways of the country dweller were still not quite the same as the ways of the townsman, it seemed.

"'ullo, Sir. Not lookin' fer Mister Trumpton I 'ope? He be gone ... 'ad a 'eart attack they reckon. Puttin' out his wheelie-bin he were when it 'appened. He were dead for 'e 'it the ground ... the ambylance bloke told I."

To Dick it was as if he was hearing a tale he knew already, these were just details that did not amount to much. He did glean however that Trumpton's death had occurred a few hours *before* he had left Dick the message describing the fate of the Paganorama crew. Trumpton would have been proud to know that his lifelong study of the esoteric was crowned with an ability to communicate from beyond the grave himself.

Any pain that accompanied the realisation Trumpton's voice was silenced forever might come later. And it did, when he returned to Clinton. He was grateful that Boswell was there to comfort him.

Deliverance may have come to Windleroot, but for others in the saga that was not to be so. The body of Goldie was discovered some weeks after he had shifted from this mortal coil – alone and unshriven. His demise led the authorities to ask certain questions, and then follow up a few leads. One led to a flat in Chigwell owned by Beans, but he was not to be found there. His fate would take a more bizarre turn.

Rover melted into the Essex landscape, as did M'bouto and Gowley, but Derek was not so fortunate and was apprehended. Of Vargle Snipe little was heard for some years, until an article in a Tennessee newspaper reported that he was living in a commune in the hills, high upon a ridge, the leader of an impenetrable creed. His end came when he was mugged and murdered in Memphis, by persons known or unknown.

Of the Windleroot crew, Zeep, freed from her obligations to the Boxer brigade, emerged as a minor celebrity in the town. Her company was quite in demand at various gatherings in the Town Hall and the Bumbly Rooms. It was rumoured that the owner of Krazy Krystles was contemplating leaving Bombalina, his long-standing partner, to set up a new life as Zeep's lover in Lead Street. For the first time in her life she would not have to spend Christmas with her dysfunctional family in Dagenham.

Rivet, disgraced and penniless, declared himself bankrupt. The land at Badcorn was repossessed, and the near shanty town sold to a scrap dealer. Rivet acquired a yurt which he pitched near Groom's Codpiece on the edge of the Isle of Teflon. There he spent his days in an alcoholic haze relieved only by visits from Boggy who brought him helpings of faggots and chips, and permitted Rivet to ogle his girlfriend.

Squiddle's eccentricities took a turn in the direction of good old-fashioned lunacy, a legacy of her family. By the thinnest of whiskers she avoided being removed to an institution in nearby Tupworth Vole. Her appearance had to be seen to be believed, and few made the effort. She had taken to dressing as Boadicea and covering herself with woad which, to the more critical eye, turned out to be blackberry jam. Having no chariot, nor the prospect of commandeering any horse to pull such a contrivance, Squiddle had gaily improvised.

Daily she rode her bicycle across the fields, while waving a toasting fork, the nearest to a trident that she could muster. Once her arch enemy, the equally insane Beans somehow became Squiddle's consort. His penance for his past impertinences was to sit in the basket at the front or alternately run alongside his mistress like a dog on a leash. Like Rivet, the pair passed into local folk lore – characters that may or may not ever have existed.

Thus the Isle of Teflon was restored to those whose feudal heritage it truly was – the ill-tempered farmers, murderous poachers and cider-swilling yokels of the Crumpled Horn.

When Janice rang the doorbell, one look at the size of the removal van parked in the middle of Richardson Gardens told Dick his new lover really meant business. In Victorian times there would have been numerous trunks and hat boxes; today it was her Apple Mac that was the first item carefully and ceremoniously taken over the threshold.

After all the cardboard boxes had been unloaded, it was agreed they would be dealt with the next day. Dick and Janice went into the garden. They looked at each other, not just with a look of love but of knowing. The bliss, once begun, would have no end. For a start, they had a great deal of kissing to catch up on.

As they stood there, Dick might have seen a flash in the sky, which could easily have been a flying saucer. He certainly glimpsed a figure in a tweed jacket, smiling and waving from behind the sundial. Isis, the Queen of Heaven contented herself with looking down from the stars upon two of her favourites.